D0671528

MISSING MR. WINGFIELD

E. CHRISTOPHER CLARK

WILLIAMSBURG REGIONAL LIBRARY
7770 CROAKER ROAD
WILLIAMSBURG, VA 23188

CLARKWOODS

MAY -- 2018

© 2017 E. Christopher Clark. All rights reserved.

Published in the United States by Clarkwoods in Chelmsford, Massachusetts.

Cover art contains elements of photographs by Marcus Selmer from *The Public Domain Review*, as well as photographs by "Gelpi" and "sozon" from Shutterstock.

No part of this book may be reproduced in any form or by any electronic or mechanical means, including information storage and retrieval systems, without permission in writing from the publisher, except by a reviewer, who may quote brief passages in a review, or by members of educational institutions, who may photocopy all or part of the work for classroom use. Scanning, uploading, and electronic distribution of this book or the facilitation of such without permission of the publisher is prohibited. Please purchase only authorized electronic editions, and do not participate in or encourage electronic piracy of copyrighted materials. Your support of the author's rights is appreciated.

This is a work of fiction. Names, characters, places, and incidents either are the product of the author's imagination or are used fictitiously, and any resemblance to any actual persons, living or dead, events, or locales is entirely coincidental.

ISBN for the Print Edition: 978-0-99940-440-9
ISBN for the Digital Edition: 978-0-99940-441-6

Library of Congress Control Number: 2017914637

For Stephanie, who came to see the very first play about Veronica on Valentine's Day 1998, then asked me out two days later

All we have to do now
    is take these lies and
    make them true somehow.
    — George Michael, “Freedom ’90”

I

THE BASTARD SONS OF BASTARDS

November 2010

I

LAURAS AND TOMS

When Tracy was called to the principal's office to answer for the pantsing of Brian Meltzer, the first question that Old Lady Standish asked was, "Is he the first boy to break your heart?"

"Oh no," said Tracy.

"There was someone else?"

"Yes," she said. "A telephone man who fell in love with long distances."

"A what kind of a man?"

"Mr. Wingfield," said Tracy, plucking one pencil from Standish's Reese's Peanut Butter mug, then another.

On the other side of the desk, the principal moved her computer's mouse around. Then, once she'd gotten her cursor to wherever it was she wanted it to go, she began to hunt and peck at her keyboard. "Wingfield, you said?"

Tracy rolled her eyes, lining up pencils on the desk, their dull points aimed at the dull old woman. "Have you ever seen *The Glass Menagerie?*" she asked.

"Is that Wilde or Williams?" asked the principal, still typing away with her index fingers. "I always get them mixed up."

"Well, they do both begin with a W," said Tracy, trying to hide her incredulity, but forgetting to mask her sarcasm in the process.

Principal Standish stopped typing, folded her hands in front of her, and stared over the glasses that sat precipitously on the edge of her nose. She was stone-faced for a moment, then two, but soon enough a smirk cracked through the veneer and she shook her head. Then she pushed her seat back from the desk, rose, and crossed to her bookshelf. She plucked a dusty old Norton anthology from the top shelf and returned to her seat.

"The pages are so thin," said Tracy, as she watched the old woman leaf through the tome.

"Just a smidge thicker than tissue paper," said Standish, "but there's a whole lot of canon to cram between two covers. Anything heavier and—"

Standish went silent, adjusted her spectacles, and read. She moved her lips for the first few words, then caught herself.

Though she would never say so out loud, Tracy was thankful that Principal Standish didn't consider her God's gift to Harwich High School. From the moment she'd transferred here, all those years ago, everyone else had treated her like some kind of golden child. How miraculous she was for having survived the divorce of her parents, the marriage of her mother to another woman. How astounding that, despite all the trouble in her life, she'd not only survived, but thrived. Tracy remembered the first spelling test she'd taken here on the Cape, back in the third grade, how the teacher had applauded the emotionally bruised child for spelling *knight* correctly on her first try. How hard it must be to string six letters together—some of them silent!—when your soul was as black and blue as hers. Tracy could still feel that teacher's hands on her shoulders, the sympathetic squeeze. She could still feel the fire in her cheeks as she tried not to look any of her new classmates in the eye.

"Which Mr. Wingfield?" Standish asked. "The son or the father?"

Tracy smirked, then thought better of it and ducked her head. Damned pompousness coming out again.

"The father," said Standish, closing the book, its two halves slapping together in her arthritic hand.

"Most people forget he's there," said Tracy.

"But he isn't," said Standish. "And that's the point."

On one of his visits home from Hawaii a few years before, Tracy's Uncle Michael had taken her into Cambridge to see a play one of his college housemates was putting on at some derelict building just outside the ivy-covered walls of Harvard. It wasn't a theater, this place; it was more like an old house. But that was perfect, Uncle Michael told her, "exactly what this guy's been imagining since the first time he read the script."

The script, of course, was *The Glass Menagerie*, and Tracy traced the abstract lines on its cover—the dog and the giraffe and all the rest—as Michael covered his ears on the Green Line, the ceaseless whine of the subway car driving him batty.

While they changed trains at Park Street, Michael, rubbing at his temples, told her about the thing he was most looking forward to. "The photo of the father," he said.

"The father?" Tracy asked him. "What father?"

Michael laughed. "Everyone forgets about the father, but my pal, the director, he wrote his whole thesis on the dude."

"But he's not in the play, Uncle Michael. The father isn't around."

"Yeah," said Michael. "And that's why he's so important."

Tracy recalled little of the forgettable production, but she would never forget the comically large portrait of the smiling soldier in the doughboy's cap, his toothy grin frozen in sepia forever. It hung above the mantle of the working fireplace, which roared throughout the show, and it was so big that the stage lights actually obscured the top of his head, his hat.

"On purpose," Michael had told her. "All on purpose."

Maybe, Tracy had thought, but she realized even then, even as young as she was, that a decision made on purpose could be a bad decision just the same.

"Do you miss your father?" Standish asked.

"I thought we were here to talk about me pantsing Brian," said Tracy, picking pencils up off the desk and replacing them in the cup.

"We are," said Standish.

"Okay," said Tracy. "Good."

Brian Meltzer was a schmuck, the kind of kid who helped a hot girl with her homework then stared at her ass as she walked away, a smug grin on his face, like he'd earned the ogle. They all went to him when they came to the tutoring center, though. It wasn't that they minded Tracy; it's just that she wouldn't do their work for them. And she'd tried to tell them, for the past four years, what kind of a kid Brian was, but they didn't care. "Do you know how you're paying for all that extra help?" she'd ask.

"It's just our asses," they'd say. "And he's not the only one. And at least we're getting something out of it with him."

Tracy would sigh, they'd wave a dismissive hand, and that would be the end of it.

"What made this morning different?" asked Standish. "What pushed you over the edge?"

"I'm mad as hell," said Tracy, "and I'm not going to take it anymore."

Standish laughed. "A great film, that one. Have you seen it, or just caught clips on YouTube?"

"Unlike the men in my family, I—"

"I thought we weren't talking about your family," said Standish, an eyebrow raised.

"Touché," said Tracy.

Standish smirked, gave a curt nod, and directed her attention to her window. Tracy looked now, too. School buses were lining up in a neat row outside. The doors to two of them opened and the drivers, one male and one female, stepped out. They chatted amiably, the woman offering the man a stick of gum.

"Years ago," said Standish, "they would have been smoking."

"Nasty habit," said Tracy. "Killed my great-grandfather."

"Do you know what kind of chemicals they put in chewing gum, Ms. Silver? Or in those Diet Cokes you guzzle like they're going out of style?"

She knows what I drink at lunch? thought Tracy.

Standish pulled a manila folder from a wire rack stuffed with them and plucked a form from it, one of those horrible triplicate things, the yellow form bound for home, the pink for the teacher who filed the complaint, the white for Tracy's permanent record.

As Standish began to write, Tracy gave an *ahem*.

"Yes."

"Just so it's clear, I had no idea Brian was going commando today."

"Commando?" said Standish.

"Commando," said Tracy. "You know: sans underpants."

Standish grinned, shook her head. "I've never heard that term."

"My mothers let me watch too many *Friends* reruns as a kid."

Standish finished writing, then handed the form over to Tracy to read.

"The surprise appearance of Mr. Meltzer's penis did not factor into your punishment," she said.

Tracy nodded, took the lone pen from the Reese's cup—you couldn't sign these things in pencil, right?—and signed. "One day's suspension seems fair," she said. "And it gives me extra time to pack for my college visit this weekend."

"I've forgotten," said Standish. "Where are you headed?"

"Hawaii," said Tracy. "To visit my uncle and check out U of H. He teaches there," she added. "Illustration and art history."

Standish nodded. "Maybe take the play with you," she said, "and re-read it on the flight."

"You think I missed something?" said Tracy.

Standish bit her thumb and considered Tracy for a moment.

"I did," said Tracy, "didn't I?"

"Are you aware of Mr. Meltzer's home situation, Ms. Silver?"

Tracy nodded. "Lives with his mom," she said, "which, if I can say, makes his behavior even more—"

Standish raised a finger and Tracy shut herself up.

"It's not just the Lauras of the world who are missing their old men," said Standish. "It's the Toms, too."

Tracy nodded again, tore off the bottom copy of the form, and then folded it into a square. She stuffed that into the front pocket of her jeans.

Standish said, "We'll see you in a couple of days then."

Tracy nodded one last time, but the gesture felt all wrong. There were words left to be said, and she had not yet mastered the art of holding her tongue. She envisioned this for a second, actually pinching the fleshy instrument of her self-destruction between thumb and forefinger, and the pause was just long enough for Standish to notice.

"Yes?" said Standish.

Tracy ducked her head and half-mumbled, "Permission to speak freely?"

"Permission to what?" said Standish.

Tracy looked up. "Don't you think your reading of the text is a little heteronormative?"

Standish raised an eyebrow.

"I mean, Laura and Tom's issues with their mother have more to do with Amanda's psychoses than the lack of a father figure. Amanda would be messed up even if her husband were still there." Tracy paused, bit her lip, tried to hold back. But she couldn't. "Not every work in the canon is centered around daddy issues," she said. "My life isn't any worse because I have two mothers, Mrs. Standish. It just isn't."

"Ms. Silver," said Standish, steepling her hands in front of her face for a moment, then unsteepling them, then smiling the smile of a woman who's just dropped a deuce in her pantsuit. "You will undoubtedly be the valedictorian of your class. Your performance here, occasional lapses in judgment notwithstanding, is so far beyond the standards we have set that our faculty struggles to challenge you. My point: you could attend any college you wanted, and I know you have been courted by a great many of them."

"Yes," said Tracy. "And?"

"And yet," said Standish, "your first choice, if you'll permit *me* to speak freely, is a second- or third-tier school whose sole perk is its proximity to the only male authority figure you have ever truly valued."

Tracy felt her brow furrow, felt an eyebrow raise, felt words ready to tumble from her mouth. But once more, just as she was about to speak, Standish raised a solitary finger.

"Ms. Silver," Standish began again. "Your mothers are among the finest parents I've dealt with in all the many years I've been at this school. This has nothing to do with them and everything to do with you."

"I don't need a father," said Tracy.

Standish gave the briefest of chuckles. "It's funny," she said. "Mr. Meltzer said the same thing. And yet, when his father came to pick him up this morning, to take him away for the Thanksgiving holiday, his face was lighter than I've ever seen it. As for you, Ms. Silver, isn't it true that your college essay is about the rise and fall of your uncle's band?"

"Yes," said Tracy, "but—"

Old Lady Standish shushed her one last time. Then she stood, crossed to the door, and made ready to open it.

Tracy stood and stepped toward the door. But Standish still hadn't opened it. "A final lesson?" she asked.

"Consider this," said Standish, her hand fiddling with the knob, "I never said you were a Laura. Maybe," she said, "you're a Tom."

Tracy rolled her eyes and sighed, "I don't think you understand what I meant by heteronorma—"

Standish shook her head and finally pulled open the door. "Good afternoon, Ms. Silver," she said. "Have a safe flight."

"I have, like, so much more to say about this," said Tracy. "It is totally unfair the way teachers start a debate and then end it before—"

Standish set a hand on Tracy's shoulder and squeezed. Then she nudged her out of the office. "Oh," said Standish with a smile, "the maelstrom your mothers have set loose upon our unsuspecting world."

And, not knowing whether to take these words as a compliment, an insult, or something somewhere in between, Tracy watched Old Lady Standish shut the door.

II

THE SNOWS OF YESTERYEAR

December 1999

2

BAILEY & SCROOGE

It began with a piano falling from the sky.

Veronica stepped onto the subway platform, guitar case in hand, and tried to shake the image from her mind. But just as the last whispers of the instrument's final cacophonous chord faded into a gentle hum, she caught sight of something that scared her even more.

It was a man, a *sales*man. He stood in his suit, leaning against a pillar, his nose in a book. It was Dickens, a collection if she'd read the spine correctly. But he didn't read, not him. She knew this man. He watched and he listened, but he did not read.

The Salesman looked up at her as she stepped tentatively toward him. He dog-eared the page he was on, then flashed her a wide smile. "Veronica," he said. "It's me. It's—"

"I don't know you," she said, turning away, stepping toward the yellow line that separated platform from track.

"You do," he said. "Or, well, you did. You did know me."

"Fine," said Veronica, listening as his footsteps grew closer. "I don't know you anymore."

"That can be fixed," he said, setting his hands upon her shoulders. "It can all be fixed."

She thought to shrug him off, so blatant was his bullshit. But he was selling her on it, the way he always did. How many times had the feel of his hands on her shoulders calmed her, comforted her? Whether it was on the swing set, each gentle push of his filling her with the bravery it took to swing higher and faster; or when she'd learned to ride her bike, and his lightest touch could right her most severe wobble; or at the piano, where even the suggestion of his hands nearby could convince her to power through the next measure.

The piano! She gestured toward the exit. "Did you see what happened out there?"

"I did," he said. "A shame. A real shame. Avoidable."

She turned on him, had to see in his eyes if he believed his own spin. "How?" she asked. "It was an accident. How do you avoid having a piano dropped on your head?"

"Stay away from high-priced high rises."

"Excuse me?" said Veronica.

"Stay away from places where a piano is likely to fall on you from an unsafe height and you are less likely to have a piano fall on your head." He smiled and ran his hands along her upper arms, giving her shoulders a squeeze as he said, "It's simple logic, sweetheart."

She stormed away from him, stared down the tunnel, squinting to see if she could make out any oncoming trains. "Don't call me that," she said. "You don't know me. You don't have the right."

"But I do," he said, his voice echoing through the empty station. "I've known you for longer than anyone else in the world, except perhaps your mother and the doctor who delivered you. Veronica," he said. "Look at me. It's me. It's—"

"Shut up," she said, frightened by the sound of her own voice, the authority it had as it bounced back at her. She looked around, disoriented. Where was everyone? Had the city shut this place down after the piano fell? But, if they had, why hadn't she and the Salesman been evacuated, too? Something was going on here. "Where am I?" she said. "What is this place?"

"It's a subway platform," he said.

"Yes, I get that," she said, crossing to the map of the subway system, which showed not the Red and Green and Blue lines she was expecting, nor the Orange or the Silver, but instead a Purple line and a Yellow and a Black. She set a finger upon the Yellow Line and followed it to its terminus, a station named Oz. She shook her head. "I get that it's a subway platform," she said. "But is this real, or is it all happening inside my head?"

"Ah," he said. "Well, to quote one of your daughter's favorite books, 'Of course it is happening inside your head, but why on earth should that mean that it is not real?'"

She turned and faced him again. "Are you messing with me?" she asked.

He held a hand to his heart, trying to look affronted. "Would I ever?" he said.

"Yes," she said. "Yes, you would."

"I am not messing with you," said the Salesman.

Veronica tried to place the quote, but couldn't. And this surprised her. There were only so many books on their shelf at home, and she had read each of them to her daughter so many times. "What book is that from?" she said. "I don't recognize it."

"Of course not," he said. "It's what—when did you go to sleep? 1999?—That book hasn't even been published yet. But once you bring that one home, you're going to read it to her. Again and again."

Veronica scoffed. "You're from the future now, too?" She shook her head, paced. "It's that Chinese food that I ate that's causing this, isn't it? I have a friend who has this theory about crab rangoon being laced with marijuana. I never believed her, but—"

"Oh, be quiet Veronica, and I'll explain."

"Please do," she said.

He pulled his book out of his jacket pocket and began to thumb through it. "I can't remember the damned quotation," he said. "I nearly flunked out of school because of my English grades. I'm sure I told you that once."

She sighed, exasperated. "You never told us anything just once, Dad."

He smiled at the sound of the word, slapping his knee with the book as he did—slapping his knee! who still did that?—and then he let out a laugh. "You said it," he said. "You called me—"

"The quotation!" said Veronica. "Get on with it."

He returned to the book, put on his rough approximation of a British accent, and spoke: "I am here tonight to warn you that you have yet a chance and hope of escaping my fate."

She sighed. "*A Christmas Carol*?" she said. "So, who are you supposed to be? Marley? My father's not dead yet."

He slipped the book back into his jacket pocket. "Allow me some artistic license, if you please."

"As if I have a choice," she said.

"I am all of the ghosts in one," he said. "So many of you have asked, over the years, to have all of us at once, that we figured we might as well acquiesce."

"That's kind of you," she said, stepping again toward the edge of the platform, looking in both directions for a train out of there. "Now, can we get on with it?" she asked. "I'd like to get some actual rest before Tracy wakes up to bitch at me about the latest wrongs I've done her."

The Salesman slipped up beside her and asked, in almost a

whisper, "Do you regret having her, Veronica? Do you often wonder what life would be like if—"

"Hey," she said. "Wait. Is this *A Christmas Carol* or *It's a Wonderful Life* that I'm dreaming here? It's not some mashup, is it?"

He strolled down the yellow line, heading toward the far side of the platform. "I was just asking a question," he called out, over his shoulder.

She stomped after him. "Yeah, a question no parent is allowed to answer out loud," she said.

He paused at the place where the platform ended and the tunnel began, unlatching a metal gate that locked up a ladder to the tracks below. "Well, you're not answering it out loud now," he said. "Are you? This is, as you say, all in your head."

"I'm still not answering it," she said.

He started down the ladder. "Oh, you will," he said. "By the end, you will."

She watched him climb down, stepping over the tracks, careful to avoid the third rail, and though she knew that she would follow him—that she *must*—she stood still, holding her ground. She shook her shoulders hard in protest, not wanting to give in, and felt the weight of her guitar case bouncing against her hip for the first time since she'd stepped onto the platform. Had it been there the whole time? She set it down. No use bringing it with her. Serenading him wasn't going to get her out of this.

"Wait up," she said, descending the ladder herself and then following him into the darkness.

3

HETFIELD, ROBERTS & PEACOCK

When she saw the light at the end of the tunnel, she did not flinch. The worst that could happen, she figured, was that a train would run her over and send her back to the waking world. And though that would leave her without an answer to the question of what the Salesman was up to, she was sure she'd see him again, that the epiphany he sought to bring her to could be dealt with at a later time.

And so, the train came. But it was riding the track opposite them, so no escape was forthcoming. It hurtled by, faster than any subway car she had ever seen, but that wasn't what stunned her most. What really got her attention was what she saw in the darkness just after it passed by, a fleeting image sprung from the shadows by the train's fading tail lights. She squinted and, almost as if the tunnel could sense what she was doing, overhead lights began to flicker to life. There was a table there, on the other side of the tracks, and chairs, a whole kitchen. She knew this place. And she knew the girl sitting at the table, the girl with the slap bracelets and the *Ride the Lightning* t-shirt, the girl staring at the overturned glass bottle that lay in front of her.

Veronica stumbled backward in disbelief, tripping over a rail as she did and then realizing, as she fell, that the third rail was behind her, that the end was coming now, just as she'd seen something worth seeing, worth exploring. But when she landed, it was not on the hard metal of subway tracks, nor on gravel or wood chips or whatever it was that lay beneath those things, but on the cold linoleum of her parents' kitchen floor.

The Salesman hovered by her side, offering a hand to help her up, a hand that she did not take. "What do you see here?" he asked. "Which night is this?"

She pushed herself up from the floor, her gaze locked on the young girl, the girl she had once been. "Fuck," she said. "This is the night I got pregnant." She looked out the kitchen window, just to make sure, and there was the snow, just as she remembered it.

Not able to bear the sight of the flakes falling, she stared back at the bottle. It was a wine cooler, the brand her mother drank, and that night it was one of only four bottles sitting amidst a castle of empty cans. The boy who had plucked it from the countertop laughed at her as he'd set it down on the table. And then he had stopped laughing, and he had said, "Silver, you are a total lightweight."

It was the first time that alcohol had ever passed between her puckered teenage lips, the first time that *any* of the girls at the table had been liquored up. Veronica watched her younger self duck her head and avert her eyes. This wasn't Vern's fault—Vern, that's what they'd called her then—but she didn't know enough not to feel guilty. Aside from the blizzard, which had stranded her parents somewhere in the wilds of Maine, this was all the boys' fault. They were the ones who had crashed the party, who had broken the tradition.

Veronica looked around the table, at the bodies that had filled the once-empty room. Then she looked at the Salesman, who was still standing beside her, his gaze shifting between Veronica and the scene playing out before them.

"What was the tradition?" he asked her, reading her mind.

Since middle school, when Vern had finally been allowed to stay up and watch the ball drop, her New Year's Eve sleepover had become something of an institution. Vern and her two best friends would crowd around the kitchen table, binge on Chinese food with her parents, and then pile into the four-poster upstairs with a bowl of popcorn, a box of tissues, and a stack of Julia Roberts tapes from the rental place down the street. That was how things were supposed to go. Amy's hands were not supposed to be massaging the crotch of some flat-topped Neanderthal—one was supposed to be entwined with Vern's hand, the other with Desiree's. And Desiree wasn't supposed to be wearing some random guy's letterman's jacket to keep warm; she was supposed to be curled up under the covers, her body balled up against Vern's. They were supposed to watch movies until the bowl of popcorn was empty, or their tear ducts were dry, whichever came first. And then they were supposed to fall asleep beside each other under the heavy down comforter, under the soft cotton sheets. They were supposed to be drinking Diet Coke, not Coors Light. They were supposed to be playing a board game, not Spin the Bottle.

"Supposed to, supposed to, supposed to," said Amy.

"Was I mumbling out loud again?" asked Vern.

Amy extricated one of her hands and set it atop the overturned wine cooler. "Rules were meant to be broken," she said, giving the bottle a spin.

"We can leave," said Desiree's Letterman.

Amy's Neanderthal nodded. "Buncha other parties'd be glad to have us."

Vern ignored them and stared at the spinning bottle. She watched it as a kitten might watch a game of tennis, her eyes moving in circles as its spin grew slower and slower. If Amy wanted to break the rules, that was fine. Vern just wished that the girl would take these interlopers and make trouble somewhere else.

The truth, Veronica remembered, as the sound of the glass vibrating against the hardwood grew louder and louder, was that this was the night she'd finally had enough of Amy's shenanigans. Ever since her first encounter with the generous johnson of her barbarous Neanderthal, Amy had become singularly obsessed with sex, and not with having it as much as possible—she'd only 'done it' once—but with *talking* about it as much as she could. She asked which kind of dick Vern and Des liked best, knowing full-well that Vern, at least, had never even seen a penis, let alone handled one. She talked constantly about orgasms, about how the one she'd had with the Neanderthal (or, well, the one she *thought* she'd had) hadn't been quite like the little earthquakes she could muster with her own finger, and about how she'd been plotting and planning to make sure that the next one was much better, how she'd stolen *The Joy of Sex* out of the public library to make sure of it, and how she was leafing through the pages of that old tome every goddamned night. And, worst of all, Amy didn't seem to think she had a problem. But she did have a problem, and the night was being ruined by it.

The long neck of the empty wine cooler swung round to a stop, pointing into the small space between the Neanderthal and his runty cousin, the third wheel that they'd brought along, ostensibly, for Vern's sake. Vern gave Desiree a look. Desiree smiled and shrugged. And then, Amy clapped her hands. "Two for one!" she shouted. "Who's first?"

The Neanderthal punched his cousin in the arm, and the Runt offered up his cheek.

"Go easy on him, Ames," said the Letterman. "Dude's a virgin."

The Runt scoffed. "Am not."

"He ain't no more," said the Neanderthal with a chuckle. "Didn't your mom tell you she took care of that?"

"Good one," said the Letterman, hurling an empty across the table at his friend.

In the shadows, still watching, Veronica shook her head. She turned to the Salesman and asked him, "Were you this much of an idiot when you played football?"

He smirked. "I made these kids look like Road Scholars."

"That's Rhodes," she told him. "Not 'road.'"

"See," he said, still smirking.

At the table, the Runt asked, "Can we get this over with?"

"Absolutely," said Amy, leaning across the table. "You ready?"

The Runt nodded.

"Okay then," said Amy, taking hold of his head and latching onto his cheek with her barracuda's mouth.

The Runt went pink, the Letterman screamed "Get a room," and Desiree said, "Quit it," but it was only when the Neanderthal gave her a sharp smack on the ass that Amy let go.

"My turn," said the Neanderthal.

Amy turned around and grabbed hold of the brute by the back of his neck, then buried his face in her bosom. She straddled him, pulled his face out of her cleavage, and then laid on him the sloppiest French kiss that Vern had ever seen, tongues going everywhere, saliva spreading across cheeks and dripping off of chins, the tip of someone's tongue penetrating the cavern of someone's nostril.

Vern went green and Veronica felt her stomach churn in memory. Maybe part of it was the Chinese food, and maybe some other small part of it was the four wine coolers she'd drunk, but a large part of what was making both the young and the old Veronica sick right now was the sheer *wrongness* of this display, of this show that Amy was putting on. These two, they didn't belong together, except in the crudest of ways, except in that 'insert tab A into slot B' way that all men and women fit together. Before this asshole, Amy had just been another flannel-wearing, clarinet-playing band geek. Before, when she liked a guy, she made him a flower out of tissue paper, doused it in fuzzy peach perfume, and stuck it onto the end of a plastic straw. Now, she did this. Her hormones had convinced her that make-believe roses weren't good enough anymore. It was time to move faster, her body told her. The clock was ticking.

Amy dismounted her boy toy and slipped back into her chair. She took off her flannel, a ratty old thing of her dad's that she never took off nowadays, except for its once-a-week washing, and she asked, "That better?"

"Much," said the Neanderthal.

Amy gulped down the last of her beer, nudged Vern, and said, "Your turn."

She resented having to do this, but she knew that there was no way out. With her hand atop the bottle, she wondered which of these idiots she minded kissing the least. She knew who she wanted to kiss *most*, but boys weren't kissing boys tonight and that probably meant that girls weren't kissing girls. Vern went over the physics in her head, trying to figure out how hard she would have to spin it to get the Runt, the lone college boy, the least of all evils, and then she spun the bottle so hard that it nearly spun off of the table.

She turned to Desiree as it whipped around and around, and Desiree must've mistaken the look on her face for panic, because she offered up a bottle of tequila straight away. It wasn't panic that Vern was feeling, though. It was guilt. This situation, this night, was the latest evidence against her, enough ammunition for any prosecutor to prove that she was just as bad as Amy, just as warped and dishonest with herself. If she were really being true, if she were really being the person she was meant to be, she would have told Desiree why she was so adamant about keeping up the New Year's Eve tradition. She would have told her just how often she'd wanted to kiss her pouty lips, or else she would have just kissed them, not even bothering to ask. That would have been the most honest thing to do.

It all went back so far, this lying. Veronica could still recall, clear as day, the moment it became obvious to her who she was. There, in her mind's eye, she saw Desiree strolling in and out of the surf at Red River Beach, down the Cape, a creature positively transformed in the two weeks since the end of school. There was something about her hair swirling gently in the sea-breeze, and something about her face too, something about the thin eyebrows, the green eyes, the high cheeks, something that seemed different than before. Maybe it was just the bikini, a skimpy string thing that the girl was nearly spilling out of, but Veronica couldn't help but stare at Desiree's breasts, which put Veronica's own endowments to shame. Veronica could still feel the heat building as her friend drew closer, a feeling that had never come from thinking about boys, the way her mother had told her it would. She remembered how she'd pulled her legs tighter together, hoping to stave off the sensation, and how that only seemed to make things worse.

But then, suddenly, she was back in the moment, back in the cold of her kitchen, drawn back by the hooting and hollering. She watched—and felt, yes *felt*, because she was no longer watching; she was there, in the seat, inside of the girl she had once been—a soft hand slip over her own.

"Let's just get it over with," said Desiree.

Every eye was on them. Veronica looked down at the table to see what had happened. She looked down to see, and she saw, but she didn't believe, *could not* believe.

"It ain't two out of three," said the Neanderthal.

"Yeah," said the Letterman. "In case you were wondering.

"No," said Veronica. "Sorry. Just spaced."

"You ready then?" said Desiree.

Veronica nodded. "Sure," she said.

Desiree leaned across the corner of the table that sat between them, knocking over the now empty bottle of Pepe Lopez that was in front of her. "You look nervous," she said, giggling, brushing a strand of fallen hair out of Veronica's eyes.

"I do?" said Veronica. *Of course I do*, she thought.

From the shadows came the voice of the Salesman. "Why were you nervous?" he said.

The room disappeared. The table was still there, and the chairs, but the people were gone, and all around her was nothing but darkness.

The Salesman came closer and asked again, "Why were you nervous?"

"Why was I nervous?" she said.

The Salesman sat down in the chair opposite Veronica, and as he did another memory flashed to life around them, then dimmed. She wondered suddenly about who had the power here. Was he the one conjuring these scenes, or was she? Could she force him to see, the way he had just forced her?

"I'll show you why I was nervous," she said, gambling. "It was another night," she said, "around another table."

Veronica picked up the bottle and tossed it to him. "You were there," she said.

As he caught the bottle, it transformed from clear glass to brown.

"Yeah," she said. "You were there and I, I was there." She pointed to her right, to another chair, and the Vern of her memory stepped out of the shadows, a game board under her arm. She sat and began to set it up.

Veronica stayed where she was, remembering who had been there, and she wondered how far she could push the magic of this place. "And Matt," she said, "my brother, your son—he was here." Veronica looked down at her hands, but they were no longer hers. Her engagement ring was gone, her wedding band too, and the fingernails she saw were not bitten, no longer covered in chipped and fading paint. The nails were immaculate now, in fact. The fingers slender and clean, if a bit hairy. Her hands had become her brother's. She looked down and saw that she was wearing the Kimball College shirt Matt that had been wearing that day. All of her had become all of him.

The Salesman shuffled back and forth in his seat, obviously uncomfortable at the sight of Veronica's transformation. He hadn't expected to see his son this night. Hadn't expected it, and wasn't prepared. He looked away, ashamed. "And then what?" he said.

Veronica watched as the dining room of her grandfather's house on Cape Cod materialized around her. As far as the Silver family went, you knew it was the end of summer when the board games came out. It was tradition on the last night down the Cape to gather for a game of Monopoly, or Risk, or Clue. She looked to her left, as the kitchen table of her parents' house elongated into the dining room table at Grampy's, and she noted, with a choked back tear, the old man who appeared next to her father. Grampy hadn't played in years by that point, since before Grammy died, but he stayed up to watch.

"Do you remember this?" Veronica asked the Salesman.

He picked up his cards from the table and mumbled. "I'd rather I didn't."

Then, as young Vern moved the token for Miss Scarlet across

the board and began to consult her detective's notepad, Grampy spoke, asking the question that would ruin everything.

"What's the name of that colored fellow who's got his own talk show now?"

"That's Arsenio Hall," someone said.

The Salesman chimed in, laughing as he observed, "Next thing you know, they'll be replacing Carson with a fag. Or a lesbian."

Veronica remembered all too well the words her brother spoke next, so she spoke them. Under her breath, just as he had. "Yeah," she mumbled. "Someone like me."

Vern kicked Veronica under the table and gave her a frown.

So Veronica reached under the table and gave her leg a rub. Then she pressed on, just as Matt had, just as older brothers often did, deciding that a little sister's discomfort was more than enough reason to keep at it. "Hey Gramp," she said, "didn't Great Aunt Dottie have an affair with another woman once?"

Grampy sighed. "My sister was a wild stallion. She did a lot of things." He reached his hand across the table and patted Veronica's. "But we loved her regardless."

Young Vern set her cards down and said, "I'm going to suggest Mrs. Peacock, in the study—"

Veronica picked Matt's blue pawn up, then set it down in the study beside Vern's piece. Then she spoke the words of her brother once more: "You don't have a comment on all this, sis? You just want to move straight to the accusations?"

"I'm *suggesting* at the moment. I'm not sure yet."

"What weapon?" Veronica asked.

"The rope," said Vern.

Veronica grunted. "I'm not man enough for the gun?

"That has nothing to do with it."

Calmly, Veronica asked, "Are you trying to say that I'm just a little bitch who'd have to use a rope to kill someone? That I'm some kind of nancy boy?"

Vern frowned. "That's not what I'm—"

"Hey," Veronica shouted at the Salesman, who was sipping at his beer again, "what if Vern's right? What if I am some gay little nancy boy?"

"My son?" the Salesman scoffed. "The Eagle Scout? The star shortstop for the Lions? A faggot?" he spat. "I don't think so."

"What if I told you," said Veronica, "that the reason I keep going back to Wa-Tut-Ca each summer is because I have a crush on the quartermaster?"

"You better cut the shit," said the Salesman.

"Grampy knows," said Veronica, waving a hand toward the old man. "He's known for a long time. You think he was gullible enough to accept that I had a sudden interest in cars, after years of avoiding the garage like the plague? No, he actually asked me questions. He pretended like he gave a damn."

"The quartermaster?" the Salesman shouted. "The Italian kid with the cars? Are you trying to tell me that when you were sleeping over there... Are you trying to tell me that—"

"Yeah," said Veronica. "That's just what I'm trying to tell you. He taught me more than just knots and camping and canoeing and cars. He taught me fellatio and rimming and—"

"Matt!" shouted Vern.

"And anilingus," said Veronica. "He helped me earn my merit badge in anal—"

The Salesman reached across the table and grabbed hold of Veronica's neck with both hands, seeing not his daughter but the son she was pretending to be. Through her tears, Veronica could see Grampy and her Uncle Albert wrapping themselves around the Salesman's hulking arms, trying to pull him off. But she was fading out. She couldn't breathe. Bursts of light were flashing before her eyes, like miniature fireworks announcing the beginning of some grand event, or the end. And then, without realizing what she was doing, she pursed her lips and spat out what little saliva she could muster.

The Salesman let go and stepped away from her. He stared and seemed to see, seemed to see what he had done and who he had done it to. Veronica rubbed at her throat and laughed a mirthless laugh as her old man retreated into the shadows.

4
EMERSON, SILVER & SILVER

Veronica stood her ground as the scene shifted around her, as Grampy's dining room disappeared and her parents' kitchen materialized once more. She stared into the shadows, waiting for the Salesman to return, because she could not bear to look at what was about to happen behind her, because this particular tableau was etched onto the insides of her eyelids. This scene was what she saw when she tried to sleep, what she'd been seeing for nearly a decade now, whenever she closed her eyes, whenever rest would not come.

"You wanted to know why I was nervous?" she shouted. "You wanted to know why, old man. That night—what you did to Matt—that's why!"

His voice came from behind her, from the opposite side of the table. "But still you kissed her," he said, meaning to make her turn, to make her see. "Despite the nerves," he said, "you still did it."

"And what good did it do me?" she said, as she turned around to watch, as she gave him the satisfaction of watching her discomfort.

Desiree tilted her head and leaned in, her face drifting toward Vern's like a luxury liner coming into port. Vern closed her eyes.

She blushed as their lips met. Veronica remembered the feeling of shame coursing down through the trunk of her body, the feel of it settling down into that part of her which was crying out for more. Desiree's lips were smooth and thick and warm, and Veronica remembered wanting to die right there, with that feeling the last thing on her mind. But Desiree was going further, feeding off of the energy of the audience, pushing Vern's lips apart with her slippery tongue. Veronica could still remember the taste: tequila and cherry lip gloss.

Alcohol and hormones conspired against them, raging through their bodies, shouting orders. Vern pulled Desiree closer and let herself go. *To hell with all of them*—that's what she'd thought. If it was a show they wanted, then it was a show they were going to get.

Vern's fingers wandered through the tangled curls atop Desiree's head, her other hand running along her friend's back, its gentle arch. One of the boys gave a wolf whistle. Desiree's hands squeezed Vern's shoulders, then ventured southward until they rested above her throbbing heart.

Veronica watched the tears welling up in the eyes of her younger self, recalled how her whole face ached from having to hold them back. Nobody could know what this meant to her. None of these people would understand. And what would Desiree do if she did know, if she felt a tear on her face that she knew wasn't her own? She would disappear, wouldn't she? That's what any sensible straight girl would do, wasn't it?

A bedroom door slammed shut, somewhere down the hall. And then, they parted. Amy and her beau were gone. The Letterman stood then, put his hands on Desiree's shoulders. And Veronica watched as Vern came to the realization that it was over, the night and the dream that she and Desiree would lose together that part of themselves which had so far remained unfound, hidden. Veronica watched a pained smile form on the face of her younger self. She watched as Vern realized that a part of Des would forever belong to the Letterman now, another patch to sew onto his godforsaken jacket. Des gave Vern's hand a squeeze, and then she was gone. Veronica and Vern, the both of them, they watched Desiree slink down the hallway. They listened to the sound of another bedroom door closing, to the sound of a heavy jacket falling to the floor. Then they turned back to the situation at hand.

At the far end of the tunnel, again on the opposite track, there was a light growing brighter. Another train on its way. The Salesman turned to see it and then seemed to spot something: the train's headlamp had illuminated. He stepped toward the nearest pillar and reached behind it. And, as he did, he said, "Could you think of no other reason to stop yourself? Sure, you'd been spurned by love," he said, pulling from the shadows, impossibly, the guitar case she'd left on the platform. "But was there no other place you could take solace?"

"Music?" said Veronica.

"Music," said the Salesman.

Veronica laughed, raising her voice to compete with the volume of the oncoming train. "Christ," she said. "I was a teenager. I had an itch, and my guitar wasn't going to scratch it."

The Salesman shook his head, then shook the guitar at her. "Some itches never stop itching," he said. "Some itches are best left unscratched."

"What the fuck does that even mean?" said Veronica. And then, she caught on. "Wait a minute," she said. "Wait just a damned minute. Are you the one that regrets me having the baby?"

The train was almost upon them now, so it was hard to tell if he was shouting because he was angry, or just because he wanted to be heard. He said, "This is and has always been about you, not me. If I regret anything, it's that your actions forced me to force you into a situation that—"

"My actions?!" she shouted, shoving him. "MY ACTIONS?!" she shouted again, pushing him across the divider between the tracks, right into the light of the train's headlamp.

The train roared as they fell into the light, but then the light changed. It faded, transformed, from bright white to pale purple glow. The guitar tumbled to the floor of what Veronica suddenly realized was a hospital room. And the Salesman, he tumbled into a chair that sat beside a bed. And in that bed, holding a baby, holding *her* baby, was young Vern, who said, with a note of concern in her voice, "Dad?"

"I know," said the Salesman, "that you're unhappy about the situation."

"That's not what I..." said Vern, trailing off. She laughed, then continued: "Yeah, what's there to be unhappy about."

"You stay with us a year," said the Salesman. "We'll help you take care of the baby, you and Tim will have time to get to know each other better, and at the end of the year I'll set you up with an apartment in Boston and you can get on with Berklee like you want to."

Veronica watched herself boiling over, a poisonous mixture of teenage angst and righteous indignation churning inside of her. Vern said, "When will I have time for Berklee with a baby to take care of? And a husband to take care of? A husband, Dad! Are you really going to force me to marry—"

The Salesman stood and set his hands upon Vern's shoulders. "We'll work something out for the baby," he said. "A nanny, or something."

"But what about—"

The Salesman started for the door. "You've done good," he said, not looking at her. "You've done everything I've asked you to do, and you deserve to be repaid for that. For your loyalty," he said, opening the door. "For your understanding," he said, leaving.

"My loyalty?" said Vern. "Ha! And my understanding?" She shook her head and then, a grin playing across her lips, obviously amused by something—Veronica felt strange, not remembering what that something might have been—Vern began to rap. "Boys are stupid," she spit, "boys are dumb. I hate dem boys so much, I kick 'em in da bum. Girls are purty, girls are sweet. Everything 'bout my girl is wicked fucking neat."

In the shadows, Veronica laughed. But Vern, she looked mortified.

"I didn't swear in front of my baby," said Vern, standing up as the baby began to cry. "Nope. Didn't happen."

The baby cried again, and Veronica felt that all too familiar feeling of being split in two, one part of her still standing in the shadows, the other part swaddled up and fussy despite her best efforts. It was a strange feeling, but not an altogether unpleasant one. The unpleasant parts were always really unpleasant—from the toe-curling pain that had come when the baby had first latched onto her breast to the time, at age 7, when her not-so-little one had flown over the handlebars of her bicycle. But, for the most part, she felt this cleaving of herself to be a natural and welcome thing. That part of her that they had pulled from her body, that she had given a name of its very own—it was the first thing she had ever really finished. Her notebooks were full of verses without choruses, of choruses without verses, but this Tracy, this tiny being she had created almost entirely on her own—she was a full song, a full album's worth of songs. And Veronica was prouder of her Tracy than she was of any chord progression she'd plunked out on the piano, than any string of notes she'd noodled out of her guitar.

Vern was trying to sing the baby to sleep now. "Oh, Desiree," she sang, and the baby seemed to respond. "You like that, huh?"

said Vern, a smile lightening her weary face. "Oh, Desiree," she sang again. "So long hoped for, so long denied. Please come and rescue my baby and I."

Veronica crept closer to the edge of her memory, wanting to see Tracy's face, suddenly possessed with the desire to see if the baby really was the sweet cherub she remembered, or if it might be the wrinkled old man she feared.

"Des," said Vern, speaking in Veronica's direction. "Is that you?"

Veronica looked down at herself and saw that the chest she had always envied was now obscuring the paunch she had come to dread. Desiree's maroon field hockey number was emblazoned there, on a white shirt. She ran hands along the pleated skirt she had never worn, except in her daydreams, and then she twirled a strand of curly hair around her finger as she said, "Yeah."

"I got your flowers," said Vern, pointing to the shelf by the window. "They were beautiful."

"Were?" said Veronica. "They're dead already, huh?"

Vern teared up a little. "I can't even keep a plant alive," she said. "Pathetic, huh? What makes me think—"

Veronica ran to Vern's side and took hold of her free hand. "Don't," she said. "You'll be an awesome mom. You'll be perfect. And I'll be there, Vern. Best friends for life, right?"

Vern pulled away, headed for the window.

"What?" said Veronica. "Did your dad say something?"

Vern turned around to face Veronica again. To face Desiree again, Veronica had to remind herself. "Never mind," said Vern. "I just... I want to tell you something, something important, but..."

"But what?" said Veronica.

"Never mind," said Vern. "Can you get me out of here?"

"Can you leave?" said Veronica. "What about the baby?"

"I've got the car seat," said Vern. "I've got everything ready."

"But what about the Runt?" said Veronica, looking around the room. "Shouldn't you wait for—"

"I'll just leave him a note," said Vern, handing the baby to Veronica, then rushing across the room for pen and paper. "Tracy and I just want to be with you right now. Just us girls. Can you do that?"

Veronica looked down into the face of her daughter. *Damn it*, she thought. *Wrinkled old man*.

"Desiree?" said Vern.

"Hell yeah," said Veronica, strapping Tracy into the car seat. "Let's go."

Vern did a little dance and gave a little *squee*, then grabbed the handle of the car seat and stepped through the door. Veronica made to follow after her, but a hand squeezed her arm and stopped her in her tracks. She turned and saw the Salesman. She looked down at herself and saw her own small tits were back. *Damn*, she thought.

"So," said the Salesman, as the hospital room faded away, "where did you go that day?"

"Hampton," said Veronica. "The beach."

"With a baby?" said the Salesman.

"I was seventeen," she told him, shrugging him off. "And you'd trapped me. Can you blame me for trying to escape?"

"No," said the Salesman, circling her, "but why is it that, whenever you tried, you failed?"

"I didn't try that often," said Veronica. "I was a good girl."

The Salesman laughed. "A good girl?" he said. "What about that play your brother wrote about you and your, uh, exploits?"

Veronica blushed, looked down at her feet. "That play wasn't about me," she said.

"Oh, he may have embellished a little," said the Salesman, "but it was about you. I may be slow, sweetheart, but I ain't that slow."

"It wasn't about me," said Veronica, noting that, out of the darkness, a familiar pair of buildings were emerging. It was her grandfather's house, in the years after his death, when the family was still deciding what to do with it. The paint job on the barn was half-finished, the sign that had once read 'Garage' replaced with one that read 'The Theatre.'

"It wasn't about you?" said the Salesman, leading her toward the barn's open doors. "Then what about the way you and Desiree looked at each other on opening night, when we all went to see it?"

He extended a hand, which she took, and he led her inside.

5

DIFRANCO-MAGUIRE

She could not recall taking a seat, nor sitting through her brother's tedious curtain speech, nor even the first two-thirds of the show. One moment, they were at the door, the next the play was reaching its climax.

And Veronica was torn, not sure which drama the Salesman had brought her here to witness: the farce playing on stage or the romance playing out in the seats. The Salesman had found them a place opposite Vern and Desiree, the stage thrust between them, but that didn't clear things up at all. The way the actors stood, the way the scenes played out, Veronica could always see her younger self off in the distance. She felt a headache coming on as she struggled to focus on foreground and then background, background and then foreground.

There was a single young woman on stage now, a blonde in her early 20s—cast first and foremost, Veronica remembered, because her hair was the opposite color of Vern's. The character she was playing, according to the photocopied program Veronica consulted, was Nica, and she was shouting.

"No!" Nica called to someone offstage. "You can't. You can't do that! You can't! You're a... and he... he..."

And then, there came a knocking, not from the door Nica was shouting at, but from another on the other side of the stage.

"What now?" grumbled Nica.

"Chinese food!" said the woman at the door.

Nica did not cross to welcome the delivery person. Instead, she remained focused on what was happening behind door number one. "I didn't order any Chinese food," she said.

"The order was placed by a gentleman by the name of Tim."

In her seat, Veronica laughed. That name hadn't been changed to protect the innocent now, had it? Then again, was the Runt really innocent? Of anything?

Nica continued her watch at door number one as she called back, over her shoulder, "All right. Come in. Door's open."

Onto the stage walked a young woman wearing Birkenstocks, a flannel, and an Ani DiFranco t-shirt. Veronica laughed at the lazy stereotype, then noted her brother's one attempt at originality: a backwards baseball cap from Intercourse, Pennsylvania that he had picked up on a family trip to that state's largest auto show the year their grandfather died. But she was sure it didn't mean anything beyond the connotation that the girl was loose and a lesbian. Her brother was inscrutable, yes, but he was also shallow and incapable of nuance.

"You're not Chinese," said Nica, sizing up the delivery person—Andi, according to the program.

"You're quick," said Andi.

"And you just lost your tip," said Nica, rifling through the pockets of her denim mini-skirt. "Cash only, I suppose?"

"Actually," said Andi, "the order was prepaid on your..."

"Fiancé?"

"Yes," said Andi, setting an enormous brown paper bag down

upon the living room table. "Your fiancé's credit card. I just need him to sign a copy of the receipt and I can get out of here."

Nica slumped into an armchair. "You'll have to wait a couple of minutes," she said, gesturing to door number one. "He's in the bedroom, fucking my best friend."

"Interesting relationship," said Andi.

"You're telling me," said Nica.

Beside Veronica, the Salesman held up his hands, and all else stopped. Veronica looked out at the stage, at the audience. They were all frozen in place. She stared at Vern and Desiree. They were holding hands now, on the sly. Not even hands, really. Just fingers, one hooked around another.

The Salesman tapped her on the shoulder. "Did Desiree ever actually sleep with Tim?" he asked.

"No!" said Veronica. "I told you, this isn't about—"

The Salesman shushed her, clapped his hands once, and everyone around them came back to life.

On stage, Nica asked Andi, "You want a drink?"

Andi said, "I don't turn 21 until October."

"Never stopped me," said Nica.

"And I'm driving," said Andi.

"Okay," said Nica. "Whatever."

From behind door number one came a comic moan and the creaking of a bed frame.

"So," said Andi, "is every Friday like this around here?"

"What do you mean?" said Nica.

Andi opened the bag as she spoke, pulling from it a white box and chopsticks. "I mean," she said, "does your fiancé sleep with your best friend every Friday night?"

"No," said Nica, tucking her knees up under her chin and running her hands over her purple leggings. "This is the first time. He's usually faithful. And she's usually gay."

"Oh," said Andi.

There came again then the sound of coming, or at least the farcical approximation of that sound. The offstage voices hollered clichés, took the Lord's name in vain, thanked Him for their pleasure, and then trailed off.

Nica leapt to her feet, stalked over to the door, and stared at it for a moment, before turning around to face Andi once more. She jammed a thumb between her teeth.

"What?" said Andi, slurping lo mein into her mouth.

Nica looked over her shoulder as she tapped her foot on the floor. Then she blurted out, "You want to fuck?"

"Excuse me?" said Andi, setting down box and chopsticks and eyeing the door.

"Do you want to sleep with me?" said Nica. "I wanna make them sorry. Maybe if they come out here and see me with you, they'll think twice about screwing with me again. So, do you want to?"

"Uh," said Andi, checking her watch. "I couldn't."

"Why?" said Nica, clutching her hands together behind her back and thrusting her chest upwards and outwards, like a good soldier, as if to make the other girl see what she was missing. "Do you think I'm ugly?" she said as she drew closer.

"No," said Andi. "I, uh, think you're very attractive."

Nica stepped behind Andi and slipped off her hat. "Then what's the problem?" she said as she ran her fingers through the other girl's curly locks.

"Well," said Andi, "you're not exactly my type."

Nica set her fingers to work on Andi's neck as she pulled her face close to Andi's ear. "Ah," she said, brushing her lips against Andi's cheek. "but you most certainly are my type."

Andi leapt up and away, stumbling. "Do you have a penis?" she said.

Nica giggled, then stopped, and then, finally, understood. "You mean you're a... No, you can't be. This is just... You're straight?"

"I told you you weren't my type."

"Wait," said Nica, flabbergasted. "You, in the Ani shirt and the flannel and the... the... You're straight?"

Andi sighed. "I tried to tell you."

"I don't believe this!" Nica shouted to the heavens as she slumped again into her chair. "Am I doing something wrong here?"

"No," said Andi. "I just happen to like dick."

In the audience, Veronica moved to get up, saying "I'm not watching this anymore," but she was startled back to her seat by two things. First, the Salesman's hand on her arm. And second, the sight, across the way, of Vern and Desiree mirroring them.

"Sit down," the Salesman told Veronica. "Sit down," Vern told Desiree.

And now, with the rest of the room on mute, Veronica could hear Vern say to Desiree, "I'm not embarrassed. Why are you embarrassed?"

"You wouldn't understand," said Desiree.

The Salesman raised a finger to his lips and all sound disappeared again, save the words being spoken on stage. Andi and Nica were both seated now, sitting on either side of the living room table, passing the box of lo mein between them.

"Do you throw yourself at delivery people often?" said Andi.

"I throw myself at just about everybody I get a chance to," said Nica.

"And why's that?"

"Because I can't be with the person I want to be with," said Nica.

Veronica stared across the way, listening to the play, but watching something else. Vern and Desiree were no longer holding hands. They sat only inches apart, but those inches might just as well have been miles.

"Okay," said Andi. "So, who do you want to be with?"

"My best friend," said Nica.

Andi gestured to door number one. "The one who's back there?"

"Yes."

"But why?" said Andi.

"I don't know," said Nica. "I guess because she completes me."

Andi scoffed, "You've seen *Jerry Maguire* one too many times."

"What?" said Nica.

"You haven't seen it yet?" said Andi. "You're not missing much. Anyway, that's what the fucking pretty boy Tom Cruise says to that Zellweger chick at the end of the movie."

"What have you got against Tom Cruise?" said Nica.

"Honey, I could write a book about what I've got against Tom Cruise."

"Okay," said Nica. "What's your point?"

"My point," said Andi, "is that you saying she 'completes' you is a bunch of bullshit. The only person who ever completes you is you. And putting that pressure on someone else... Man, that's some fucked up shit. God, do you know how many unoriginal, over-sappy, under-attractive men have tried to use that one on me since that movie came out?"

"A lot?" said Nica.

Andi stood, working herself up, stalking back and forth between her chair and the edge of the stage as she spat the rest of her monologue. "You bet your ass," she said. "I say, to hell with all this completion crap. Just come straight out and say you want to fuck and get it over with. The direct approach is so much more honest, and so much easier to deal with. If more men came up to me and said shit like, 'Nice shoes. Wanna fuck?' instead of this 'You complete me' bullshit, I'd be giving head a lot more often."

"Well," said Nica, pausing as the audience roared with laughter, "thank you for that insight."

"You're welcome," said Andi, sitting, flush from her speech. "Now, back to the problem at hand. You want to be with your best friend, but your fiancé is the one keeping a roof over your head."

"Actually," said Nica, "it's my dad who's paying the bills right now, though Tim has all these prospects, or something. Or so they tell me."

"Well, whatever," said Andi, gesturing to door number one again. "Those two have been off doing their thing for a long time now. Your fiancé and your friend," said Andi, "not your fiancé and your dad, of course. And they're going to keep doing their thing. The real question is, when are you going to start doing your thing, and when are you going to realize that whoever comes along for the ride is just—"

Veronica leapt to her feet and shouted "STOP!" and the audience was gone, the theater empty, except for the two actors on stage.

Nica and Andi cast glances at the Salesman, as if looking for instructions. Veronica turned to look at him herself and saw him nod them off. By the time Veronica looked at the stage again, they were gone.

The Salesman stood and made his way toward the door.

"It doesn't matter who's along for the ride?" said Veronica, stomping after him. "I'm no romantic, but that's a pretty fucking bleak outlook on love."

The Salesman shook his head as he stepped outside.

Veronica followed him, stumbling as she stepped out, not onto grass as she'd expected, but back onto the subway tracks.

"Why do you place such high stock in Desiree?" said the Salesman. "Why?"

"Do you know how deep it runs between her and me?" said Veronica. "Do you know how far back it goes?"

"To the beach?" he said, a note of disgust in his voice. "To you wet with desire for a girl in a bikini too skimpy for fourteen year old to wear? I see inside your head," he said, tapping a pair of fingers hard against his temple. "I know it all."

"No," she said, searching the darkness for the right place to take him, knowing it must be out there. "It goes back even further than that."

"Really," he said, snorting back a laugh. "Okay then. Show me."

6

ELIOT, TALLARICO & HOOK

The trains had stopped running for the night, so they made their way there on foot, emerging from the tunnel just outside Kenmore Square, then trekking down Commonwealth Avenue as the sun rose on an empty Back Bay.

"This is eerie," Veronica said to the Salesman as they made the turn near Packard's Corner, "like some movie about the end of the world."

The Salesman pointed to the sky. "No mushroom clouds," he said.

"Not with a bang but a whimper," said Veronica, smiling despite her aching feet.

"That's from *The Stand*," said the Salesman. "Right? From the mini-series they did on ABC?"

"It's from T.S. Eliot."

"Yes," he said, "but it's also from *The Stand*."

Veronica shook her head and sighed. Then she told him, "You're really nothing like him, you know."

"Who?" he said.

"My father," she said. "You're what I wish he was. Like the second draft of a song," she said, "after I've cut all the shitty parts, or at least most of them. After I've cut it down to three-oh-five."

The Salesman had nothing to say to that. No comment about her Billy Joel reference. No nothing. Whereas the real version, her father out there in the waking world, wouldn't have been able to shut up. Instead, the Salesman just kept on. And kept on keeping on. It wasn't until they got there, to 1325, that the Salesman said another word.

It began with a smirk, something so small she might not have noticed it had she not been staring at him the whole time and waiting for something. Anything.

"What?" said Veronica.

"I made good on my promise, didn't I?"

"Yes," said Veronica, as they started up the stairs. "You did."

"Do you know who used to live here?" asked the Salesman.

Veronica groaned, then decided to play along. "No," she said. "Who?"

"The Bad Boys of Boston," he said. "Aerosmith, that's who! And my brother, your uncle, he opened for them once upon a time."

"Did he now?"

"Sure did," said the Salesman. "Played bass. I think it was up at Canobie Lake, or somewhere around there."

"I never knew that," said Veronica, rolling her eyes, hoping he could not see what she was thinking right then and there.

"At any rate," he said, as they made their way into the apartment, as they blended into the bustling crowd within, "what day is this? What have you brought me here to see?"

Veronica took his hand and brought him into the living room, and then she tucked them away in a corner to watch.

Vern sat on the center of the couch, with Tracy on her lap, as laughing children circled around the two of them, and around the birthday cake that sat on their coffee table. The adults stood around Veronica and the Salesman, on the opposite wall, armed with cameras and camcorders. And as the crowd began to sing "Happy Birthday," Vern huddled close to her daughter. "Make a wish," she told Tracy, as they leaned toward the cake. And then they blew at the candles in unison, smoke blowing back at them, the scent of melting wax in the air.

All around Veronica and the Salesman, there came one flash after another. It felt like overkill, Veronica remembered, like she'd been thrust onto the red carpet of the Grammys in a tattered old set of pajamas. But for Tracy, who at three was already becoming something of a diva, it was heaven. She hammed it up, loving the attention, posing for this camera, and then that one, never noticing, as Vern did, that one of the paparazzi had stopped shooting altogether and had lowered her weapon.

Veronica and the Salesman looked, with Vern, at a frowning Desiree. Vern tilted her head and frowned back, and Des seemed to catch herself then, forcing a big, bright smile onto her face. But Vern knew there was something wrong.

The Runt crept up behind Vern and rubbed at her shoulders, while Tracy leaned forward on Vern's lap to swipe at the cake's frosting with a pair of eager fingers. Across the room, Desiree was slipping through the crowd, past Veronica and the Salesman, down the hallway, toward the bedrooms. And that was when curiosity got the best of Vern. She pulled herself out from under the Runt's grasp, set Tracy down on the couch beside her, and followed after her friend. Veronica took the Salesman by the arm and followed, too.

In the bedroom, Desiree stood by the window. She ran her fingers along the lacy fringe of the curtains that the Runt had picked out on that day, a little over three years before, when Vern had finally told him about the baby, when the size of her paunch had basically forced her to. He'd wanted to celebrate, and so he'd bought curtains at a K-Mart across the parking lot from the McDonalds where they'd been having lunch. "To remember this moment forever," he'd said, showing her the ugly things. And she had remembered. She didn't think her brain would ever let her forget.

"You didn't have to leave the party just to check on me," said Desiree.

Vern rounded the bed and took hold of friend's hand. "Are you okay?" she said.

Desiree turned and faced her, facing also the two onlookers she could not see. Her eyes were swollen and red. She leaned back against the wall, managing a weak smile. "Do you ever think about that night?" asked Desiree. "About New Year's Eve?"

"What about it?" said Vern, holding Desiree's face in her hands, wiping at the tears with her thumbs.

Desiree looked away, looked down. She tapped her fist against the window pane. "It was probably even earlier than that," she said. "Do you remember that canoe trip when we were twelve, when your dad took us way up into Maine?"

Vern nodded. "It was wicked cold."

"And he said, 'If you girls don't want to do this...'"

"But we'd already slipped into our life jackets, had already started arguing about who got which oar."

Desiree smiled. "We were a day into the trip, miles and miles away from the car, and away from civilization. It was so peaceful," she said. "I remember we saw a moose on the side of the river, just grazing."

"And then we hit those rapids," said Veronica, shaking her head.

"I fell overboard," said Desiree. "And it... it gets fuzzy from there. But on New Year's a few years back, when you kissed me, and ever since, I... I've started to remember."

Veronica felt a real physical change in her body then, could see that Vern felt it too, their pulses quickening, chests rising and falling with greater speed. "My dad thought you might have hypothermia," said Vern, picking up the story. "We set up the tents and he told me to go inside, strip us both down, and then to curl up with you in a sleeping bag, to keep you warm."

"For years," said Desiree, "I thought it was just a dream. But it was the safest and best feeling I'd ever had, you pressed up against me, holding me. And when you kissed me on New Year's..."

Vern looked like she was beginning to hyperventilate, and Veronica struggled to breathe right along with her. They inhaled deeply, trying to keep control.

"Calm down," said the Salesman.

"What?" said Vern to Desiree, unable to say more, hoping that Desiree would answer the question, would answer this question that Vern had been asking herself for more years than she could remember.

Desiree grabbed Vern by the back of the neck and pulled her close, pressing her lips to Vern's. And it took a moment for Vern to respond, took almost too long in fact, for Desiree was already pulling away by the time Vern opened her mouth to kiss her back. Suddenly, there were tears streaming down Vern's cheeks, but Veronica couldn't tell—couldn't remember—whether they were Desiree's or her own.

"Do we have to stay?" said the Salesman. "Haven't you proved your—"

But Veronica clapped a hand over his mouth and held him there, wanting him to see, wanting him to see it all.

Fingers tore at the buttons of Vern's blouse till it hung open at her sides. And Desiree seemed surprised that Vern's breasts were bare, though they must've gone shopping together a hundred times, though she must've known what she'd find. Veronica closed her eyes, could feel herself in Vern's body again, could feel Desiree's hands on her. They were uncertain hands, and cold to the touch, but they were soft, and careful, and they felt like they belonged there.

Veronica opened her eyes in time to see Vern pull Desiree away from the wall, in time to see them falling against the bed. She closed her eyes again as she watched Des's anxious fingers pushing Vern's skirt up, then she felt those fingers slip up along her legs, her thighs, her hips, and then finally, mercifully, to that warmest of places.

The Salesman struggled against her grip and Veronica opened her eyes. She tried to keep the Salesman's mouth shut, to keep him from saying whatever words might stop this. Together, they watched as Vern wrapped her legs around Desiree's back and squeezed, as Vern slipped her own hands underneath Des's turtleneck while a pair of lips pressed hot against her neck.

"ENOUGH!" shouted the Salesman. His voice was muffled by Veronica's fingers, but it was, apparently, clear enough, for everything went black once again, and they began to fall through the darkness.

"Don't you see?" said Veronica, as they dropped. "It could have been her and me! Did you ever even consider that?"

The wind around them was picking up now, as they sped along, but the Salesman's voice boomed over it. "Don't you remember what she said to you?" he said. "Before the baby was born? Don't you remember what she said to you, and where she said it, and where you were going?"

They landed in the back seat of a car, of Desiree's car, just in time to see Vern grab hold of Desiree's forearm and squeeze.

"Pull over," said Vern, closing her eyes, leaning her head back into the soft leather of the Cabrio's passenger seat. "I think I'm going to be sick."

Des flicked on the directional, and they all listened to the thing click and then pause, click and then pause, as they waited to turn. Veronica recalled that moment in *Peter Pan* where Captain Hook begins to hear the ticking and tocking that signal the return of his nemesis, the crocodile, come back to finish what it started with the mauling of his hand. The click of Desiree's direction was like that, these days—every time they turned in somewhere, it was to give Vern a chance to throw up without ruining the upholstery.

The car turned—a little too sharply, Veronica thought, the whole of her body sliding into the Salesman's, the whole of Vern's sliding into Desiree's—and then it rolled to a stop. Veronica stared through the windshield at the red brick and white woodwork of St. Mary's Church. Desiree shifted the car into park, pushing the stick forward with such force that Veronica thought she might break off the handle.

"Why are you so angry?" Vern asked her.

Desiree tapped her lacquered fingernails on the steering wheel.

"I'm feeling sick," said Vern, reaching to turn the heat down and the fan off. "Okay? I'm not fibbing."

Desiree stared down at the dash. "I know you're not fibbing. It's just that, if we could get to the doctor's office and get this over with, we wouldn't have to... *You* wouldn't have to deal with this anymore.

Vern slid her hand underneath her sweater and rubbed at her stomach. She pinched the loose roll of flesh just above the waistband of her sweats. Veronica remembered how her tummy had never felt so soft before, so pudgy. With her free hand, Vern plucked her can of Chelmsford Ginger Ale from the cup holder, the maroon and yellow aluminum glistening with condensation. The cup holders were positioned right in the path of the heater's vents, and Veronica could still remember the taste of the warm soda, could still remember wishing she hadn't left it there so long.

Desiree glared at Vern, shaking her head.

"What are you looking at me like that for?" asked Vern.

The car shuddered for a moment from the assault of the fierce February wind. Vern twisted the knob for the fan, bringing it back up to full blast.

"You know you're not supposed to eat or drink anything beforehand, don't you?"

"I could throw up all over your car," said Vern, sipping some more of her soda. "Would you prefer that?"

"I'd prefer that we get to the damn doctor's office before you have any more second thoughts."

Vern stared into the mirror on her side. Veronica stared too, watching gray puffs of exhaust rising up from the back of the car. "Second thoughts," Vern mumbled. "I'm on third thoughts now, and fourth thoughts..."

Vern unbuckled her seatbelt and shifted, turning her back to Desiree and leaning her side into the soft leather.

A pair of hands—cold, Veronica remembered—slipped up under the back of Vern's sweater, thumbs kneading at just the right spot. Vern exhaled, let go a low, soft moan.

"Don't you want to be done with this?" asked Desiree.

"It's not that bad," said Vern, grimacing and wincing, though Desiree could not see.

"I mean, why would you even want to have his—"

"It's not his," snapped Vern, twisting herself around. "It's mine."

Desiree slumped back into the driver's seat, rubbed her expert thumbs along her own furrowed brow.

"You know," said Vern. "I was on the phone with the nurse at the doctor's office, listening to all of their instructions—don't eat anything after midnight, bring someone to give you a ride home—and she started to sound like the teacher in Charlie Brown, her voice like an out-of-tune trumpet. But then, at the end, she says this one thing, and it's this one thing I can't get out of my head."

"What did she say?"

"She said, 'After the procedure, we'll remove the products of conception.'"

Desiree turned away, stared out through the windshield at the church's vast parking lot.

Vern clasped her hands over her stomach. "Doesn't that make it sound like they're taking out the garbage?"

"They've got to be clinical about it," said Desiree.

"But what do they even do with it when they're done, Des? Throw it in the trash with the half of their tuna fish sandwich that they couldn't finish? Flush it down the toilet like we did with goldfish when we were kids?" Veronica yelped, "What are they going to do with my baby?"

It was a question that Desiree couldn't answer, or didn't *want* to answer. She sat silent, her hand on the stick shift, waiting for instructions.

"You don't have anything to say?" said Vern, wiping at her eyes, her nose.

Desire wrapped one of her amber curls around a finger and began to twirl it. She bit down on her lower lip, closed her eyes.

Vern swatted at Desiree's hand. "Stop twirling your hair and say what you want to say!"

"You've made your decision, Veronica. What am I supposed to say?"

"I haven't made—"

"Yes," said Desiree. "You have."

"And you think it's the wrong one," said Vern.

Desiree shook her head and shifted the car into gear. "What does it matter, what I think? It doesn't matter," she said. "And it never will."

The Salesman opened his door and slipped out of the car. Veronica thought to stay, hoped they would take her away, but when the car didn't move, when the girls in the front said nothing further, she got out and she stomped over to the Salesman, who was walking toward the tree line, toward the shadows, his work here nearly done.

7

ODBODY & MARLEY

Into the woods he went, and into the woods she followed. But they weren't long amongst the trees. Soon enough, the sky darkened over them and all light seemed to fade out of the world. "It did matter," she yelled into the void. "It did!" But he said nothing back.

Out of the darkness then, there came one final flash, and Veronica saw herself climbing into the four-poster, beckoning the Runt to climb on top of her. She felt her soul swoon as he drove himself into her, breaking her open for the first time. She watched Vern wince, her brow furrowed, and she remembered how badly it had hurt, the Runt burying himself into her, the words of her Grampy's motto—"Honesty breeds happiness"—falling away like dust from the drill-hole.

The silence of the scene was eerie, but that was the way it had been. He didn't make any noise at all, the Runt, not even as he squeezed hold of her shoulders, his whole body convulsing against hers, that throbbing, awful piece of him seeping into her.

Neither of them said anything when it was done. He simply lay on top of her. And she, she turned away from him, her eyes focused on the nightstand, squinting, seeing something she was sure she wasn't seeing: the small square he'd taken from his wallet, the package unopened, untorn.

Quiet. It was so quiet that, like in the book her brother had sent her for Christmas, she could hear the snow falling faintly through the universe and, like herself, faintly falling.

The next few weeks were a blur, a video cassette on fast-forward. She watched herself pick up the phone and hang it up, pick it up and hang it up. God, he had called so many times.

And then there was the stainless steel bowl she kept by her bed, the one they used to make pancakes with, the bowl she seemed to fill at least twice a night when the nausea came.

And, of course, there was the trip to her Aunt Michaela's office for the test, a test that a pediatrician in their prim and proper town rarely had to give. All of it was like a blur until that afternoon in Desiree's car, on the way to another doctor's office, on the way to a doctor who would Wite-Out the mistake, who would give her one more chance to pass the final exam of her adolescence. It was all a blur until that moment of truth when she grabbed hold of Desiree's forearm and squeezed, until she asked Des to say what she wanted to say.

Once again, Desiree shook her head and shifted the car into gear. "What does it matter, what I think? It doesn't matter," she said. "And it never will."

Veronica closed her eyes. "It did matter!" she shouted again, into the darkness.

"I know it did," said the Salesman, stepping out of the void and back to her side, a flashlight in his hand.

"It mattered," said Veronica, "because she was the one who held my hair back during every hurried trip to the toilets at school. It mattered because I knew, even then, that she'd be the one holding my hand in the delivery room, the one reminding me to breathe. And it mattered because, even though I knew you were going to force me to marry the Runt, even though it would be his chapped lips that pressed against mine when the preacher said so, and not hers, it was she who I loved. She was my partner. She always has been. She always will be."

"But what a dangerous partner to have," said the Salesman. "Look what she almost made you do."

Veronica jabbed a finger into the Salesman's chest. "She almost made me see that she loved me!" she said. "She almost made me admit that I loved her. And what the hell would have been wrong with that."

"She almost made you kill your daughter."

"Is there a point to all this?" she asked him.

"Always," he said.

"You want me to say it," she said. "You want me to say it out loud."

"Yes," said the Salesman.

Veronica looked down, unable to look him in the eye, or maybe just unwilling. "Okay," she said. "Fine. I wonder. Every once in awhile, I wonder what it would be like if my daughter had never been..."

But she trailed off as she noticed the light rising around her, the subway platform materializing again before her very eyes.

"Yes," he said. "Go on. Had never been what?"

Veronica stared across the platform at her guitar case, sitting there all by its lonesome.

"You know," she said, "in all my time at Berklee, and all the time since, I only ever wrote one song worth keeping, one song worth a damn."

"But that wasn't what you did," said the Salesman. "Your thing was reinventing songs. There was the venomous dirge you made out of 'Here Comes the Hotstepper,' the contemplative cover of 'Freedom '90'—"

"But there was that one song," she said, turning from the guitar to face him.

"Which one?" he said.

"I don't remember much of it," she said. "I wouldn't let anyone record my originals because, you're right, they weren't my thing. But there was something about it," she said, pausing for a moment to listen to a guitar tuning in the distance, then deciding the sound was just a lie of the mind. "I'm sure the lyrics were dumb," she said, "but the meaning behind them..."

"Was what?" said the Salesman. "What was the meaning?"

"I wrote it for my little girl," she said. "It was a distillation. Of all this stuff, everything I wanted her to know about my mistakes, everything I wanted her to learn from them. And I don't know," she said. "Maybe it didn't work. Maybe it was terrible, but—"

The Salesman pressed a finger to her lips, then nodded over her shoulder. She turned around in time to see Vern begin to play the guitar, an empty pickle jar standing at her feet, a sleeping baby strapped to her back.

"You can't be president," sang Vern. "You can't be the boss. You can't make the rules, cause you don't know the cost."

And then came the chorus, and Veronica sang with her, "So, just sing, Angel. Sing, when you can't do a thing. When you can't do a thing, you just sing, Angel. Sing."

On either side of them, trains rolled into the station, the morning's first commuters making their way. A small crowd gathered as Vern delivered the next verse. "You can't hit that ball," she sang. "You can't make that toss. You can bear a child," she sang, and then she belted, pouring everything she had into the last line, "but you can't bear the cross."

All of them sang the chorus now, Veronica reaching for the

Salesman's hand as she did, intending to squeeze it, to thank him for this moment. But he was gone. She whirled about, looking for him amongst the onlookers, but he was nowhere to be found.

Vern finished the song. The crowd showered her with applause and her cup runneth over with tips. Then the people were gone, onto their trains, and then the trains were gone too, and just the two of them remained, Vern and Veronica.

"What are you waiting for?" said Vern, as she packed up her gear.

"What?" said Veronica.

"Which train?" said Vern. "Where are you going?"

Veronica raised an eyebrow. "Are you speaking in metaphors now, too?"

"No," said Vern, emptying the pickle jar of its bills, its change. "I'm just making small talk."

"Oh," said Veronica, confused, wondering if Vern recognized her or not, if this were memory or something stranger. "I, uh, I suppose I'm heading home."

"And where is home?" said Vern.

"You *are* speaking in metaphors, aren't you?"

Vern smirked. "Aren't we all?"

Veronica leaned against a pillar and sighed. "I'm supposed to tell you it's all going to get better, I suppose."

Vern laughed as she picked up the guitar case. "Sure. Maybe," she said. "That'd be a lie, and I'd know it. But that's what we're good at, you and me. So, go ahead."

"Okay," said Veronica. "It's all going to get better."

Vern smiled, then mocked, "You almost sounded convinced."

"I've got years more practice than you," said Veronica.

"True, that. But here's a question for you: better than what?"

"Excuse me?" said Veronica.

"It's going to get better than what?" said Vern, setting her free hand on Veronica's shoulder, looking her dead in the eye.

"Than life right now," said Veronica. "I mean, we're going to leave the Runt."

"I know we are," said Vern. "It's a matter of time. But that's just going to be different, right? Not better."

"Life without the Runt is way better than—"

"For you," said Vern, shaking her head and walking away. "But what about for Tracy?" she said, reaching a hand behind her back to rub the sleeping infant. "What about for your daughter? What is life going to be like for her, without her dad around?"

"I'll still be there," said Veronica. "And Desiree, too. And there are plenty of men in our life to play the father figure if she needs one. My brother, my cousin Michael. Things will get better, as she gets used to it."

"And when she gets used to it," said Vern, "what then? You don't think something else will come up? What about puberty for her, middle-age for you?"

"Watch it," said Veronica, offended.

"What about the stress of trying to cram all the years you should have spent with Desiree into the few years you have left?"

Veronica sighed. "Things will never get better," she said. "Is that your point?"

"No," said Vern, exasperated. "My point is that things are just things, that life is just life. It's never better or worse. It just is. And the sooner you realize that, the sooner you remember that—"

Veronica pulled herself out of her slouch, pulled herself away from the pillar that was holding her tired body upright. "Remember that?" she said. "Remembering that implies that I ever thought that to begin with."

"You have," said Vern. "In the quiet moments. In the, for lack of a better word, 'best' moments."

Veronica ran a hand over Vern's cheek. "When did I lose you?" she said. "When did I lose this part of myself, this hopeful, smiling part?"

Vern took Veronica's hand in her own. "You didn't," she said. "I'm still here."

"So," said Veronica. "What do I do?"

Vern stomped over to the station's exit. "To begin with," she said, pointing up the stairs with the guitar case, "you stop waiting for the piano of death to fall on your head. Instead, you leap up into the air to meet that son of a bitch and you play the shit out of it until you both come crashing down together!"

Veronica chuckled. "Did you just mix your metaphors?" she said.

"Hellifiknow," said Vern. "Our brother was the English major, remember? We just write silly pop songs," she said, crossing to stand in front of Veronica once more. "Don't ever think too hard about what they mean, or they'll stop meaning anything."

Vern set the guitar case between them, then pushed it gently into Veronica's hands. She gave her older self a bear hug and a peck on the cheek, and then she ran for the stairs.

Veronica slung the guitar case over her shoulder and followed the lead of the girl she had once been, the woman she would strive to be again.

III

BETTER OFF THAN THE WIVES OF DRUNKARDS

July 2000–April 2001

8

THE SECOND MAN ON THE MOON

The roller coaster came to a full and complete stop just after they'd slid past the loading area and the control booth, just as they'd descended the small slope that would take them into the ride proper. Ahead of their train, Veronica saw the tunnel of pulsing blue lights grow suddenly dark. She heard the sounds of the Space Mountain "energy surge" fade into silence. And then she turned around in her seat, as best she could with the T-bar restraint keeping her in place, and she asked her cousin, "What the hell is going on here?"

Michael shrugged and said, "Dunno."

The overhead lights came on, washing out the attraction's eerie ambience. A few moments later, one of the ride attendants came bouncing down the set of stairs just to the left of their vehicle, a heretofore invisible set of steps which descended down the slope and into the now bright white light of the tunnel.

"What's going on?" cried Veronica to the attendant.

"Nothing to be worried about, ma'am," he said with a smile. "You'll be on your way shortly."

Veronica groaned.

"Chill out," said Michael. "I'm sure they'll figure it out soon."

Veronica held her left arm up, twisted her wrist back and forth. "You see what time it is, Michael?"

"Oh, Jiminy Cricket," said Michael. "Not the damn schedule again."

"We're supposed to be leaving for the next park in twenty minutes, and we haven't even gotten in line for Dumbo yet, let alone ridden the stupid thing."

"If you were that concerned about Tracy getting to ride flying elephants, why didn't you have Des and Jenna take her over there while we were in here?"

"Because I want to see her on the ride," said Veronica. "You don't understand, Michael. Getting your kid on all the rides she wants to ride is only part of it. The other part, the bigger part, is being there to watch her enjoy them. That's what makes the interminable flight and the hellish heat and the exorbitant price of the watered-down soda all worth it. Otherwise, what's the point?"

"I think the point is to enjoy yourself," said Michael. "If you didn't want to ride this ride, we could've—"

Veronica turned her head to look him in the eye as best she could. "I wanted to ride Space Mountain, Michael. It was the one thing I wanted to do for myself. I've told you that."

"Okay," said Michael. "I'm just saying... If you wanted to do Dumbo instead, we could've come back another—"

Veronica sighed and turned away from him again.

"What is it about Space Mountain anyway?" asked Michael. "You've avoided every other thrill ride in the place."

This was true, Veronica thought to herself. She was much more of a "It's A Small World" kind of girl than a "Big Thunder Mountain Railroad" chick. But there was something about Space Mountain, something she wasn't quite sure she could articulate to Michael, not because it was all that difficult to explain, but because it sounded so silly when she explained it to herself.

Summer trips to Disney World had been something of a tradition for Michael's family. They'd gone four times that Veronica could remember, and they had the overstuffed photo albums to prove it. But for Veronica's family, the Disney experience had been a one-time thing. It was 1988, the summer before the Great Schism. Mom and Dad were doing their best impression of a happy couple, even carrying their act into the evening so that, after the first night, Veronica didn't bother to stay awake waiting for the sounds of their fighting to break through the thin hotel walls. Her brother Matt's performance wasn't so convincing, at least not to Veronica, who saw the glum expression that he wore at night, saw the ghost of that glumness in his face even when he smiled and played the part of the favorite son during the day.

Her most solid memory of that week—the rest of it was a blur of bright colors and the cheery sounds of children at play—was of the ride she and Matt took on Space Mountain, and of the aftermath of that ride.

She supposed now, with the power of hindsight at her command, that she should have known what was going on between the ride attendant and her brother as they snaked forward through the line. She remembered how odd it seemed to her that they kept staring at each other, but she also remembered writing it off as nothing more than boyish machismo.

"You nervous?" her brother had asked her once, or twice, or a half a dozen times. And now she realized, again through hindsight, that it had been as much a question for himself as it had been for her. As the attendant directed them to their car, there had been one last look shared between the two boys. And then Matt was back to his old sullen self. He made his way up front, and she sat behind him. They'd lost track of Mom and Dad, who'd probably been shunted off into a train on the other side.

It wasn't until they'd descended the slope, made their way through the tunnel of flashing blue light, and rocketed into the ride proper that Matt changed, changed for the moment and for good. As they rocketed through the darkness at thirty miles per hour, she heard a distinct change in his screams. They went from shrill yelps of terror to deep, guttural, almost primal bellows. He'd lost it. That's what she'd thought at the time. He'd flipped his lid. Matt screamed, "That the best you got?" as they hurtled down an unseen drop.

Veronica felt as if the very soul of her had lifted up out of her body for a moment, as they tumbled down, a heavy, leaden weight rising up out of her stomach and into her throat. And, for a moment, she was lost to the world. But then that weight came crashing back down into her, and she was back in that car, with her screaming sibling in front of her, and, try as she might to scream, she couldn't make a sound.

When they found Mom and Dad again, out in the center of Tomorrowland, Matt, breathless, told the lot of them that he was going back, that he wanted to ride it again.

It wouldn't be until later that night that Veronica would get the truth out of him. There had been no second ride. Instead, there had been a stolen kiss in a Tomorrowland bathroom, and a promise to meet up again before the week was over. Matt came back to the hotel room that night and confessed to Veronica who he was. "I like guys," he'd said. "And there's no use denying it anymore."

"Does this have anything to do with all that screaming you did on Space Mount—"

"Yes," he'd said. "A hundred times, yes. I mean, how many different ways could that ride have gone wrong, Veronica. And if you and I had died in there—"

"Died? Who dies on a roller coaster?"

"—if we had died in there, Veronica, think of how much in life you would have missed out on. And all because you were afraid, or because you were playing by someone else's rules about what you were allowed to do as a teenager, or as a girl, or as a boy who liked boys."

"You're a weirdo," she'd said. But the truth was that, even back then, she'd thought he might be right. There had always been so much to be afraid of in their family. Fear seemed to be the motivating factor in every decision their parents made. And she wasn't sure she wanted to live like that. She wanted to be rid of fear in the same way that he appeared to be. Or, well, if not in exactly the same half-crazed way, then in some way, in some other way.

And yet, here she was, twelve years later, still quivering.

From behind her, Michael said, "So, it's that Space Mountain fills you with a Zen-like sense of peace, is that it?"

"I was just thinking," she told him. "Did you know that the summer before Matt came out to the family, he came out to me?"

"I always figured that you knew before the rest of us," said Michael.

"It was after we rode Space Mountain," said Veronica.

"Well, listen," said Michael, "I hate to break it to you, but I kinda figured out the truth about you and Desiree a long time ago. You know, even if you've never come right out and said it, a straight girl can only go to so many Ani shows before she's a gay girl."

Veronica smirked back at him.

"So, you're hoping what?" said Michael. "That you'll somehow find the courage to run away with Des just as soon as we're done here? That she and you will take Tracy and go hide away in some lesbian coven in Idaho or some damned place?"

"I'm not sure Idaho is the first place a group of gay girls would think of to hide out."

"Why not? All those potatoes..."

"Potatoes?" said Veronica, not following.

"All natural, easy to carve, come in all different sizes..."

Veronica laughed. "Cuz, you've got problems."

"Hey," he said. "apparently, it runs in the family."

She sighed. "I have the divorce papers in my purse, Michael. Or, well, Desiree has them, because she's got my purse. And I kind of figured that if I was ever going to find the courage to sign on the dotted line, it might be here. Right here, after this ride."

"Oh," said Michael. "Well then, I'm gonna get out and push, because there is no way I'm letting them give you enough time to change your mind about this."

Veronica reached a hand back toward him, as far as it would go.

"Are you trying to hit me?" asked Michael.

"Grab my hand, idiot," she said, and he did.

She squeezed his hand and said to him, "It's going to be hard for Tracy, without a dad around."

"The Runt was never much of a father to begin with," he said.

"Do you think," said Veronica, "that you...?"

"What about Matt?" said Michael.

"He's got his own issues to deal with," she said.

"Father figures are overrated," said Michael. "Two women, you guys'll do it much better."

"But," said Veronica. "If she needs someone."

Michael squeezed her hand back, but didn't say a word.

The overhead lights went off with a quick flash.

"Oh boy," said Michael. "Here we go."

"You know what to do, right?" said Veronica.

"No," said Michael. "What?"

"When this thing gets going, you've got to scream. You've got to scream your damned lungs out."

"Ah," he said, sounding unconvinced, "the people who scream on these things—"

"Don't be judgmental, Michael. Give it a try. Scream like there's no tomorrow. Scream like you have nothing to lose. And then just scream because you feel like screaming."

"Okay," said Michael.

"Ready?" said Veronica, pulling her hand back. The tunnel of blue light began to pulse again.

"Sure," said Michael.

"Hands in the air?"

"Okay," he said.

The train slipped forward, down the hill. Light and sound pulsed around them. And then, as they rocketed forward into the darkness, they began to scream.

And it felt good.

9

THE OLD M'AM AND THE SEAMS

Veronica stood on a pedestal, chewing on a piece of bubblegum that had long ago lost its flavor. She watched the storefront window shudder in the November gale that raged outside and she sighed, wishing with all of her heart for just a moment of that breeze. Sweat dripped down along her bare back and down between her breasts. A spaghetti strap was sliding down her slick shoulder. On the couch in front of her sat two girls she hardly knew and the daughter who was becoming more of a stranger to her every day, each of them sweating as well, sleeves rolled up, sweaters discarded. And at her feet crouched a bony old seamstress, shivering in a shawl, fretting with the hemline of a dress that refused to fit, mumbling some kind of curse in some kind of old world tongue, the only kind of profanity which carried any weight anymore. Veronica gritted her teeth and swallowed her gum. It was going to be a while yet.

She was twenty-five years old, a tall shapeless mother-of-one in a slinky lilac gown that wasn't doing her worn-out body any favors. The same dress which had looked good on Mellie, the pleasingly plump sister of the bride, the same dress which the seamstress assured them, based on the measurements provided by email, would look stunning on Veronica's cousin Ashley, this dress seemed to want nothing to do with Veronica. A child-sized version of the ensemble even managed to make Tracy, Veronica's bookish tomboy of a daughter, look like some sort of princess, the heiress to the throne of the Purple Kingdom. But on Veronica, the dress just did not work. It hung on her like an undersized drape thrown carelessly over a coat stand. She had no hips to fill it out, and barely enough chest to hold it up. And yet, Tracy and Mellie would not cease showering her with compliments. "You look wonderful," said Mellie. "The most beautiful mom I know," said Tracy. Only Jenna, the bride-to-be, remained undecided.

"Jenna," said Mellie, "don't you think she looks good?"

Jenna frowned. "It's just not flattering on her, is it?"

Veronica could have kissed this girl, so relieved was she to finally have an ally.

The seamstress rose to her full height, her creaking joints crackling and popping as she did. She stepped backwards, away from Veronica, and sat on the arm of the couch.

"Do you see what I'm saying?" asked Jenna.

The seamstress chewed on the end of a pin. "I am not one to admit failure," she said.

"Oh," said Jenna, taking the seamstress's hand in her own, "that's not what I'm saying."

"But if ever I was to admit that my magic has left me," the seamstress continued, trailing off into a mumble.

Mellie frowned. "I still say she looks good," she said. Beside her, Tracy gave an exasperated sigh. The little girl picked up Veronica's pocket book, and began to rifle through it.

"What are you looking for, Trace?" Veronica asked.

"Nothing," said Tracy, continuing to dig. "Didn't you bring the Game Boy?"

"Auntie Ashley's old thing?"

"Yeah," said Tracy. "I was gonna play Tetris."

"We're almost done," said Jenna, smiling a weak smile at Tracy. "I promise."

Tracy pulled an envelope from the pocket book. "What's this?" she said.

"Put that back, please," said Veronica.

Tracy squinted, examining the return address. "This is from daddy's lawyer, isn't it?"

Veronica stepped down from the pedestal, and snatched the envelope away from her daughter.

"So," said Tracy, her face clenched into a frown. "That's it then."

"We've talked to you about this," said Veronica.

"You ruin everything," said Tracy, as she ran for the door, as she stormed out into the tempest.

HAIL FELL FROM THE SKY, each stone ripping into the gooseflesh of Veronica's arms like a spitball sent from the mouth of Heaven. She stomped through the muck on the side of the road, calling out her daughter's name, imagining the worst. Cars blazed by, hydroplaning here and there, kicking up a spray of cold, dirty water as they passed. Veronica stumbled in their wake, caught herself, and then continued on. Tracy would not have been so lucky. She was too small, too frail. In her mind's eye, Veronica saw a tiny body flying up over the hood of an SUV.

"Tracy!" cried Veronica, picking up the pace. "TRAY-CEEEEEE!!!"

She shook her head to try and get the image out, tried to

imagine Jenna and Tracy sitting at the snack bar of the Roller Kingdom again, the two of them splitting a plate of fries. It was an image that Mellie had painted for her while they worked to free Veronica from the shackles of her gown. And it was an image that made sense, she had to admit. It was right down the road, and Tracy did love it there, and, you know, why wasn't it possible that Jenna had found her before tragedy struck? Jenna had begun her pursuit before Veronica could even ask her for the favor. They were safe. That's all there was to it. And yet, Veronica couldn't help but sigh as she raced down the hill and toward the roller rink. She couldn't help but pause a moment before she opened up the door. Even if Tracy was alive, damage had still been done. The rift between them seemed more like a chasm now than ever before: deep, jagged, unbridgeable. Like the gash her brother had torn in the fabric of their family all those years ago, Veronica's attempt to be true had brought about a great schism of its own.

She opened the door and stepped backwards in time, back into the place that she herself had fled to so often, so long ago. The hall was dark and cavernous, the rink itself a halo of neon light at the center of the windowless purgatory. There were a dozen patrons, or thereabouts, and most of them were crowded around the outdated arcade games, the dusty old snack bar. Just like old times, there were only a handful of people on skates, and two of them, it turned out, were the two that Veronica was looking for. She leaned against the side of an out-of-order Pac-Man machine and watched them from the shadows.

Tracy whipped around the track as if trying to outrun the truth, or, as if, like Superman flying round and round the planet, she might be able to turn back time if she skated fast enough, hard enough. Veronica watched her daughter, and saw herself. In Tracy's eyes, there was such determination, such stubbornness, and such frustration. Tracy knew that this wasn't going to do any good, but she was going to do it anyway.

Jenna rolled off of the rink, and into the shadows. She came to a stop and bent over, hands on her knees, panting.

Veronica sighed. "She hasn't stopped since she got the skates on, huh?"

Jenna shook her head.

Veronica took a look at the skates. "We're the same size, right?"

Jenna nodded, rolling toward the nearest bench.

"She'll get over it," said Jenna, as she handed over the skates. "I know I did."

"How old were you?"

"Five, when my dad left. It was sad, but once I realized that there wasn't going to be any more yelling..." Jenna trailed off, managed a weak grin.

Veronica smiled, lacing the skates onto her own feet.

Jenna laughed. "Of course, with my mom's lousy taste in men, I've been through it three times now. So maybe I'm not the best person to ask."

Veronica stood, arms held wide at her sides, trying to keep herself upright. Tracy whipped by, a scowl on her face.

"Did you hate your mom?" asked Veronica.

Jenna sat silent for a second, and then she sighed heavy and hard. "I hated myself," she said.

That was worse, Veronica decided, so much worse. As she made her way out onto the rink, she couldn't shake Jenna's words from her mind. What if she, Veronica, had already done that kind of damage to Tracy? That would be unforgivable for certain, and maybe even unfixable to boot, and she didn't think she could live with herself if it were true.

Her little firecracker whipped up next to her, fuse burnt down almost to nothing. There was a little explosion in Tracy's high voice as she said, "How come you can't skate? Didn't you, like, live here when you were a kid?"

"I came on metal night," said Veronica. "Nobody ever skated. We sat in the booths, argued about the black album, head-banged to 'Bohemian Rhapsody'."

"Who's we?" asked Tracy. "You and daddy?"

"This was before I met him."

Tracy huffed and skated away. Veronica lowered her arms and stumbled forward. Before I met him—those were the magic words, and Veronica couldn't believe she'd been stupid enough to utter them. "Tracy!" she shouted, pushing forward hard, tripping, falling onto her face. It took her breath away, the impact of her body hitting the floor, the sight of her daughter continuing on as if nothing had happened.

They were in the backseat of Jenna's beat-up Chevette before Tracy uttered another sound, and, once again, it was nothing more than an exasperated sigh. Up front, Jenna and Mellie stayed quiet. And though she knew that now was neither the time nor the place, she couldn't help herself.

"What do you want me to say?" she said.

"I want you to explain something to me," said Tracy.

Veronica glanced over at her daughter, surprised at how much venom an eight-year-old could muster, wondering if she herself had ever sounded so mean when she was so young.

Tracy frowned, gulped something down, and then spoke. "If you and daddy were a mistake, then what does that make me?"

Veronica reached for Tracy's hand, but the little girl pulled it away.

"That's what I thought," said Tracy, turning away.

Veronica felt her eyelids grow heavy and hot. How could she make her see? How could she get her to understand?

When they got home, the Runt wasn't the only thing that was missing. Their apartment was empty, barren. All that was left was Tracy's bed, a single down comforter, and three boxes labeled 'Veronica's shit.' Tracy didn't say a word. She didn't throw Veronica so much as one nasty look. The little girl simply went to her room, sat on her bare mattress, and stared at the place on her wall where a poster of Sarah McLachlan had once hung.

Veronica read the note he'd left on the refrigerator without really reading it. She picked up her cell phone, ordered Chinese, and went back to her daughter's room to see how the kid was doing.

Tracy had opened one of the boxes. A photo album lay open on her lap.

"He brought most of your stuff to his new place."

Tracy nodded, flipped another page.

"He says the landlord expects us out by the end of the week."

Tracy looked up, her eyes a little swollen, a little red. "Where are we going to go?"

Veronica sat on the floor, leaned back against the wall. "Down the Cape, I think. The family's old summer house. Your grandfather will say no, but I think my Uncle Albert will overrule him."

Tracy gave her a little smile, then cast her gaze downward, her hand running over a crinkly page of the old photo album, smoothing it out.

"I'm sorry," said Veronica.

Tracy shrugged. "Whatever."

The doorbell rang and Veronica leapt up to answer it. By the time she returned with the enormous brown paper bag, Tracy had set the photo album aside and was examining a single snapshot. Veronica set their food down and sat down next to Tracy on the bed. She looked at the photo, a photo of Veronica and Desiree in their high school graduation gowns. Vern and Des were all smiles in the photo, the only evidence of their turmoil the glistening diamond on Veronica's ring-finger and the pregnant belly beginning to make itself known.

"Is it true that you're in love with someone else?" asked Tracy.

"What?" said Veronica.

"Daddy says that the reason you two don't get along is because you're in love with someone else. Is that true?"

Veronica bit down on her lower lip. She sat still and silent for a moment, but then, finally, she nodded her head.

"For how long?" asked Tracy.

"A long time," said Veronica.

Tracy ran a thumb over the photograph, left it hanging above Desiree's face. "Why didn't you marry that person then, instead of Daddy?"

"Because I'm a coward," said Veronica. And for a second, she thought of taking it back, she thought of revising her answer. But instead, because she knew it was true, and because she felt a weight lifting from her shoulders just by being honest, she said it again. "Because I'm a coward."

Tracy tossed the picture back into the open box, then slid to the floor. "Let's eat," she said. "Before it gets cold."

⁂ 10 ⁂

YOU'LL NOT BE BURIED IN MY TOMB

Veronica crouched at the foot of the Christmas tree, reaching under its lowest branches for the red metal stand that held the dying fir upright. Pine needles hailed down on her bare arm as she fumbled around for the first screw, her hand scraping against the trunk and slipping into the stand's soupy reservoir before she finally found it. She turned her face away from the shaking tree, squeezing her eyelids closed and biting softly on her extended tongue, and then, finally, she began to turn the screw.

Her father's heavy boots clunked along the living room floor. She felt the tree steady when the clunking came to a halt just to her left. And then, she heard his voice admonishing her. "You can't do that alone," he said. "The tree's going to fall on top of you. You'll get yourself killed."

"I was just getting it started."

"And besides," he said. "You're a guest here now. It's not your responsibility to clean up after your old man anymore."

Veronica sighed. She moved to the next screw.

"How is Tim?"

"I wouldn't know."

Robert grunted. "You can't even speak to the father of your child?" His voice trailed off. Then he grunted again. "What about when you drop Tracy off with him on the weekends? Like yesterday. Did you talk when you dropped her off then?"

Veronica shuffled herself around to the other side of the tree to work on the final screw.

"You don't even talk then?"

"We talk," she said. "But it's not exactly what you'd call a conversation."

Robert sighed. "Where did I go wrong in raising my kids? I mean, the two of you, you just... you seem determined to fuck up every good thing that's thrown at you."

"Done," said Veronica, ignoring him. "You can pull it out now."

"Oh," he said. "Okay. You just hold the stand then."

Robert groaned as he hoisted the tree out of the stand, and Veronica could hear him panting as he leaned it up against the wall.

"You want help carrying it out?" she asked him.

He looked up at her, then back down at the floor, and then he nodded.

They set the tree down on the curb, in front of his three overflowing garbage barrels, and beside the heap of flattened boxes they'd stuffed into his blue recycling bin. Robert put his arm around her, the first time he'd done that in years. And Veronica didn't like it. His glove, sticky with pine sap, clung to the shoulder of her pea coat. "I'm glad you came," he said. "I do wish you'd brought Tim, but—"

Veronica groaned. "I'm divorcing him, Dad. Please just get over it."

Her father wrenched his arm away from her and tended to a barrel in danger of tipping. "I like Tim," he said. "He makes an honest living. And he dotes on Tracy like any good father should."

"He's not her father," she said. "Michael is closer to a father than the Runt has ever—"

Robert stalked back toward the house. "I hate it when you call him that," he said. "He is your husband and the father of your—"

"He's neither!" she said, trudging after him through the snow. "Not anymore."

"And Michael? He's your cousin, not your... not a... and..." Robert trailed off, stopped to center himself, then found his heading again. "Michael is too young to be a father figure. And, besides, he's getting married, starting a family of his own with..." He trailed off again, his brow furrowing as he searched for her name. "That girl from Maine," he said.

"Jenna."

"Jenna," said Robert. "Sure. So, you can't count on Michael. And Veronica, you don't need to," he said, taking hold of her shoulders.

"Let go," she told him, trying to shrug him off.

"You've got Tim," he said as he let go of her, catching her drift a little later than she'd have liked. "You tell me: what's wrong with Tim."

"I'm not in love with him, Dad."

He stomped off again, reached down into the high snowbank as he passed it, balled up a clump of the stuff, and hurled it at the garage.

Veronica rolled her eyes and hurried after him.

The roar of the vacuum cleaner greeted her as she came in from the cold. Her mother was in her purple bathrobe, maneuvering the old Dirt Devil around the fireplace, getting it into every corner and crevice. The bathrobe was a plush, furry thing that hadn't fit her in five years. Lydia's body, which had never been what one would call trim or fit, at least not in Veronica's lifetime, had not withered, as Robert's had, as much as it had expanded. Like the overfull bag of the vacuum cleaner that she handled so deftly, it truly seemed as if she were about to burst.

From the kitchen came Robert's voice. "Coffee?" he shouted.

"You should buy her a new bathrobe," Veronica told her father. She took a steaming mug from him. "I mean, if you guys are going to pretend to play house again, why not go the whole nine?"

"You know, when I was running around the damned mall doing the Christmas shopping, I couldn't think of a damned thing. Not a damned thing." He sipped from his own mug and peered around the corner. "How could I have forgotten that she needed a new bathrobe?"

Veronica sipped at her coffee, but pushed it away almost as soon as it had touched her lips. One tiny slurp had been enough to scald the tip of her tongue, and it was bitter besides. "Dad," she asked, setting it down, "could I get some cream and sugar?"

"Did I forget?" he asked, picking up her mug for examination. "Christ, I'm sorry about that."

"It's okay."

He set down her mug on the countertop and opened the refrigerator. "Lot on my mind, I guess. You know how that goes, right?"

"I sure do," she said. "That said, I'm wondering if you've been to the doctor lately."

He scoffed. "I'm not losing my marbles, Veronica." He pinched open the top of the carton of cream and began to pour. "Tell me when," he said.

She held up her hand when he'd poured enough. In the living room, the vacuum stopped.

"Vern?" Lydia called. "Robert?"

"In the kitchen, Mum," Veronica shouted.

Lydia waddled in, smile on her face. She was much bigger since she'd quit the cigarettes, and Veronica saw that her father found it an effort not to frown. Closing the door on one bad habit, Robert had confided in Veronica, had just opened the doors to others. Lydia bought a donut with her morning coffee now, and at dinnertime she always made room for dessert. The holidays had been one night after another of pie and cookies and giggled "just one more"s. But what her father saw as folly, Veronica saw as good fortune. She remembered all too well the emphysemic hacking and wheezing of her grandfather near the end, and Veronica would much rather he had made the same trade her mother just had. After all, it was hard to hug a tombstone.

"Coffee?" Robert asked, holding up the pot.

Lydia waved a hand at him. "No, no, no. It's my New Year's resolution to start losing some of this weight," she said, rubbing at her belly. "I've put my mind to it."

She reached into the cavernous refrigerator and produced a gallon jug of spring water. Then she took her coffee mug—World's Best Grandma—down from the rack that hung above the stove, and she filled it to the brim.

Lydia came to the table, and sat beside her ex-husband, an exiled queen taking the throne beside her once and, perhaps, future king. And together, the two of them looked at their daughter, the princess who refused to play out the fairy tale ending they'd written for her, and they began to speak in unison, like some kind of Greek chorus trying to narrate for her how it was going to be. But before they could get a word out, Veronica backed away, dropping her mug into the sink, looking for an exit.

"I'm not going to listen to it," she said. "I should have known," she said. "I should have fucking known."

"Veronica," said Lydia. "All we're asking you to do is think of your daughter.'

"Think of Tracy," said Robert.

"I am thinking of Tracy!" shouted Veronica. "What you want me to do is repeat your mistakes, instead of learn from them."

"You think it was a mistake for me to stay with your father until you kids were grown up?"

"That wasn't a mistake," said Robert. "That's the way things should be done."

Veronica growled.

"Who's going to pay the legal fees?" Robert asked calmly.

"What?" said Veronica.

"Tim knows about you and..." He trailed off, seemingly incapable of saying Desiree's name. "Tim has evidence of adultery, Veronica. He'll bring that to court. He'll use it to win custody."

"He doesn't love her," said Veronica. "He doesn't want her."

"He does love her!" shouted Robert. And then, after a breath, he said, in a more measured tone, "And even if he doesn't, he'll take her just to spite you."

"To spite me?" said Veronica. "And that's the kind of man—"

"That's the kind of man you'll turn him into," said Lydia. "Believe me, Veronica. I know what the scorn of a woman can do to a man." She squeezed Robert's hand. "You're going to break the poor boy to pieces. He does love you."

"But I don't love him!" said Veronica. "I've said it again and again."

"Then who do you love?" asked Robert.

"I don't..." stuttered Veronica. "You know you don't want me to say her—"

"That's not allowed!" he shouted as he stood, knocking over his stool. "You can't... You..." His face was turning red as he struggled to find the words. "Not the both of you," he said. "Your brother, I can't do anything about him anymore. But you... No, not the both of you."

"I'll find the money myself," said Veronica. "If the Runt wants to make this a war, then Desiree and I will—"

"Stop!" he said.

"Stop what?"

"Don't say her name in front of me," said Robert.

"Robert," said Lydia, wrapping her hands around one of his forearms. "You should calm down."

"I'm bringing her to Michael's wedding," said Veronica. "She and I are—"

"You and her are nothing!" he screamed. "And you'll never be anything. This world won't let you be. And I—"

"This world, Dad? It's the year 2000."

"I won't let you be!" he shouted. "I want better for you, Veronica. I demand better of you."

"Can't you just accept—"

"The day I accept that is the day that I..." He trailed off. "You won't just be breaking Tim's heart," he said. "You'll be breaking mine, too."

"That's not fair," said Veronica. "That's not what I want to—"

"Love is never fair, Veronica. You should know that by now."

And with that, he walked away, sliding open the glass door behind him and stepping out onto the deck. Lydia, still in her bathrobe, still in her bare feet, stepped outside to join him.

Veronica watched her mother wrap an arm around her father's waist. She watched him return the favor. And then she felt sick to her stomach.

"The house," she said finally, because that was the whole reason for the visit, for the show she'd tried to put on. The performance she'd obviously bombed. "The house down the Cape," she repeated, clarifying.

"You moved in a month ago," he said, still not looking at her.

"Uncle Albert gave us the key," she said. "And yes, we've been living there. But I guess, I guess I wanted your blessing."

He grunted, then said, "What am I supposed to say?"

She stared at his back and imagined he was the Salesman instead, the version of him that she'd dreamed up a year ago. The Salesman might not have given her a blessing, but he would've found some roundabout way to let her know that he at least wasn't saying no.

"Are you going to try and kick us out?" she asked him. "I guess that's what I want to know."

"It's a long drive," he said, but did he mean that it was too long for him to drive to evict them? Or did he simply mean that she had a long drive ahead of her, and that it was time for her to go?

Veronica didn't ask. She turned and headed for her room, itching to pack, dying to get out of there.

11
WHAT AN ARTIST DIES IN ME

There were five naked blondes on his living room floor, all of them clustered around a solitary brunette, fully clothed, with a missing tooth.

"Hey Tracy," said Veronica, as she stepped into her ex-husband's apartment, "why are they all—"

"Slumber party," said Tracy, cutting her mother off.

"A naked slumber party?" asked Veronica.

"Why not?" said Tracy. "You and Desiree have been having naked slumber parties for years. At least that's what Daddy says."

Veronica looked over her shoulder, back at Desiree, who was still standing in the hall. Des shrugged. Vern gave her a frown.

"You almost ready to go?" asked Veronica.

Tracy nodded, reached for her backpack, and then began to pack the dolls away.

As Veronica moved to collect Tracy's dirty clothes from the arm of the couch, her sleeping bag from the floor, and her books from the coffee table, she looked around for signs of her ex. "Where is he?" Veronica asked.

"Hiding," said Tracy.

From the doorway, Desiree asked, "He get you anything cool for Christmas?"

"Yeah," said Tracy. "A new doll. A really big one."

"How big is big?" asked Veronica. "We don't have a lot of room in the car."

"Oh, she's not coming with us," said Tracy. "She was a present for both me and Daddy."

"You're sharing a doll with him?" asked Desiree.

Tracy nodded. zipped up her backpack, and slung it over her shoulder. "I'm ready to go," she said.

Veronica looked at Desiree. Desiree arched an eyebrow as she looked back.

"Do you mind," said Veronica, "if we see the doll before we go?"

Tracy shrugged. "Sure," she said. "She's in my old room."

Veronica and Desiree followed Tracy down the hallway, whispering to each other as they went.

"Why is it her 'old' room now?" asked Desiree. "Why was she sleeping on the living room floor?"

"Why do you think?" said Veronica. "The Runt doesn't want her here. He never did. He only moved her things here in the first place to inconvenience me."

In front of them, Tracy pushed the bedroom door open, then stepped aside to let them in.

When Veronica saw what was inside, she had no words.

Desiree had three: "What the hell?"

"Isn't she pretty?" said Tracy.

The doll was not just big; it was life-size. It reclined on the bed that had once been Tracy's, head resting against the wall, a cowboy hat angled down over its face. It was a blonde, the doll, just like Tracy's toys. But, mercifully, it was not nude. It wore cowboy boots, a denim mini-skirt and a light blue tank-top pulled taut over a pair of enormous tits. Its skin was smooth and tanned and—Veronica couldn't resist—soft to the touch.

Desiree had knelt down beside the bed, was holding one of the doll's hands in her own. "It has a French manicure, Vern. I mean, a real French manicure. These look like real..." She trailed off, stared at the thing's chest. "And look at those things!" she said.

Veronica stepped around Desiree, toward the thing's head. She lifted the brim of the hat up, gasped, and took a step back.

"Ow!" yelped Desiree. "You stepped on my—"

"Did you see her face?" asked Veronica

"It," said Desiree. "It's an it, not a her."

"Can you take Tracy outside?" asked Veronica.

"Absolutely," said Desiree. "This is creeping me the hell out."

"What's so creepy about her?" said Tracy, as they disappeared down the hall.

Veronica peeked out after them, made sure they were gone, then lifted the hat off of the doll's face once more.

It was so real, so eerily real, except for that docile face. That was the sort of look that only happened in fantasies, the sort of look that said, 'Do with me what you will.' Veronica shuddered to think of what the Runt had done.

She ran her hand over the doll's blushed cheeks, through her blonde hair, across her pink lips. Then she stopped. She pushed gently on the lower lip, just to see, and the doll's jaw moved; her mouth opened. Veronica slid a finger over the tongue. It was wet.

"Christ," said Veronica.

She looked back at the door, then at the doll.

"Fuck it," she said, closing the door.

She kneeled down at the side of the bed and pushed the skirt up the doll's hips, revealing a pair of plain cotton panties to match the tank top. Then she pulled them to one side and found herself gasping again. There was a small triangle of pubic hair and beneath it a pair of perfectly sculpted labia.

"No way," she said to herself as she ran her fingers over them. "No way," she said again as she parted them. "Oh my God," she said as she slid two fingers inside.

Behind her, the door opened.

"I assure you," said her ex-husband. "She's not your type."

Veronica stood and shook a slick finger at him. "This is nuts."

"Which part? The part where I've replaced you with 'the world's finest love doll' or the part where your daughter had a tea party with her this morning."

Veronica plowed past him into the hall.

"Yeah, go ahead and run away," he said. "Don't finish it."

"Finish what?" she asked, searching the living room to make sure that Tracy had not forgotten anything.

"This," he said.

"It is finished," she said. "We're finished."

"Oh no, we're not. There's still one thing left you have to say to me. And if you've never had an excuse before now, now you do."

"What, Tim? What am I supposed to say?"

The Runt laughed. "Tell me I'm not allowed to see her anymore."

"I don't get to decide that," said Veronica, heading for the door. "The judge—"

"Fuck the judge!" he said, getting in her way. "You know what the judge will say when you bring this to him, when you tell him I let our daughter play house with a sex doll. You know what he's going to say. So, say it yourself. Stop letting other people do the talking for you."

"Get out of my way," she said, balling up a fist, just in case.

"Say it," he said.

She swung at him, fist connecting with ear, and he went down, runt that he was.

"It's not just the judge's decision," she told him, as he lay prone, whimpering. "It's Tracy's. I can't make that decision for her. I won't."

She stepped over him and headed for the stairs.

THAT NIGHT, in bed, Desiree turned to Veronica, shaking a book in her general direction, and asked, "Have you read this?"

Veronica gave the book's dust jacket a once-over, then nodded. "I grew up with an uncle who was obsessed with that band, then I lived in their old apartment for eight years. So, yeah, I've read it."

"Listen to this," said Desiree. "This is gross. And I quote, 'The album title worked on two levels. The first was the old biker ritual where a guy had to go down on his menstruating old lady before he could get his wings.'"

Veronica smiled. "It's pretty obscene, I'll give you that."

Desiree feigned a shiver, then closed the book. "I mean, how did they even prove it to the guys? Did they have to come out of the back room with a red mustache? And who was to say that they didn't use fake blood? Was there some sort of arbiter who checked the woman beforehand just to make sure?"

"I think you're overthinking this," said Veronica.

"All I'm saying," said Desiree, "is that you better not come near me when I've got mine."

"I know," said Veronica, with a chuckle. "Besides, we're all synced up now anyway. When I've got mine, I'm not even thinking about sex. Can't even stomach the thought of it."

"Good," said Desiree.

"You have to admit," said Veronica. "It's not nearly as gross as fucking a souped-up mannequin, though, is it?"

They chortled, collapsing against each other. Veronica pressed her face against Desiree's chest, felt her lover's laughter pound through her tired brain like a balm. She closed her eyes.

"Why didn't you tell him it was over, Veronica? That he wasn't allowed to see her anymore?"

"It's not my call," said Veronica.

"But he's dangerous, Vern. He shouldn't be around her."

"He's disgusting," said Veronica. "But he's not dangerous."

"He doesn't even want to be her father," said Desiree. "You said so yourself."

"But she wants him," said Veronica. "And as long as he's still Daddy to her, that's all that matters."

THEY WERE HEADED NORTH on Route 3 and driving past Plymouth when, from the back seat, Tracy asked, "Why didn't Desiree come with us today?"

"Well," said Veronica, "because we'll need the extra room for the ride home."

"For what?" asked Tracy.

"Your doll," said Veronica.

"You mean the big one?"

"Yep," said Veronica.

"But it's Daddy's, too."

"You don't think he'll let you borrow it?"

Tracy didn't answer. Veronica adjusted her rear-view mirror to get a look at the back seat.

"You think he won't share like he said he would?" asked Veronica.

"I think he likes the doll more than even I do," said Tracy. "Is that weird?"

"I don't know," said Veronica. "Do you think it's weird?"

Tracy was silent again. Then she said, "Maybe. Just a little."

"Well, I guess all you can do then is ask and cross your fingers."

"I hope he says yes," said Tracy. "Oh, and if he does, do you think Desiree would let me borrow one of her bikinis so I could take the doll to the beach?"

"It's January, sweetheart. Nobody's going to be at the beach."

"Oh, but the kids from the neighborhood, they'll see. And they'll come. And it'll be so cool. We'll all take pictures with her, us in our snow pants and her in the bikini!" Tracy began to laugh.

And because it was her daughter, and because that girl's laugh was as infectious as any plague the world had ever known, Veronica laughed with her.

BEFORE VERONICA LET Tracy out of the car, she made her promise to ask about the doll first thing.

"Will do," said Tracy. She pecked Veronica on the cheek and skipped up the steps of the apartment house. "See you in a couple of hours," said Tracy, waving over her shoulder.

"Bye!" called Veronica, checking the dashboard clock, then sighing. "Let's hope old habits really do die hard," she said to herself.

It took ten minutes for Tracy to come running back down the steps, her face pale except for her red eyes. She opened the front door and slipped into the shotgun seat, something she never did, even when Veronica gave her permission.

"Let's go," said Tracy.

"What happened?" asked Veronica, as Tracy slammed the door,

as The Runt raced out of the building. He was shirtless, his hair disheveled, a pair of plaid boxer shorts all that covered him.

"He was on top of her," said Tracy. "And he was... He was moving up and down. And..."

The Runt stopped at the foot of the stairs and stared at Veronica. She watched his shoulders tense, his chest rise and fall. He clenched his fists. Come get us, Veronica dared him in her mind. Come and get us.

"I don't think he was expecting me, Mum. Was he expecting me?"

"I don't know what he was expecting," said Veronica. *But he got what he deserved*, she thought to herself. He got what he deserved.

"I don't want to see him anymore," said Tracy.

"Okay, sweetheart," said Veronica, buckling Tracy in. "If that's what you want."

12

IN THE MOOD FOR A MELODY

That year it was Veronica's job to deliver the flowers to Grammy's grave. Everyone else was busy with preparations for her cousin's wedding and she was the one living in the Cape house anyway—the house that had been Grammy and Grampy's—so it just made sense. But her car was the worst, and there was a snowstorm on the way, so she couldn't wait for Desiree to arrive that evening with her everlasting Honda, and that was how Veronica and her daughter ended up broken down in the parking lot next to the Congregational Church, God's steeple casting a shadow over her as she took the Lord's name in vain.

"Mum," said Tracy. "Am I going to miss school? How am I going to hand out my valentines?"

Veronica laid her head down on the steering wheel.

"Do we have money for a tow truck?" said Tracy.

Veronica cast a glance over at the dozen red roses sitting on the passenger's seat. Then, she sighed. "Not anymore," she said.

"How about breakfast?" said Tracy.

Veronica sat up and searched for change. She dug between the car's seat cushions, plumbed the depths of the glove box, and fished around the cubby next to the cigarette lighter. "We've got enough for Dunk's," she said.

In his last months, her grandfather had made a request of the family that he called "simple": every Valentine's Day, place a dozen red roses on the grave of his late wife, their grandmother. It was a tradition he had begun early in their courtship, that he had continued on with after her death, and that he didn't want to imagine ending when he was gone.

"But isn't the snow just going to kill them?" said Tracy as they lay the flowers down.

"Yep," said Veronica.

In the coffee shop, they ate donuts and shared a hot chocolate. Tracy had a jelly and Veronica had a chocolate honey-dipped. There was a song on, coming over the shop's speakers, and Tracy sang along.

"How do you know the words to this?" said Veronica.

"I don't know," said Tracy.

Veronica frowned at her. "You don't think it's a little inappropriate?"

"Why?" said Tracy.

"Well, for one, your love doesn't cost a thing because it's not for sale yet."

Tracy sighed, kept singing.

"And for another," said Veronica, "do you have any idea what 'all the things' are 'that money can't buy'?"

"Love, Mum. Love. That's what The Beatles say, anyway."

Veronica smiled. "Well, I'm glad you've got taste some of the time."

They walked back past the car on their way home. Tracy's music player lay on the back seat. It had been a Christmas gift from the Runt, a costly piece of plastic about the size of a CD player that stored a hundred hours of digital music. Digital. What did that even mean? Veronica wondered, suddenly, how mixtapes would work with a thing like that. In seven or eight years, when boys were trying to woo Tracy, what would they do? Email her a bunch of files? What would they do for liner notes? Type them? Where was the romance in that?

"You want to bring your Nomad with us?" said Veronica.

"Oh my gosh," said Tracy. "I can't believe I forgot it."

The first flakes fell during their walk down Chatham Road, but it wasn't until they turned onto Deep Hole that things got miserable.

"Those poor flowers," said Tracy.

"I know," said Veronica.

"It's really romantic, though," said Tracy.

"Sure is," said Veronica.

"What's the most romantic thing you ever did for Desiree?"

Veronica smirked and snickered. Leaving the Runt when it made no financial sense to do so, she thought.

"What made no financial sense?" said Tracy.

"Did I just say that out loud?" said Veronica.

"You mumbled something," said Tracy.

"I guess I've never made a real, big, romantic gesture," said Veronica. "Got any suggestions?"

"You should write her a song," said Tracy. "A really good one."

At the piano that afternoon, in the cold dark of Grampy's living room—her living room now, she had to remind herself—Veronica played in circles, searching for the next chord. Each time she came round to it, the place where the bridge should have been, she found herself going back to the beginning. It grated on her, this timidness. She had never been this tentative with her guitar, and though it had been ages since she'd sat on this bench and plucked away at the old upright, since those summer days when Grampy would break out his trumpet to accompany her, she couldn't remember ever being so scared.

She slapped both hands down on the keyboard, her lead foot lowering the boom on the sustain, and she closed her eyes, letting herself be swallowed up by the wall of noise. She leaned her forehead against the rough wood, unpolished for almost a decade now, since before Grampy died. It was cool against her skin and it was only then, as she felt her flesh slip into the piano's ornamental grooves, that she noticed the sheen of sweat that had covered her. Down the hall, a door slammed open and the hall light flashed on. A pair of feet shuffled toward her.

"That was it!" said Tracy.

"That was it?" said Veronica. "That was garbage."

"Nuh-uh," said Tracy. "It was pretty, except for the end. Just needs words."

Veronica turned to face her daughter, straddling the bench as she did. "The words are the hardest part, Trace. There's a reason I only do cover songs."

"What about that one you sang to me when I was a baby?"

"That was one song," said Veronica. "One song out of ten years worth of trying."

Tracy gave a heavy sigh, shook her head, and stalked off toward her bedroom again. Once the door slammed shut, Veronica got back to it.

Desiree walked in ten minutes later.

"Hey," she said. "Why'd you stop playing?"

"I don't know," said Veronica.

"That was one of my favorites," said Desiree. "I haven't heard you play that in years."

Veronica lifted an eyebrow at her lover.

"What?" said Desiree. "That was the one you wrote for your brother's play, right? The one back in high school?"

"You've heard that song before?"

"Yes," said Desiree. "It was the song the troubadour sang to Sleeping Beauty to try and wake her up."

"After all the kisses had failed," said Veronica.

Desiree sat down beside her on the bench. "I loved that play so much," she said.

Veronica set her fingers back on the keyboard, trying to remember the rest of the song.

"I think most people were too dim to figure it out," said Desiree. "But not me. I got it. And when the princess woke up for that moment, just after the singer had admitted defeat and left. God, that got me every time."

"Every time?" said Veronica.

"Yeah," said Desiree. "I went every night the weekend it played."

Veronica ducked her head. Then she took Desiree's hand in her own and squeezed.

"What?" said Desiree. "What's wrong?"

"You don't have to work at it," said Veronica. "You don't have to work at loving me."

Desiree gave a brief laugh. "And you have to work at loving me?"

Veronica looked up. "That's not what I meant," she said. "It's just that... it's so hard sometimes to do the right thing, to say the right thing. And then I look around at people like you, like my grandfather—as hokey as it was, his roses, they were his thing, and he believed in them, and it worked."

Desiree worked her hand free of Veronica's, then placed Veronica's hands back into their positions on the piano. "Play me the song," she said.

Veronica shook her head. "I don't know it. I can't remember the bridge."

Desiree hummed the tune. She was off-key, but she got the point across.

"That was it?" said Veronica. "That's so damned obvious. How did I not—"

Desiree set two fingers to Veronica's lips. "Just play," she said.

"But the words," said Veronica.

"Make them up," said Desiree. "Those I can't remember."

So, Veronica played. She looked out the window, at the snow falling faintly and faintly falling, wondering where those words were from, that turn of phrase. It wasn't hers, she knew, but she sang it anyway. Always cribbing from somewhere, always propping herself up with the work of someone else. She shook her head, and was about to stop. But then Desiree laid her head upon Vern's shoulder. And that was enough to keep her going.

13

GLORY, THE GRAPE, LOVE, AND GOLD

At seventeen, somewhere between four and five months pregnant, as a great big fuck you to the rumor mill, Veronica closed out a talent show with a scorching guitar solo she played whilst standing atop her high school's grand piano. And her life as a musician had been pretty much downhill from there. A few months later, she married the sad sack—*the runt*—who knocked her up. Sure, her father paid for four years at Berklee in exchange for her "loyalty"—whether to the Runt or to her dad's heteronormative stance on love and marriage, she was never sure—but she'd never had enough time to really learn anything, despite how much she was taught.

"It was actually the middle school's piano," Veronica told her daughter as they loaded her gear into the auditorium.

"You mean that one up there?" Tracy asked, pointing at the stage.

"Yep," said Veronica, as they walked the aisle. "When they built the high school across the street in the seventies, they forgot to build an auditorium. Or else they were being cheap and figured they could just keep on using this one over here."

"So, wait," said Tracy, huffing, straining under the weight of a guitar case she shouldn't have tried to carry herself. "Did this building used to be the high school?"

"Yes," said Veronica, plucking the case from her daughter's hands. "Until 1974. My Uncle Albert was the last class to graduate here."

"So," said Tracy, collapsing into a seat in the front row, "the piano could still technically be the high school's, depending on how old it is."

"The piano's not that old," said Veronica, hoisting her stuff up onto the stage. "It would have to be older than me."

"Oh," said Tracy. "And that's pretty old."

Veronica did not correct her.

Up on stage, Vern's cousin Michael was giving instructions to the members of his old high school band. They were reuniting for what would be the penultimate event of Wedding Week: a concert on the same stage where they'd played their first gig many moons before. In her head, Veronica did the math. Tracy had been two and a half then, and Veronica's biggest accomplishment to that point in her career at Berklee was the venomous dirge she'd made of Ini Kamoze's "Here Comes the Hotstepper."

Veronica slumped into a seat beside her daughter.

"You know," said Tracy, "they're pretty awesome."

"You've heard them before?" asked Veronica.

Tracy dug around in her backpack and produced her Nomad, headphones coiled around it. "Yep," she said, patting her music player. "I have their demo tape and their seven inch."

Veronica turned to face her daughter. "And how, may I ask, did you come upon those? Napster?"

"No way," said Tracy. "Too dangerous over there now. I'm using Kazaa these days."

"So, you stole your uncle's music?"

Tracy groaned. "How could I steal it if it's not for sale anywhere? You're crazy sometimes."

Veronica mussed Tracy's hair. "It runs in the family," she said, as she watched her cousin descend from on high to mingle with the commoners.

"Hey," said Michael.

"Hey yourself," said Veronica.

"What you listening to?" asked Michael.

Veronica turned to look at Tracy, who had slipped her headphones on. "Tracy, take those off. That's rude."

"How's it rude?" said Tracy. "I'm listening to his band!"

"But we're about to play," said Michael, chuckling.

"Really?" said Tracy, pressing play on her Nomad. "Because it looks like you're about to talk."

TRACY'S favorite song by Gideon's Bible, Uncle Michael's band, was the one they rehearsed first with Veronica. It was called "Mistake," and though she wouldn't know what it was really about until years later, when she wrote an explication of it in high school, she had a sense, even at eight years old. The growl of her uncle was what got that across, the palpable anger in every hiss and snarl. "He was a mistake," roared Uncle Michael, "she was a mistake," he continued, "and I was a," he screeched, trailing off as the guitars kicked in.

And oh, those guitars. Veronica's was solid, a foundation on which to build upon, but the other girl on guitar, she was fierce. Her name was Robin, and Tracy had heard she and Uncle Michael used to date. Tracy looked around the auditorium for Jenna, the girl

Michael was going to marry, to see if she looked jealous. She didn't. She had a smile on her face, was nodding her head to the beat. Nope, she didn't look jealous at all. But she should have. Dancing was cool—that's what Jenna did; she danced—but to shred on a six-string, that was something else.

When the band broke for fifteen, Robin grabbed the seat beside Tracy and sat down. "I hear you're a fan," said Robin.

Tracy ducked her head, nodding. She was sure she would cry or faint or otherwise embarrass herself if she looked Robin in the eye. She had listened to little else besides Gideon's Bible since finding their stuff online a month before. Aside from "Mistake," the songs Robin sang were the ones she listened to the most.

On stage, Veronica sat at the piano and noodled away at the song she'd written for Desiree back on Valentine's Day. She looked at her fingers as she played, then looked up at the ceiling, but never out into the empty auditorium, never at any of the people lurking in the wings.

"Your mom has no idea how good she is," said Robin. "Does she?"

"She says you put her to shame," said Tracy, focusing her gaze on the screen of her Nomad, on the flashing battery indicator.

"Really?" said Robin, with a chuckle. "Before you showed up, I was telling the guys how jealous I was of her, how nervous I was to be playing next to the one and only Veronica Silver."

"Nervous?" said Tracy, finally looking at Robin. "You?"

"Oh yeah," said Robin. "The whole thing makes me nervous, really."

"Because you and Uncle Michael used to date?"

Robin looked at Tracy, gave her a smile. "That's part of it, sure."

"Hmm," said Tracy.

"Hmm?" said Robin.

"I'm trying to decide something," said Tracy.

"What's that?" said Robin.

"Who's the Desiree in this story? That's what. Is it you, or is it Jenna?"

Robin raised an eyebrow. "Is Desiree the good guy or the bad guy?"

Even after all these months, Tracy hadn't decided the answer to that question yet. So, she said, "Neither. She's the Desiree."

WHEN VERONICA LOOKED up from the piano, Tracy was in deep conversation with Robin. It was a strange sight, Robin sitting sideways in her chair, knees tucked up under her chin, listening intently to the story Tracy was telling her. Even in her street clothes —torn jeans, a red flannel, and an *Appetite for Destruction* tank top— she looked like a rock star. But sitting the way she sat, nodding along as she stared into the eyes of the little girl holding court before her, Robin also looked like she might just be a cool babysitter, the kind you hoped to get as a kid, but were scared to have hired as a parent.

"What do you suppose they're talking about?" Michael asked Veronica as he sidled up beside her.

"Surely, they're addressing the injustice of Janet Jackson topping the charts again," said Veronica.

"Good call," said Michael. "I was thinking they might be tackling the sociopolitical realities of electing a crackhead President of the United States."

Veronica laughed.

"You ever worry," said Michael, "about the world we're leaving behind for her?"

"I ain't leaving shit behind yet," said Veronica. "I'm not done with the world myself."

"You know what I mean," said Michael.

Veronica wrapped her arm around Michael's shoulders and gave him a squeeze. "I do," she said.

Out in the front row, Robin was waving them over. "Michael!" she shouted. "Veronica!" And then she turned, searching the seats for someone else. "Jenna!" she cried, waving her over, too.

They congregated around Tracy, who was biting her lip and tapping her sneakers against the seat, her knees tucked up under her chin now, just like Robin's.

"What's up?" asked Veronica.

Robin looked at Tracy and nodded to her, as if to say, go ahead. But Tracy said nothing.

"Trace," said Michael. "Did you want to tell us something?"

"She wanted to ask us something," said Robin.

Tracy shook her head in a silent no.

"Okay," said Robin, looking at Tracy, as if for approval. "You want me to say it?"

It took Tracy a moment, but she did nod.

"Okay," said Robin. "Tracy is wondering who the Desiree is in Michael's story: Jenna or me."

Veronica felt her jaw drooping. She looked over at Jenna, wanting to apologize, but not wanting to hurt her daughter's feelings by saying "I'm sorry" out loud. It was a valid question, she supposed, just phrased poorly, and perhaps not something Tracy should have asked one of the parties involved.

"Wow," said Michael, leaning back against the edge of the stage. "I'd never thought about my story having a Desiree in in it."

"Well," said Veronica, attempting to lighten the mood, "your story does have a Desiree in it, but that's a whole other chapter."

She looked around, waiting for a chuckle, but none came.

Jenna sat down in the seat one row behind Robin's and leaned toward Tracy. "You're worried Uncle Michael might be marrying the wrong girl?"

Tracy looked down, bit her lip harder. A tear rolled down her cheek as she nodded.

Michael crouched down in front of Tracy, lifted her chin up. "Honey," he said. "That is the sweetest..." he said, then trailed off, crying a little himself now. "But you needn't worry. Let me tell you a story."

He told the kid-friendly version of it, but Veronica knew this story, knew it well, so her mind filled in the blanks as he went.

MICHAEL'S FAMILY hadn't had to set the leaf into the middle of their dining room table in years, not since Grammy and Grampy were both still alive and still living upstairs, not since Veronica's family had moved from across the driveway to across the town. But that night, the night that Robin met Jenna, the night Jenna met everyone in fact, there were six of them. And though they had been cramming five around the unextended table for years—thanks, of course, to Robin—six just wasn't possible.

Jenna was, at that point, just a college housemate of Michael's, a friend crashing in the spare bedroom. Her work-study job had offered her extra hours over spring break, and it was an offer that she, like many a poor scholarship student, could not refuse. The dorms were closed, and commuting from her home in Maine certainly wasn't an option, so Michael had offered her a room. It was as simple as that. Or, well, it should have been. But things were never simple when his little sister got involved. Ashley loved drama, and she was constantly looking for ways to pull people's strings.

"It's lucky you live with Michael," was how it began. "He's never been able to say no to a pretty girl in his life."

"Ash!" said their father, as Jenna gave an uncomfortable chuckle, ducking her head and pushing a stray lock of her auburn hair behind her ear.

Robin went scarlet. And that was all it took for everything to unravel. Two girls who might have gone through the entire evening without so much as an indifferent glance toward one another were now adversaries. Ashley was excused from the table, her mother glaring after her.

"It's too bad you have to work through your break," said Robin. "That's so sad."

Jenna forced a smile. "I don't mind really. Spring break's never really been a time to party for me. My mother's never been able to afford that luxury."

Robin frowned and gave her a supercilious little nod. "Michael and I were supposed to join some friends in Cancun," she said. "He says he decided against it because he has a lot of painting to catch up on. But we both know what the truth is, don't we?"

Jenna shook her head. "I'm afraid not."

Robin smirked. "The truth is that Michael decided against it because he has no idea how to have a good time." Robin laughed, and then added, "At least, not like he used to."

Michael stayed quiet, as was his wont. Speaking up wasn't going to prove anything. And it might just make matters worse. The real truth of the matter was not that Michael didn't know how to have a good time. The truth of the matter was that Michael's idea of a good time and Robin's idea of a good time were two paths slowly diverging from one another in the increasingly frosty woods of their relationship. Booze and bongs and hot bods—those were Robin's turn-ons. There was always some new beer to try out with her, some new drug she'd gotten from a friend of a friend of a friend. And lately, there were the constant hints that another body crammed into bed might spice up their lackluster love life. But up at the college, away from Robin (she was in Boston, at Berklee), Michael had been discovering, or, rather, rediscovering, that those things weren't his cup of tea. He'd learned that a quiet afternoon at the pond, with a couple of issues of *X-Men* to read, was far more enjoyable for him than a hit of X at some kegger in some Boston dorm room, obnoxious drum-n-bass blaring in the background. He'd decided that the *Rent* sing-a-long parties at his townhouse were a lot more fun than the stressful gigs that Gideon's Bible had been putting on these past few months. And he knew, in his heart of hearts, that a girl like Jenna, a girl he could talk to, a girl who was as comfortable with silence as she was with a roaring stereo, was the kind of girl he should be with. He kissed Robin. He fucked Robin. He played hard-nosed, kick-ass rock and roll with Robin. But he couldn't remember the last time he'd had a conversation with her about something other than kissing, or fucking, or rock and roll.

That night, the fucking happened in the back row of theater number four at the old Route 3 Cinema across town, the dingiest, most filthy room in the place. Screwing at the cinema was something she had always wanted to try, and though they had fooled around back there before—French kissing, heavy petting, et cetera—they'd never gone all the way. To sate her, and to hopefully put an end, at least temporarily, to all her talk about threesomes, Michael had consented to give it a try. But he was still nervous about the whole thing. Yes, the construction of the new movie theater down the street had given the staff at Route 3 a kind of "Screw it. What's the point?" mentality when it came to rules enforcement, but fucking in the back of a movie theater was still fucking in the back of a movie theater, and Michael didn't like the idea of being caught, regardless of whether or not he was going to be punished for it.

She rode him while facing the screen, so the both of them could still watch the movie. And, as his sneakers stuck and then unstuck themselves to the floor, it occurred to him that the sticky residue there might not be entirely the fault of spilled soft drinks and discarded chewing gum. It was an unpleasant thought, but, thankfully, not one he had to focus on for long. From the time she hiked up her skirt and shimmied onto his lap until the time that she shimmied off and headed for the bathroom, no more than three minutes could have passed. The more risqué the situation, the quicker she was done. And, of course, that was part of the problem. They were running out of things to try. Doing something while driving: that was next. And maybe, he found himself thinking, they would crash and burn, and it would all be over, all of it.

While he was driving her home, Robin wound herself tight around his free arm, squeezing his hand between her thighs. She purred against him, warmer than she should have been on this cold night, in this cold car, with its busted heater. "What about Jenna?" she asked, as they turned off of the main drag and onto her road.

"What about Jenna?" Michael asked, trying, gently, to extricate his hand from the prison of her legs.

"Well," said Robin. "You like her. That's obvious."

Michael shook his head and turned away from her.

"What?" said Robin, pulling herself off of him as they pulled up in front of her house. "Tell me you haven't imagined it."

Michael turned to face her again, rubbing the numbness from his freed hand. "I haven't imagined it, Robin. I don't imagine those kinds of things."

"Sure you do," she said, opening her door. "You just won't admit it."

"This is a fine way to say goodnight," he said.

And then, Robin stepped out of the car, and slammed the door behind her. And somewhere, deep inside, he knew that, finally, this was the beginning of the end.

There was a light on in the upstairs living room when he got home, and Michael felt his shoulders loosen up at the sight of it. Just as it did up at school, the warm glow of a second story window was all it took to set him at ease. Jenna was still up, and that meant that, for once during one of these horrible sojourns back home, he was going to have someone to vent to.

He let loose a heavy sigh once he'd reached the top of the stairs. Jenna looked up from the pages of *Dance Kinesiology* and gave him a smile. "That bad, huh?"

Michael plopped down onto the couch next to her. She set her book down on the floor and patted two hands on her lap. Sighing again, he laid back, resting his head on her legs. She ran her fingers through his hair, rubbed at his temples. "Spill it," she said.

"Why am I still with her, Jenna?"

Now it was Jenna who sighed. And then groaned.

"You said you wanted to hear it," said Michael.

"I think I changed my mind," she said. "A woman's prerogative, you know."

Michael chuckled.

"Okay," she said. "Go ahead."

He spilled the beans on the whole evening, up to and including Robin's latest proposal for a ménage à trois. And he felt no remorse for being so open, for sharing. Because this is what they did at the college. They were honest with one another, and they leaned on each other when they needed to. Like a family. That was what was at the heart of it. Kimball College and Jenna, most of all, had reminded him what a family was supposed to be like. Up there was not like down here, in "greater" Lowell, where the lies came as fast and furious as the Merrimack came over the Pawtucket Falls, where you were on your own from start to finish.

At the end of his story, Michael felt Jenna's taut belly ripple with laughter against the crown of his head.

"What's so funny?"

She collected herself, then said, "That she'd want to share you with me."

Michael gave her a smirk. "You think she wasn't serious?"

"Oh," said Jenna, "I'm sure she was serious. That girl feels like she's got something to prove. But, you believe me, Michael: if I ever got ahold of you, you'd never go back. I wouldn't let you go back, and you wouldn't want to."

Michael felt a rush of blood away from this face, away and down, toward a lower place. He hoped she wouldn't notice.

"You're a great guy, Michael, and your girlfriend's an idiot for not knowing that. She's always seen you as having the raw material to be a good man, as someone she would have to shape and mold, and she's thrived on that. But now that you're coming to the realization that you are a good man—no assembly required—she's getting desperate."

Michael frowned. "How desperate, do you think?"

Jenna was silent for a moment. And then she asked, "Are you sure you want my opinion on this?"

Michael nodded.

"It's only a matter of time before she finds someone, Michael. If you won't be shaped to her liking anymore, then she's going to go find someone who will. That's what girls like her, women like her... that's what they do." Jenna stopped rubbing his head. "That's why my mom's had kids with three different men, why she's been through two divorces and is working on her third."

Michael reached up, squeezed her hand.

"Most women I know, Michael... they want a man they can fix." She sighed again, looked down at him. "Even me, I guess."

Michael sat up, turned around to face her, grabbed her other hand. "Don't," he said. "You know that he's a good guy, deep down."

Jenna's gaze remained fixed on her lap. "How deep, though?"

They looked at each other and sighed.

"Some other time," said Michael, wistfully.

"Some other place," she said, finishing the familiar refrain of their friendship. And then she hugged him. She hugged him closer and longer than she ever had before.

They parted, she stood, and then she ruffled his hair. "It'll all work out in the wash, Michael."

He nodded, and smiled at her mixed cliché. "I guess so."

TRACY WAS CONFUSED. "SO," she said, "you should be with Jenna because she likes kissing less than Robin does?"

Everyone looked at Michael, who was sitting on the floor now, each of the women giving him a puzzled smirk. It was like they were wondering how he was going to answer the question, too.

Michael stared at Tracy, a warm smile on his face, but she focused on his eyes, because the eyes were where the truth was; she'd read that somewhere. His were hazel, or so he'd told her when she asked him time and time again, and though she'd never known before what hazel meant, now she had an idea. His eyes were a greenish brown, but there were flecks of blue in there too, of gold. She was sure, if you stared deep enough into Uncle Michael's eyes, you could find any color you were looking for. But she wasn't sure whether that was good or bad, or what it meant about him and the truth.

"No," he said. "That's not it. What I'm trying to say is that, we meet a lot of lovely people in our lives, Tracy. Sometimes, it's the first person that we're meant to be with. And sometimes it's the last one. Does that make sense?"

"Kinda," she said. "But," she said, and then trailed off, thinking about something. There was this photograph of Robin and

Michael, back in their high school days, singing into the same microphone, smiles cracking through the masks of their serious rock and roll faces, and Tracy, she had just seen them do the same thing up on stage. They had just looked at each other in the same way, like they loved each other, like they each knew that there was no one else in the world who could make them feel like they did in that moment.

"What about when you sing those songs to each other?" said Tracy. "The songs you wrote to each other in high school?"

"Well," said Michael, "you've heard those songs. We were angry at each other, most of the time."

Robin laughed. "That we were."

"Most of the time," said Tracy. "But not all of the time."

Jenna put a hand on Tracy's shoulder and Tracy thought to shrug it off, because she was still pretty sure Jenna was the bad guy here, and she didn't want her ears filled with Jenna's lies. But she stayed still, because there was something she wanted even less than that, and that was a scene. So, she let Jenna speak.

"Tracy," said Jenna, "you've seen the plays they put on in the barn down the Cape, right?"

Tracy nodded.

"When we sing to each other now," said Robin, "it's like that. We're pretending. We're playing the people we were years and years ago."

Veronica crouched down to say something to Tracy now. "And that's what I was doing with the... with your father, Tracy. Pretending. Putting on a show. If you want to know who the Desiree is in Uncle Michael's story..."

"I get it," said Tracy, standing up, tired of all their words and explanations, ready for the scene now, if it was going to come. "I just want to be alone for a while."

She picked up her Nomad and her headphones, then walked up

the aisle and out of the auditorium. She cast a glance or two over her shoulder, to see if anyone was following her, but all she saw was Michael holding Veronica's hand as she stood, maybe to move, maybe to come after Tracy, before she sat down again and let Tracy go.

VERONICA COULD HAVE PUNCHED her cousin right then, but maybe he had a point. Maybe the kid needed some space. The school was a safe enough place. She couldn't get into too much trouble there. And the band had a few more songs to run through anyway, the covers in particular, and "November Rain" chief among them.

Veronica was flabbergasted when Michael mentioned the song by name, the song she'd made her one fleeting mark with, but Robin was taken aback by Veronica's disbelief.

"That solo," said Robin, "that solo you did, it's legend. Better than Slash's."

"Now you're just being ridiculous," said Veronica, shooting her cousin a glance, to see if this were all for real.

"Veronica," said Michael, "we are not going to pass up this chance for you to relive your glory days."

"Glory *day* is more like it," said Veronica. "Singular. And really," she continued, "it's not the same without the orchestra."

"Which is why," said Robin, "we've invited them to join us this evening."

"Chelmsford's finest," said Michael.

Her cousin really was too much. This was supposed to be his moment, his last fling before settling down. That he'd taken the time to make this happen, to make this happen for her, that was... Veronica looked out into the audience, searching for Jenna, who was all smiles as usual. That was one lucky girl, Veronica thought.

Michael brought Veronica her guitar, the one she'd played on this stage, on that song, nearly nine years before. She didn't mess with it much these days, because of its wonky pick-ups, its tendency to fall out of tune after three minutes, and the high E's fondness for snapping mid-performance.

"This one's temperamental," she told him.

"But would you play it on any other axe?" said Robin.

Veronica shook her head in a silent no.

"Good," said Michael, as Veronica slung it over her shoulder. "Now, if you'll excuse me, I'm going to leave you two to sort out who plays which solo. I've got a little girl to cheer up."

"I thought you said she needed space," said Veronica, as Michael leapt off stage, then bounded up the aisle.

WHEN MICHAEL FOUND HER, Tracy was sitting halfway up the lobby's grand staircase, the monstrosity that led to the second floor. Her Nomad was blaring "A Toast to the Duplicitous" through her headphones, and it was only when he sat down beside her that she noticed he was there.

She paused the song, asked him, "Whatever happened to David?"

"David?" said Michael.

"The other founder of Gideon's Bible," she said, clarifying.

Michael sighed. "Love triangle," he said, and when she just stared at him, waiting for more, he added, "It's a long story."

Tracy grunted. "That's the only kind of story grown-ups ever have," she said. "And they never tell them."

Tracy set her gaze on the the road just beyond the enormous two-story wall of windows that rose from the floor in front of her, that imposing tower of glass. Michael was rambling on about something that was supposed to make her feel better, but what she found herself thinking about were the friends she was making back home in Harwich—for that really was home now, she had to admit. She found herself thinking about which of the boys she would fall in love with, which of the girls would be her best friends, who she would betray first, and who would betray her.

"Tracy," said Michael, "I didn't mean to make you cry again."

"Why can't people just be nice to each other?" she said, wiping with her long sleeve at the tears she didn't realize she'd been crying.

"I don't know," said Michael. "And I realize that's a shitty answer, but..."

Tracy looked at him, wide-eyed. He didn't seem embarrassed at all about the word he'd just used. He was just staring off through the windows now, like she had, as if searching for his next thought. Tracy thought to admonish him for his potty mouth, the way she did Veronica and Desiree, but she didn't. Uncle Michael was supposed to be like her father now—she'd overheard her mother saying as much to Desiree—and he kind of was, the way that he tried to make her feel better, the way he felt the need to keep talking until she was distracted from her pain, or whatever she'd been complaining about. But he also kind of wasn't. He also kind of didn't have to be. She had two parents already, or three, depending on who you counted. Uncle Michael was free to be something else, free to be the guy who said "shitty" when that was the best word for the job.

"Are you going to break up with Jenna," said Tracy, "because of what I said?"

"What?"

She sniffled. "Because I didn't mean to do that," she said. "I just like it when you're happy, Uncle Michael."

He put his arm around her, lifted her up onto his lap. "And I like it when you're happy," he said, tickling her sides.

She giggled, then smiled.

Michael held her close. "Listen," he said. "I can't say for sure that Jenna and I will always be happy together. Your mom can't say for sure about Desiree, either. Once upon a time, we were all happy in different places, with different people. And who's to say that someday there won't be some other person, when we're in some other place?"

"But that's not fair," said Tracy. "That's not right."

"You're right," said Michael, "but we can't control the future, and we can't rewrite the past, no matter how much we'd love to. All we can do is enjoy the here and now."

"I guess," said Tracy. His answer wasn't good enough. No grown-up's answer ever was. But it would do, for now.

"So," he said, standing up and hoisting her up as he went, "you want to go see a concert?"

VERONICA HAD FORGOTTEN how boring the song was. At nearly nine minutes long, and minus the epic video starring the epically gorgeous Stephanie Seymour, there were long stretches of piano playing and oohing and ahhing from the backup singers where she felt herself stifling yawns. But, when the final guitar solo drew near, when the band stripped the opus down to its core, just the piano and the drums, when it was time for her to climb the steps that led to the top of the piano, she was ready.

She focused on the guitar as she began, drowning out everything but the music, which she let envelop her. But in the middle, in the middle it occurred to her that there was something more she wanted to see in this moment than her fingers bending the disobedient strings to her will. She was nervous to look out into the crowd, because splitting her focus, especially during a solo, had always seemed like hubris to her. But then, suddenly, she remembered her dream, remembered the message her younger self had tried to impart. Veronica looked down. She was standing on top of the piano. On top of it! She would have laughed, if laughing were allowed in a serious rock and roll moment like this. Instead, she turned her gaze to the front row, to the little girl who sat—no, stood!—there.

Tracy's mouth was agape when Veronica locked eyes with her, still not comprehending that this was her mother up there, wailing away. But then Veronica said something to her daughter with the guitar, something crazed and filled with passion, a plea: "Let go."

That was when Tracy began to headbang, along with everyone around her. People pointed, as if to say "Look at that bad-ass kid," then got back to their own raucous response, recharged by her exuberance.

Look at that bad-ass kid, thought Veronica. My kid.

Atop the piano, Veronica lost herself in the music, playing the shit out of her guitar—playing *the shit* out of it—until they all came crashing down together.

IV

THOSE WORN-OUT RECORDS

September 2001–November 2010

To: Michael Silver
From: Tracy Silver
Subject: George Michael
Date: September 21, 2001

Uncle Michael,

I have so many questions. Like, first, why am I supposed to write Dear before your name? We learned how to write letters in school this week and the first thing the teacher wrote on the board was Dear, and I was like why do we write dear? And she wouldn't answer. She rolled her eyes at me, told me I'd already asked my share of questions for the day, and asked me to be quiet. Then she turned her back on us and started scratching the chalk across the board again. The noise made my teeth hurt. Back in Boston, we had these really nice whiteboards and the teacher used markers which didn't make any sound at all and they smelled like strawberries. Down the Cape, it's like the ancient century or something. It's like that show Little House that Mom watches at the end of a long day, when she's curled up under her grammie's old afghan and trying to go to sleep. Mom had a crush on the girl on that show. Did you know that? She told me she tried to count the girl's freckles once, and that she called her dad Pa for a whole week, just to see what he would do. He never answered to it, never took his eyes off NESN until she said it like sixty billion times.

Anyway, why am I supposed to write Dear Uncle Michael? You're the one who knows these things. That's what Mom says. We were eating macaroni and cheese the other night, the two of us with spoons eating it right out of the pan because Desiree was at work and Mom didn't want to make any extra dishes, and she says to me: Michael is our fountain of useless information. Ask him. But

I think that's dumb. You always have the answers to my questions, and my questions aren't useless.

Second question: why does your email address end in 669? I heard my gramps say once that 666 is the sign of the beast, whatever that means, but yours is 669. So what does it mean? I was on Google, googling, and nothing came up. I thought of asking Mom why nothing came up, but I knew she'd just tell me to use Yahoo instead, because she's a yahoo. At least that's what Desiree says.

Oh, and Mom let me get an email! But you probably figured that out, since you're reading this right now.

Okay, now the important stuff: what is it with Mom and George Michael? Is it just the pretty girls in the videos? Is that why she only watches them when Des is at work? And why are the girls always in their underwear? I mean, except for when they're in those suits with the huge shoulders?

Mom got mad at me on Sunday, when I was supposed to be in bed. I couldn't sleep and I could see the light of the TV from under my door, and then I heard it: George Michael singing about being someone's father figure, and that's what everyone tells me you are to me, my father figure, so I thought, maybe this one is appropriate. Mom and Des are always telling me, when they want me to go to bed so they can watch grown-up things, that this show isn't appropriate. And this show isn't appropriate. And this book. And that email isn't appropriate (until now). But this was a song about father figures, about you I figured, so I decided to check it out. I got out there and on the TV the girl was in her underwear, her back up against the wall, and it looked like George Michael was going to kiss her, but then she slapped him. And I was like, is he her father figure? Is that what the song's about? But if that's what it's about, if she's me and George Michael is her Uncle Michael, then why is she in her underwear and why is he trying to kiss her like that. So I ask mom and she jumps off the couch, says a bad word, and hits the eject button on the VCR so hard that she says another bad word and starts shaking her finger.

And she's kissing the finger, sucking on it like a baby, when I notice what's on the TV now, now that the VCR is off. It's the planes flying into the towers again. And Mom is too busy with her finger to realize that I'm not crying because she scared me, or because she yelled, but because, well...

Anyway, then she notices. She turns around, she sees the great ball of fire exploding out of the building, and she flicks the knob on the TV to turn it off. Then she gets down on her knees and holds her arms out wide so I can have a hug.

And I ask her what would have happened if you and Jenna had waited an extra week to move to Hawaii like I wanted you to. What if you had listened to me, Uncle Michael, when I was crying over my hot dog and my Doritos on Labor Day after you told me you were leaving the next day, that you had to? Boston to California, early on a Tuesday morning, so you could make the next flight from L.A. and be in Honolulu for dinner. If Uncle Michael had listened to me, I told Mom, if he'd waited a week, he'd be dead. Dead, dead, dead. And Auntie Jenna too. And I'd never have any cousins. And

I had to stop typing there. But I'm not crying anymore. I'm brave now. You don't have to worry about me.

Anyway, that's why she let me get an email finally. I said, Uncle Michael is my father figure and if I don't get to talk to him then I'm going to slap him the next time I see him. Except not in my underwear, because that would be weird.

Love,

Tracy

P.S. It took me a week to write this, even though Ms. McCorkle says I'm defiantly the most precocious eight-(ALMOST NINE)-

year-old she's ever met. I had to shout out to the living room a bunch of times to ask Mom and Des how to spell stuff.

P.P.S. When I let Mom read parts of this—I covered up some of it with my hand—she laughed when she read defiantly precocious. She tells me that's not how you spell defiantly, that it has all Es and no As, and that spell-check is messing things up. But that is defiantly how you spell defiantly. Right?

To: Michael Silver
From: Tracy Silver
Subject: The Romantics
Date: May 17, 2004

Dear Uncle Michael,

So, they did it. They did it without you. And I know you know this—you're on speaker with Mom in the other room, you have been for a while now, and the two of you have singing about measuring life in love for what feels like 525,600 minutes—I *know* you know that they did it without you. But they're leaving stuff out. Like all the important stuff.

I was up before both of them this morning, slumped back into the cushions of our lumpy old couch, and I was scrolling through comments on my latest LiveJournal. Des' dinosaur of a computer was heavy and hot in my lap, but I kept scrolling because I didn't want to work on the extra book talk that Mrs. Carlson is making me do to show the rest of the class "how it's done."

Their voices were quiet at first, as if they were trying not to wake me. But I could tell that, whatever the deal was, it was not a good deal. So I closed the lid of the computer and set it on the coffee table next to the plate of toast I'd been nibbling on. Then I tip-toed toward their bedroom and leaned my head against the wall.

"Yeah," Des was saying, "okay, but are you saying we take her out of school just so we can be the first?"

"You want to take a chance and wait until after school?" asked Mom.

"What chance?" said Des. "You think they're going to be all 'Just kidding' and it'll be illegal again by three o'clock?"

And, of course, that's when I knew what they were talking

about for sure. So I stomped over to their door and pounded on it with my fist.

The door creaked open, Mom hiding behind Des and wrapping a sheet around herself. She sleeps naked, my mom. Maybe I'm not supposed to tell you that. Maybe you didn't need to know that about your cousin. But I'm mad, so I'm telling you everything.

"Did we wake you?" asked Des.

"You said!" I said, shaking a finger at them. "You said you were going to wait until Uncle Michael could be here. And Aunt Jenna and Uncle Matt and Auntie—"

"I know," said Des, nodding slowly, giving me that mom look that Mom is totally bad at.

Actually, it was kind of a dad look. So I said, "You're patronizing me" and they looked aghast that I knew the word, their eyebrows raised, Mom holding a hand to her mouth to hide a laugh. "There's not supposed to be any patriarchy in this house, but, but you're patronizing me!"

"Those two words," Des was saying, "they aren't—" but I wasn't listening.

"You said you were going to wait until the whole family could be here," I reminded them. "You said Uncle Michael was going to go online and become a priest so he could do the ceremony, and that would be so funny because he doesn't even believe in God."

"It would be funny," Des told me, again with the look, but now taking hold of my shoulders too, running her cold hands over my arms. "It would be lovely. But your mom and I have waited a long time already."

"And why would Uncle Michael want to be here anyway?" Mom asked. "Remember," said Mom, a smirk on her face, "I stole Des away from him. She was his first crush. Think about it: do you want to be there in twenty years when Lincoln marries Brian Meltzer?"

I screwed up my face and stuck out my tongue. You know how I feel about Lincoln. I cried when he told me he only likes boys, but now it's our mission—we shook on it—to find each other the perfect boyfriends. "Lincoln Baker is too handsome for dumb Brian Meltzer." I said. "And," I added, "Brian only likes girls."

"Really?" they said at the same time, casting a sideways glances at each other and looking surprised.

"Every time a girl gets her boobs," I told them, "Brian is the first to notice. And he, like, never stops noticing. The way he looks at Alicia in health class..." I shuddered, stuck out my tongue, and pretended to gag.

"Get dressed," Mom said.

I rolled my eyes and told her "You get dressed!" Then I stormed off to my room.

And then, and then—guess what?!? We weren't even the first in line at town hall. The two old guys who power-walk down Old Wharf every morning, the ones where Mom has always been like "They are" and Des has always been like "No way," they were standing there holding hands. They smiled at us as we got out of the car and Des smiled back, but Mom couldn't look at them. She looked at me instead, rolled her eyes, and mouthed "I told her."

So, they're married. They got married and we went out for breakfast at a diner over in Dennis that Mom said your grandparents used to take you to during the summers, and that was it. We came home, we crawled under their covers, and we watched Julia Roberts movies until they decided it was late enough in the day to call you in Hawaii. They let me have the laptop when I said was bored halfway through *Steel Magnolias*, which is when I started to write this and the LJ that I'm totally posting when I'm done sending this to you, but they wouldn't let me leave. It's their wedding day. Aren't they supposed to kick me out and do married people stuff? Isn't that how it's supposed to work? You and Aunt Jenna didn't hang out with all of us after your wedding. I remember how much gravel your tires kicked up as you peeled out of the driveway that afternoon. I remember how you guys waved once and then set your eyes on the horizon, driving off into the sunset. You guys knew what was what. But not Mom and Des. They sat in bed, with me, and watched old movies.

My mothers are like the least romantic people ever.

Don't you think?

Love,

Tracy

To: Michael Silver
From: Tracy Silver
Subject: Fleetwood Mac
Date: September 30, 2006

Dear Uncle Michael,

I'm 14 now, and it's one of those 5 days a year when you're 14 years older than me instead of 15, and I don't know why I'm telling you this, except that I tell you every year right before I ask if you're mad at me for stealing your birthday thunder.

I imagine you in the hospital, 14 years ago, waiting your turn to hold me, lurking in the shadowy corner of the room as they pass the new baby around. You're hoping they'll forget you in this particular game of hot potato. I imagine you wondering if your mom will still take you on your annual shopping spree at the comic book store, or if this will be the year she finally says no, that's enough, it's time to grow up.

If I close my eyes, I can see you slouching your way to your locker on that Monday morning, a few days after they made you hold me, made you hold me until they could snap a twentieth photo just in case. I can see you standing there, forehead pressed against the locker's grates as you fiddle with the combination. And I can see Des put her hand on your shoulder, and you turning to see the first girl you ever crushed on hard. I can see you finally seeing the truth in the tears she has cried over me, cried and wiped hastily away in her car that morning. She wishes you a hurried "Happy birthday" and then rushes off. You knew then that she was in love with your cousin after all, in love with my mom just like everyone tried to tell you. I can you see you shouting to her, "It's going to be okay!" and everyone staring at the two of you in the suddenly silent hall—the red-eyed senior and the sophomore with locker slits carved now into his forehead. They stare, then they hide behind their hands or their lockers or each other to giggle at your earnestness.

I think of all that, then I think of how unfair it was that someone so kind had to wait so long for another person to love. You didn't meet Robin for another two and a half years, right? Unfair.

Not as unfair as the news yesterday, though. Not anywhere close.

I know you're in love with Aunt Jenna now, that you have been for a long time, but how could you not be dying inside after yesterday? When you saw the headline, the photo of the guy with the gun in his hand and Robin's record under his arm, how could you have stopped yourself from weeping?

I've seen every video that was ever taken of Gideon's Bible. I've seen you singing "Go Your Own Way" with Robin at your senior talent show more times than I can count. And if mp3s wore out like records used to, I could totally be a cliché right now. But they don't, so I'm sitting here typing this with my headphones in, my iPod warm on my leg as it blares "Two Roads Diverging" for the two-hundredth time. I'm sitting here typing this and I'm counting the cracks in your voice, in your thin veneer, as you say goodbye.

Has Aunt Jenna ever listened to this stuff? I hope not, because I'm sure she would hear it too. Girls are smart like that. And she probably wouldn't even let you know she was hurt. But she would be. Maybe that's what she's hiding behind her big old sunglasses in this photo Mom has on the fridge. It's of your fifth anniversary, I think, from earlier this year. You two are on the beach by your house, you tan and Jenna more freckled than I've ever seen her, and you're both hiding: you behind a smile full of too-polished teeth and she behind the sunglasses. Have you ever peeked behind her façade, Uncle Michael? Have you ever looked to see if she has seen what I see? You should.

I suppose, in some way, you must still love Des too. Right? I mean, that was puppy love or whatever, but still.

And, I mean: do you ever stop loving the people you've loved anyway? Ever completely stop, that is? I mean: how could you? Love is like a horcrux, isn't it? You know what I'm talking about, right? Horcruxes are those awful left-behind bits of bad guy we found about in the latest *Harry Potter*. Love is like a horcrux, I say, only not as evil. You carve off a piece of yourself for every person you love and you leave it behind, just like Voldemort does when he kills someone. A souvenir that's forever. That's what love is. At least I think so.

Anyway, I'm so sorry that Robin is gone, Uncle Michael. I guess that's all I wanted to write you about. I know we'll talk on the phone tonight, but I know you'll move right past the uncomfortable stuff and into wishing me a happy birthday and reassuring me that I didn't steal any birthday thunder from you, none at all. I know that's what you'll do, and I wanted to get this out while I was feeling it as hard as I'm ever going to feel it. After all, that's what she would have done. Right?

Love,

Tracy

To: Michael Silver
From: Tracy Silver
Subject: Nancy Sinatra
Date: November 22, 2010

Dear Uncle Michael,

Attached is the essay I wrote about your band last year. I'm sending it now because I know, when I arrive in Honolulu this week, you're going to do nothing but pester me until I hand it over. And, apart from visiting the college and prepping for my interview and all that, I don't want to look at a screen for the entire time I'm there. I want to lie on the beach, perpetrating a tan, so that a brother with money might be my man. In a manner of speaking. I hope Jenna can get some time off to come with. A wingwoman is always appreciated, especially to keep overbearing uncles from ruining innocent fun.

And, before you ask: no, I am not packing my one piece. The bikini is all I'm bringing. And you can just get over it.

Anyway, look at me avoiding the subject.

About the essay: the truth is, even though I'm using it as my writing sample, I'm not sure it's very good. I'm not sure anything I've written is very good. Des tells me to shush when I say these things, but she's not an artist. And I can't go to Mom, because she might tell me that I'm right. She might put her hands on my shoulders, look me dead in the eye, and tell me that I suck. Just to spare me the life of the tortured artist, the life she longed for when she was raising me but that totally exhausts her now.

So, I'm coming to you. And I want you to be as honest with me about my writing as you are about the angles of my Instagrams.

Am I any good?

And I know right now that you're like: where is this coming from? I have never suffered from a lack of confidence. In fact, I've made others suffer *because* of my confidence. But, see, that's the thing.

You remember Brian Meltzer? I got suspended for pantsing him today. Right in the library, after I caught him checking out the ass of a girl we'd just been tutoring. And maybe it wouldn't have been as bad, maybe I would've gotten just a slap on the wrist, if the dumb asshole hadn't been going commando today.

That's right, after I pulled his pants to the floor, what I found myself staring at as I crouched there behind him, hoping the girl would turn around and see him in his tightie whities—what I found myself staring at was the dumb asshole's dumb asshole.

Or, well, it was really the hairy crack of his lily-white ass. But I'm a writer, so I couldn't resist the repetition of dumb asshole. I mean, could you?

Maybe you could. Maybe that's what makes you a better artist than I'll ever be. I mean, I've watched you stare at a canvas for an hour before making a mark. And when you were doing that portrait of my mothers a couple years back, I remember how you stood there after they told you it was done, just stood there before breakfast every day for a week, your English muffin going cold as you tried to figure out what was missing. Then, on the last day of your vacation, while Jenna was packing up your rental, you picked up your brush and made the bags under Mom's eyes just a smidgen darker. I was standing in the doorway, and you turned to me, and I was ready to tell you that you'd done it, that you'd captured her exhaustion just right. I was ready to reassure you that you hadn't fucked it up, that it was just the right amount.

But you didn't ask. You smiled, you gave me a quick hug, and you said goodbye.

And you know what? When Mom and Des came back inside

from waving you and Jenna off, they looked at it and they couldn't tell the difference. Which made me wonder if I could tell the difference. So I sat there the rest of the morning looking at it, until my stomach started grumbling and the smell of the grill outside called me out to lunch. And it was only as I was digging into one of Des' famous double-stuffed cheeseburgers, it was only then that I realized it didn't matter if any of us noticed. You noticed. You knew it was done. And that's all that mattered.

But I'm sitting here, Uncle Michael, staring at this screen, pausing between each paragraph to click CTRL + A like you taught me (because people who need a mouse to Select All are wasting precious, precious time). I'm sitting here, thinking about how the principal made me feel like an idiot today when I tried to lord it over her about Mr. Wingfield's role in *The Glass Menagerie*. I've only read that play like a hundred times, but she schools me without breaking a sweat? I'm a pompous bitch. Pompous and totally dumb. I don't know what I'm talking about, even when I know what I'm talking about.

So now, as I nibble the nails on one hand, the index finger of my other hovers over the Delete key. And I'm thinking about what I'll do after I delete all of this, about how I'll go to the airline's website and cancel my flight, how I'll go to the college's application portal and withdraw myself from consideration, how I'll withdraw myself from every goddamned thing. I'm thinking about how all I want to do is curl up in the attic above the barn, hiding amongst the costumes and the props until I become someone else through osmosis.

A month ago, we put on Uncle Matt's play about the day he came out. It starts with the hide and seek scene, the one where you're hiding beneath the couch, the last to be discovered. And Mom's hiding in the closet, because Uncle Matt is nothing if not on the nose. And Auntie Ashley is "it." And she finds the two of them first, but she can't find you, not until you sneeze from the dust of a thousand Silvers gone to ghost. Ashley leaps up onto the couch then and bounces up and down until you reveal yourself. "You should be nicer to your brother," Mom and Uncle Matt tell her. But she doesn't stop until you're all called down to dinner, to the dinner where the whole family is going to fall apart.

In the play, Uncle Matt lingers on you for a moment after everyone else is gone. The critics didn't get it, and said as much in their reviews. But I loved it, because the actor playing you, the little boy, he sat there and, just as he was about to cry, he gave his head a violent shake and pulled a sketchbook from his backpack. I'm not sure that's the way it happened, but I like to think it is.

But when I think about that scene, it makes me cry. Because I don't have anything like that. I don't have any moment I can point to where I *became* a writer. And I'm worried that's because I'm not a writer, because I never will be.

The new one that Matt's finishing, the one that'll be playing when you and Jenna come to visit next spring, it's about Old Silas and his goddamned boot. You know that old chestnut? The one about our ancestor who was lost at sea and the son who was terrified of the ocean as a result? Well, Matt's put zombies and witchcraft and a murder most foul into it. Really juicy stuff, going for a *grand guignol* feel. And he asked me to take a look at it, give him some feedback. Which I suppose says something. But does it say that he's pitying me, which is what the voices in my head want me to think, or does he trust my judgement as a fellow wordwright, which is what I'm sure you'll say? Who knows?

All I know is that, whenever I read it, I get this sneaking suspicion that it's trying to tell me something. That I'm not brave enough to put on the boot.

And maybe I'm not. And maybe that's the problem.

You'd put on the boot, wouldn't you? Maybe not now, now that you're a husband and a professor and a father figure and all that. But your band was a boot, right? And all the adventures with Jenna before you got married. And maybe even moving to Hawaii was a boot. You might have drowned at any moment, but didn't, and you didn't care.

What's my boot, Uncle Michael? Have I already thrown it away?

Love,

Tracy

P.S. Stop laughing. You were melodramatic when you were 18, too.

P.P.S. You have to change your password, dude. I sent an earlier version of this by mistake and totally hacked in to delete it before you could see it.

V

WHAT TO LOOK FOR IN A MAN

March 2011

18

THE WEIGHT OF YOUR WORLD ON HIS SHOULDERS

Once upon a time, they used the old barn as a garage and nothing more. But these days, the creaky old outbuilding was whatever they needed it to be. In the past year, it had been the office of a gesticulating attorney, the apartment of southern woman and her crippled daughter, the drawing room of an English manor, and, of course, an uninhabited island on which a Neapolitan ship had just wrecked. Tonight, this weekend, it was an approximation of the house that had once stood just up the hill, of that house's parlor in particular. And tonight, more than any other night—and that was saying something—it seemed haunted by the spirits the actors had conjured. All was quiet, and all were gone, but Tracy Silver did not feel alone.

She crept across the stage with a milk crate, tidying up. So many props in this one: there was an opened box on the coffee table, an overturned tea cup and saucer next to that, and a discarded apron beneath the ornate Victorian chair that sat center stage. Off to one corner rested a bloodied and muddied boot, the kind a mariner might wear—*the* boot her own ancestor had worn, it turned out.

Tracy picked it up last, set her crate on the table, and then slumped down into the chair.

She held the boot the way she might hold Yorick's skull, if her mothers ever gave her the chance, and she looked upon it the way she imagined the Dane might look upon the final remains of that infinite jester: with puzzlement and melancholy and then, just at the end, with a hint of righteous anger.

Tracy slipped off her own shoe and made to fit the boot upon her foot, but she was stopped short. Just outside the theater, there were voices approaching, four of them. She dropped the boot and hurried toward the back of the stage, making for the alcove that led upstairs to the dressing rooms and the attic. But she did not flee to the upper levels, not yet. She hid behind the door and listened.

"What I've never understood," said Desiree, "is why your grandfather's sister—"

"—Great Aunt Dottie—" said Veronica, yawning.

"Yes," said Desiree. "The cartoonist! That's the one. I've never understood why she needed an alias in the first place."

There was another voice now, a man's, Michael's. He said, "Did you read my book?"

"I tried," said Desiree. "But, y'know, Professor Smarty-Pants, we needed something to replace the coffee table's broken leg and—"

There was laughter then, even from Michael, who went on to say something about lesbians breaking into comics in the 1940s. Tracy stopped listening, tried to tune him out. It was one thing to see him from across the way, as she had tonight,—and as she had, unbeknownst to him, on the night in Hawaii when he ruined everything—but it was another to hear him speak. She wasn't ready for that yet, not after what had happened. Soon—the nip bottle in the cooler out back had been prepared especially for this confrontation, after all—but not now. Tracy looked down at her feet as she tried to summon a song, something to drown him out, but before even one note had hummed its way through her brain, another damned thing grabbed her attention. Her right foot, it was bare. Her shoe was still on stage.

Without thinking, she raced back to grab it. And that, of course, was when they spotted her.

"Hey," said Michael. "There's the girl of the hour."

"Hi," said Tracy.

"Where are you off to?" said Michael.

Jenna nudged him with her elbow. "Can't you see she's striking the set?"

"There's not someone else who can do that?" said Michael.

Tracy knelt to put her shoe back on. "It's my job," she said as she tied her laces.

"Says who?" said Michael.

"Says Mum," said Tracy, pointing at Veronica, who had slumped into the chair, eyes closed.

"Veronica!" said Michael.

"Nnnwhat?"

"Did you tell Tracy she had to clean up this mess?"

"It's her job," said Veronica.

Michael turned to face Desiree. "C'mon, seriously, you let her saddle the kid with—"

"I'm just the stepmom," said Desiree. "Veronica gave birth to her. She makes the rules."

Tracy stood, brushing dust off the knee of her stage blacks. "We run a theater out of our barn," she said. "Everyone has to do their part, Michael. It's fine."

"It's not fine," he said. "You've been busy over here since the moment Jenna and I got to town. I haven't even had a second to congratulate you on—Hey, wait, did you just call me Michael?"

Jenna chuckled. "That is your name, dear."

"No," said Michael. "I know. But... what happened to the Uncle part?"

"Technically," said Tracy, "you're not my uncle."

"Excuse me?" said Michael.

"You're my mother's cousin," said Tracy. "Technically, that makes you my first cousin, once removed."

"You've been calling me Uncle Michael your whole life."

Tracy sighed, exasperated. "Can I go now? Please?"

Veronica waved her off as she curled up into the chair again. "Sooner you're finished," said Veronica, "sooner we can all get to bed."

And with that, Tracy picked up her milk crate and made her exit. But this time, she didn't hang around to eavesdrop. This time, she hurried up the stairs, taking them two at a time, and made straight for the dressing room, dropping the crate onto the props table along the way.

She rifled through the costume rack, searching for the outfit she'd hidden there, in plain sight, in a place neither mom would think to look. There was no telling how long it would take them all to clear out, but they wouldn't wait for her forever, and the chances of them coming up here instead of just calling for her—if they even bothered with that—were slim. So, she might as well get dressed, get ready.

Downstairs, a door opened. Tracy peeked out the window and saw Veronica, Michael, and Jenna step out onto the lawn. That was good. It was all good.

She changed, transformed herself. The stage blacks were balled up on the floor now, replaced with jeans that hugged her hips, a sweater that bared one shoulder, and a pair of sunglasses so big they gave her back a sense of mystery the other garments gave away.

"Sunglasses at night?" said Desiree, suddenly behind her.

"What?" said Tracy.

Desiree stood silent for a moment, sizing her up.

"What?" Tracy said again.

Desiree put a hand to her mouth and began to shake her head.

"What?"

"You're pregnant," said Desiree, falling backwards into a chair. "And don't lie. I can tell. I was with your mom when she found out she was pregnant with you."

"I'm not—"

"How did it happen? Did you use a condom? I mean, seriously, given the family history—"

"For serious, Des! I'm not," said Tracy, sitting now herself. "I'd cross my heart, but it's two sizes too small and awfully hard to find."

"Are you having sex?" said Desiree.

"And what if I was, Mother Abigail?"

"Who is Mother Abi—"

"Never mind," said Tracy. "Point is: I'm older than Mum was when Dad—"

"That man is not your father," said Desiree, leaning forward, shaking a finger at her, looking more like a mother than she ever had before. Every gray hair, all dozen or so of them, seemed to glint in the light as she shook that finger.

"I'm sorry," said Tracy, trying not to laugh at the beauty queen aging before her very eyes. "*The Runt*. I'm older than Mum was when the Runt knocked her up. And, anyway, I haven't had it yet. I'm just thinking about it."

"Well, stop thinking. It is way too early for you to—"

"This coming from the Handjob Queen of Roller Kingdom. Tell me again: how many pairs of leather pants did you stroke on metal night for free French fries?"

Desiree ducked her head. "We were stupid when we were kids," she said. "Our job as parents is to make sure you learn from our mistakes, not repeat them."

Tracy sighed a heavy sigh. "I did not choose wisely on this one," she said.

Desiree looked up again, her eyes wide, her jaw drooping. "You were going to tell me and not your mom?"

"That was the plan, Jan."

Desiree set a hand on Tracy's knee and squeezed. "You are too smart," she said, "and you know this family too well to think you can get away with secrets like that."

"I came to you because I thought you'd understand," said Tracy.

"No," said Desiree. "You came to me because you thought I'd give you permission."

And that was true. Desiree was the parent you brought your first speeding ticket to, the one you sought out at the mall when you wanted the credit card for something you didn't really need.

"This guy," said Tracy. "I don't want to marry him. I don't want to be with him forever. Hell, I might not even see him again after tonight. His family's just renting a place down here for the weekend. But I like him."

"That's fine," said Desiree. "Like him all you want. But from a distance. Pining's good for the soul. Getting pregnant at 18, not so much."

Tracy stood and stomped over to the other side of the room, aware, even as she stomped, of how childlike this response was, aware of how much this would just calcify Desiree's stance that she was too young. Aware, but too pissed off to care.

"Tracy," said Desiree. "Do you think you're on some kind of timeline here? Because you're not. You can... Waiting isn't... You..."

As Desiree trailed off, Tracy wanted to turn and see what clues the look on her face might give, but she also felt certain that now was the time to stand her ground.

"Your Uncle Michael was right," said Desiree. "There is definitely something weird in the air tonight."

"You know what?" said Tracy, giving in and turning, unable to bear the sound of that asshole's name without some kind of a response. "You know what?" she said. "Fuck Michael."

"Whoa," said Desiree, standing. "Hold on. That's your uncle you're talking about. He's the closest thing you have to a—"

"He is not my uncle. And he most certainly is not my father."

"Tracy," said Desiree, "where is all this coming from?"

Tracy thrust her hand toward the door, toward the props table just beyond it. "The boot," she said. "The goddamned boot!"

"The play?" said Desiree, looking confused.

"It's like he's wearing it one moment and then not wearing it the next."

"Okay," said Desiree, "now I'm lost."

"It's a metaphor," said Tracy. "The boot represents everything our family's struggled with for over a hundred and fifty years. It's the call to adventure, to danger, to frivolity, to the sea from whence we came. And you can either wear it or not wear it. You can't do both. But Michael? He wants to do both. And, maybe you can for a while. But you can't forever. Eventually, you've got to take it off or keep it on. Eventually, you've got to choose!"

"Okay," said Desiree. "Slow down."

"No," said Tracy. "I'm not slowing down. Not yet. It's my turn to wear it. And I'm going to wear the shit out of that boot until there's nothing left."

And with that, with nothing left to say, Tracy pushed past her stepmother and made for the stairs, for adventure and danger and frivolity, yes, but also for all of the other things that were waiting for her, the things she did not know and could not yet name.

19

DUDES LINING UP CAUSE THEY HEAR YOU GOT SWAGGER

They crept in through the side door a few hours later, Tracy and her two best friends in the world. Tana came first, buxom as Brünnhilde, with a voice to match, only the missing valkyrie's helmet keeping her from looking the spitting image of that archetypal fat lady. Then came Tori, a lean and sinewy Odette, a self-described ugly duckling that, now that she had the love of Tana, felt like the swan she dreamed of dancing on stage.

"So," said Tana, "where did whatshisname—"

"Tucker," said Tori.

"Where did Tucker run off to?"

It had all been going so well, from the moment he had pulled his parents' SUV into Tana's driveway to the moment, on their way back from Provincetown, when Tori had volunteered to take the wheel so that Tucker and Tracy could sit in the back. And then it had been going even better, in that backseat, as they drove home down Route 6, as they rolled by Tracy's house with the lights out and the car in neutral and parked down at Red River Beach. It had all been going so well, until:

"He forgot the condom," said Tracy.

"Oh my God," said Tana. "Seriously, you cannot do this."

"He went to go get it," said Tori. "It's not like she was going to—"

"No," said Tana. "She can't do it at all. If he's too dim to remember the condom—"

Tracy groaned, exasperated. "Has it occurred to you I picked him *because* he's dim?"

Tana sank into the center-stage chair, rolling her eyes. Tori still stood, dumbfounded. "Oh, Trace," she said, "that's not why, is it?"

"You're the smartest kid in our class," said Tana, "an amazing writer, and a sexy-ass bitch to boot. You deserve better than insert tab A into slot B."

Tracy sat on the coffee table, leveling with this girl she'd known since the move down the Cape all those years ago. "Yeah," she said, "well, if I don't start with tab A, I'm never going to get to X, Y, or Z now, am I?"

Tori asked, "Did you really pick him because he's dumb?"

"I picked him," said Tracy, "because he's here. And because he's not *from* here. Because he saw the sexy-ass bitch before the virtuous valedictorian."

Tana reached for Tracy's knee and squeezed. "Give someone some time and they'd see the sexy, too."

Tori sat behind Tracy on the table and wrapped her arms around her friend. "I mean," she said, "I understand where you're coming from, but—"

"Wait," said Tana. "How do *you* understand where she's coming from?"

"What I meant was—"

"We've been sleeping together," said Tana, "since the sixth grade."

"We were not 'sleeping together' back then," said Tori. "We

were just sleeping together."

"Oh my god," said Tana. "Speaking of dim."

"Guys!" said Tracy. "Tucker and I is going to happen. Please get over it."

"Okay," said Tana, "fine. Your funeral. But where?"

"Where?" said Tracy.

"I believe," said Tori, "she wants to know which floor of the theater you'll be using, so that she and I can abscond to the other."

Tana smiled. "That would be correct."

"Of course," said Tori, leaning in closer to Tracy and whispering conspiratorially to her, "she's assuming I'm still going to give it up after she called me dim."

"But baby," said Tana, "your naïveté is one of the reasons I love you."

Tracy gave Tori's arms a squeeze and extricated herself from her friend's embrace. "We'll be down here," she said, standing.

"So," said Tana, "we can have the attic, with all the props and set pieces?"

"As long as you mind where you place those props," said Tracy. "You don't know where they've been."

Tana stood, extended a hand to Tori, and then dragged her off toward the stairs, the two of them pausing only long enough to each give Tracy a peck on the cheek, a silent wish of good luck. And then, then she was alone.

She was about to tidy up when she realized that all the tidying was done. So she paced instead, the sound of heels clicking against the floorboards keeping her company. It was such a strange sound, so disconnected from her understanding of herself. Tracy Silver didn't wear heels, especially heels that went click and clack. But, then again, she didn't wear jeans this tight either, or sweaters that showed off bare shoulders. And she didn't bite her nails, Ms. Tracy Silver, but here she was: biting them just the same.

Behind her, the outside door creaked open and the boy's voice called out, "Got it!"

Tucker was all muscle and hair gel, his body a carefully manufactured machine, his coiffure a calculated mess of brown hair. Only his glasses, square-rimmed and too hip for their own good, did anything to soften him. But that was okay. Tracy wasn't interested in anything or anyone soft, at least not tonight.

"You sure you didn't forget anything else?" she asked him.

"What else could I possibly forget?"

"I don't know," said Tracy. "You could be rocking a King Missle situation over there."

Tucker squinted. "A what?" he said.

"King Missle," said Tracy. "They had a song called 'Detachable P —.' Never mind."

Tucker nodded and headed for the chair, running a finger along it. "So," he said, inspecting his finger, as if for dust, "how was the play tonight?"

"The old man finally nailed his monologue," said Tracy.

"Which one?" said Tucker. "Doesn't he spend the whole play giving speeches?"

"The one at the end," said Tracy, "when he's strangling her."

"Oh yeah," he said, sitting in the chair, then propping his feet up on the table. "That was awesome."

"Excuse me?" said Tracy. "What is awesome about him choking the life out of the mother of his child?"

Tucker laughed. "But it ain't his kid; it's the demon's. Right?"

"If you believe the demon was real and not a figment of his psychotic imagination."

Tucker laughed again. "Oh, that demon was real, alright. Did you see the size of his—"

"I did," said Tracy, cutting him off. "But whatevs. What was so awesome about Silas killing Ada?"

"It was the passion in his eyes," said Tucker. "The only other time he looked that into something was when he walked in reading Shakespeare."

Tracy said nothing, not because there was nothing to say, but because he was right and she couldn't bear to concede the point. Though she supposed she was conceding, just by being silent. And so, maybe—but she cut herself off and went back to listening to him before she could finish the thought.

"That was the scene where I first noticed you," Tucker was saying, "lurking in the shadows, a death stare on your face. You may have hated him, but you were into it too. There was some part of him you liked, despite yourself."

Tracy stomped over to him, straddled him, and then pressed her face toward his, ready to kiss him when he said:

"Shit! I just remembered the other thing I forgot."

"What?" she said.

"My car," he said. "I forgot to lock it."

She ran her hands along his shoulders, let a few fingers slip under his neckline. "You're fine," she told him. "The hooligans of Harwich are fast asleep by now."

"It's my parents' car," he said. "I gotta go check. If it got stolen—"

She stood and moved out of his way, then watched him go. "Girls!" she shouted, once he was gone.

There was a rush of footsteps overhead and then Tana and Tori appeared in the doorway once more. Tracy stifled a laugh at the sight of them, and actually had to turn away to hold herself together. Tana was dressed in a devil's costume, Tori in an angel's. Tracy cast a glance over each shoulder to see if they were in the right places, then joked:

"I'm having a total *Animal House* moment here."

"*Animal House*?" said Tori, standing off to the left.

Tana chortled, getting it, then said, "Fuck him. Fuck his brains out. Suck his dick. Squeeze his buns. You know he wants it."

Tori said, "I thought I was the one advocating for this hook up."

"*Animal House*, darlin'. I'm just playing the part I'm dressed for," said Tana.

"I thought you guys were headed for the attic," said Tracy.

"We were," said Tori, "but when we passed the costume racks on the second floor, Miss Thing couldn't resist."

"Cosplay pushes my buttons," said Tana. "Sue me! We're in a theater."

Tracy sighed. "What am I going to do?" she said, as she turned to face them.

"Do?" said Tana. "You're going to *do* him. You wanted adventure. He'll give you a good ride, at the very least."

Tori rolled her eyes. "How can you tell?"

"He's an idiot," said Tana. "He can't carry on a conversation about anything other than sportsball. So, he's got to be good at something. Right?"

"Right," said Tracy, nodding as if she were sure.

The outside door creaked open again and Tucker crept back in. He looked as if he were about to say something, then paused and simply smiled at the sight before him.

"We'll be up in the attic," said Tori. "First and second floor are all yours."

The girls slipped upstairs while Tucker drew ever closer.

"So," he said, "what's it going to be? The halo or the horns?"

Tracy put a finger to his lips to shush him. "Please stop talking," she said, taking his hand in her own, "before I change my mind."

And, because he was obedient, because he wanted his bone, so to speak, he didn't say another word. Not one, not until she begged him to say her name and he said it.

Again and again.

20

NOT LIVING UP TO WHAT HE'S SUPPOSED TO BE

They slept on the ratty taupe loveseat that was tucked into the alcove beside the lighting booth. Many a technician had napped here during tech week and many an actor had fucked here during cast parties (or at least those were the stories she'd heard). But this was the first time Tracy had been on this couch in years, and she didn't understand how anyone could even sit on the collapsing old thing, let alone perform some other more vigorous act. It was true that they, both of them, had slept on it, but only Tucker was still asleep. Tracy's rest had been fitful at best.

But maybe it wasn't even the love seat's fault. Maybe it was the fact that his chest, so pleasing in its hardness when looked upon, didn't make a great pillow. Or maybe it was the layer of sweat between them that kept drying then coming back, drying then coming back. Or the ache between her legs. Or the place where her groin clung to his hip, all sticky, as if her labia didn't want to let go. Was that her, the stickiness? It must've been, right? Because the condom had worked; she'd seen how he'd filled it.

Whatever substance it was that glued them together, she had made it.

But what did that mean? That she wanted him again? Because she didn't. She knew that now. She didn't regret the one time. No, no, that had been fun, if a bit awkward, if a bit painful. But she didn't want to do it again. She was glad he'd only brought one condom, despite the gentle kiss she'd given him when, after they were done, he lamented his decision not to bring more.

Tracy crawled out from under him, the sounds of their bodies parting louder than she'd imagined they'd be, louder than she could stomach. Her tummy turned and she braced herself against the wall, her legs wobbling. But the moment passed and soon she was standing up just fine, searching the floor for her underwear, her bra, her jeans.

She was dressed except for her top when, beyond the curtain that hid the alcove, she heard the outside door open. She tried not to breathe, but that only made every breath sound louder. Tracy heard footsteps headed for the stage as she peeked from behind the curtain to see who it was. But before she could see him, she could hear him.

It was Michael, with headphones on, singing.

Tracy put a hand over Tucker's mouth and nudged him awake. His eyes shot open in panic, then quickly narrowed as he listened to Tracy's instructions. He nodded along, looked calm. It was almost as if he'd been through this routine before.

While he dressed, Tracy stepped up into the lighting booth, climbed the ladder that led to the second floor, and peered through the darkness for any sight of the girls. As luck would have it, they were creeping down from the attic at that very moment, back in their street clothes.

"Is someone singing down there?" whispered Tana.

Tracy nodded, put a finger to her lips.

They drew closer.

"You have a plan?" whispered Tori.

Tracy nodded again. "You guys go and wait by the stage-right alcove; Tucker's over in the stage-left one. When I give the signal—"

"What signal?" said Tana.

"I'm going to throw on one of the lights to disorient him." said Tracy. "As soon as you see it, you run. Tucker's going to do the same."

They nodded in agreement, then took their places. Tracy ducked out of the booth to give Tucker a thumbs up.

"Will I see you again?" said Tucker.

Tracy shrugged. "It's a mystery," she said, quoting from a favorite film, though one he'd probably never seen. She was about to joke with him and say "Places," but she figured he wouldn't know what that meant either. So, she simply waved him goodbye and slipped back into the booth.

It was hard to see where Michael was in the darkness, with nary a work light to illuminate him. But then, out of nowhere, the screen of his phone lit up his face. It was perfect. He was standing right beneath the special that was set to illuminate the center-stage chair. Tracy flipped on the lighting board, waited a second to hear the telltale hum of the instruments overhead, then threw up the slider for the special.

A harsh circle of bright white light shone down on Michael out of the darkness and he looked up at the sight of it, startled. On cue, Tana and Tori booked it past him. Then Tucker did the same. Michael spun around to see who was racing by, but he was squinting and probably—*hopefully*—unable to pick out a face from the darkness.

Once her friends were clear, Tracy slid up the work lights, a gentle purple wash filling out the darkness around Michael. She crouched down and threw open the cooler the tech kept back in the booth for drinks, searching for the nip bottle she'd stashed there. It was time. There was no denying that now. Tiny bottle in hand, she found her sweater, put it on, and stepped out toward the stage.

Michael, mug in hand, shook his head at her as she drew closer.

"Isn't it a little early for your morning cocoa?" she asked him.

"Isn't it a little late for you to be sneaking around?"

"Touché," she said.

He set down his mug and began to wrap his headphones around his phone. "I couldn't sleep," he said. "What's your excuse?"

She almost told him. A few months ago, before she'd seen what she'd seen, Michael was almost on par with Desiree in the cool parental figure department. But not anymore. No, instead of telling him, she pled the fifth.

"Fair enough," he said.

"So, what'd you think of the play?" she asked him, looking for a way to distract him, to get closer to the mug without him noticing.

"I enjoyed it," he said. "It was helpful."

"Helpful?" she said, circling, trying to see if he would counter. "How so?"

"Well, it was about my great-grandfather, wasn't it? I always wanted to know how our family got so fucked up, and now I know."

"Well," she said, "only some of the story was verifiable fact. Uncle Matt embellished the rest."

"Oh, so he's still Uncle Matt, is he?"

Man, he was insufferable. Tracy sighed, then said, "Seeing as he's actually my mother's brother and not just her cousin, yes."

"Semantics," said Michael, still not moving, still not turning away.

Get him talking about the play, she thought. *Get him pontificating. He'll pace. You'll get your chance.*

She asked, "How much did you know about Old Silas before seeing the play?"

"The basics," he said. "I knew he was a Civil War vet, that he married a whole bunch of times before he met my great-grandmother, that he was in his seventies when they tied the knot. I knew he was an asshole to his two kids."

"What did you know about the boot?" she asked.

"Not a lot," he said. "And I still don't get why it was so important."

He didn't get why it was so important?!? How could he say that he finally understood how the family got fucked up without also understanding the metaphor of the boot?

"The boot was a metaphor?" he asked.

Shit, she thought. *How much of that did I say out loud?*

"For what?" he said.

"God," she said, "you really are hopeless."

"OK then, Ms. Valedictorian, illuminate your poor, uneducated uncle."

She sat on the table, beside the mug, exasperated. And then, when she realized where she'd sat—beside it instead of in front of it—she was even angrier. A few inches to the left and she could have done the deed behind her back before he was any the wiser.

"The boot belonged to his father," she said, "a mariner who preferred the adventure of the sea to the quiet comforts of his family."

"Yes," he said, "I knew that."

"When his father drowned at sea, the boot was all that washed ashore. It was a warning, but it was also a promise."

"A promise of what?" said Michael.

"A promise of possibility without boundaries, of—"

"Death isn't a boundary?"

"You know what I mean?"

"I don't think I do," said Michael.

Tracy rose, looked him in the eye. She said, "Our family broke and continues to break because we can't make choices. We want the adventure the boot promises, but we also want the safety that comes when the boot is under the bed instead of on our foot."

"I don't think that's fair," said Michael. "To your mom, or to anyone else who—"

"This isn't about my mom," she said. "This is about you."

Bingo! That got him, hurt him. He glared at her for a moment, his eyes wide. His lips trembled, the corners of them twitching, as if caught between a smirk and a frown.

He asked, "You don't think I've made choices in my life?"

"I know you haven't," she said. "I know you can't."

He made to open his mouth and say something, but then seemed to stop himself short. Then, he walked toward the exit, mumbling, "You have no idea, kid. No idea."

While his back was turned to her, Tracy slipped the nip bottle out of her pocket, unscrewed its cap, and poured its contents into his mug. She gave the mug a swirl, pocketed the empty bottle, and then said, "Don't forget your mug."

Michael turned around, faced her again. "My mug?" he said.

"Yeah," she said, "I'm done cleaning up in here for the night."

He came back to the table, picked up the mug, and took a swig.

"Does it really help you relax?" she said. "The cocoa?"

"I wake up pretty panicky, most mornings. This has always done the trick."

She smiled, gave a light laugh. "Chocolate always hypes me up," she said.

"Don't I know it?" he said. "All the times I babysat you as a kid..." He trailed off, sipped at his cocoa again. "You really think I can't make choices?"

"Don't beat yourself up," said Tracy. "Mom couldn't either, not until she had that *Christmas Carol* dream of hers."

Michael chuckled. "I'll never forget when she told me about that. Sounded like she was high as a kite. But whatever the three spirits showed her, it did the trick. Within a year, she and the Runt were through and she and Desiree were together at last."

Tracy slipped her phone out of her pocket, checked the time, and then said, "She had a little help getting that dream going, I have to admit."

"What do you mean?" said Michael.

"Well, Uncle Matt was getting sick of hearing her bitch about her plight, so one night he asked me to slip a little something into her evening tea. I was young and angry and he promised it would make things better, so..." She trailed off, waiting for him to catch on.

"Really?" said Michael. "He did that? You were, what, seven or eight? What was it?"

"An old family recipe," said Tracy. "Or, well, it was something one of Old Silas' wives cooked up. The Wiccan. The one he strangled to death in the play.

Michael shook his head, finished his cocoa, and set it down on the table again. Tracy checked her phone. It was almost time.

"Christ," said Michael, "I can't believe he got you involved in that."

"It was all for the best," said Tracy.

"Yeah," he said, "because she was going to sleep. But what if she'd gotten up in the middle of the night?"

"I don't know," she said, showing him the nip bottle. " I guess we're going to find out."

"Tracy," he said, rubbing his stomach, then clutching it as he winced. "What did you..."

He stumbled as he came toward her, tried to steady himself on the chair. But it was no use. *O true apothecary*! she thought. *Thy drugs are quick*.

"I know the truth about you," she told him, as he began to twitch. "It's time to make sure you know it, too."

From the second floor, she brought mannequins. From the attic, she brought a table, chairs, and props. And then, once everything was set, she went back to the lighting booth. From the cooler, she withdrew another nip bottle, with a less potent brew, and she downed that herself. She had to drink it quick. It was the only way, according to Ada's notes, to induce a collective hallucination, to join Michael on the trip which he was about to take.

When she began to see things out there on the stage herself, things that weren't there but were, she lay her hands upon the lighting board and got the show on the road.

21

GUILTY FEET THAT GOT NO RHYTHM

The courtroom was a sort of mashup. On the one hand, it looked the trial scene from *The Undiscovered Country*, Michael's favorite Star Trek film: a big circular room with a beam of light shining down on the platform where stood the accused. But, on the other hand, it was too colorful to be Klingon. The jury, seated all around them, was comprised of every female comic book, cartoon, science fiction, or fantasy character Michael had ever crushed on, each of them done up in the most audacious outfit they'd ever been seen in. They all looked annoyed to be there, everyone from Slave Leia to *Little House*'s Laura Ingalls, from The Little Mermaid to *Lost*'s Charlotte Lewis. There were six copies of Scarlett Johansson seated behind seven variations of the X-Men's Jean Grey. And Dana Scully was there too, chatting it up with what looked like a Vulcan and looking quite pleased to be rid of Mulder for the evening. *God*, Tracy thought, as she looked around, *I have never seen so many redheads in one place*.

Michael was still out cold, though clad now in an orange jumpsuit. *Fitting*, Tracy thought, given that orange was Michael's favorite color. She thought of how happy he'd be, under different circumstances, to have found something to wear in that shade besides his ratty old Reese's t-shirt.

And what was she wearing, Tracy wondered, looking herself over. Judge's robes, of course. Simple black. Nothing crazy. No powdered wig, or anything like that. She sat behind a tall podium, looming high above the scene, like the Queen of Hearts in *Alice in Wonderland*. A banner hung down the front of the bench, a rather severe looking Venus symbol stitched into it.

Tracy took up her gavel and banged it down three times. "All rise!" she called out. And when Michael still did not stir, she waved to the shadows at the foot of her bench and two bailiffs stepped out, one done up like a swordswoman of old, the other like a gunslinger from beyond the apocalypse. The two women pulled Michael to his feet as Tracy repeated herself: "I said, 'All rise!'"

Michael squeezed his eyes together, shaking his head. "Where am I?" he said.

"Michael Silver," said Tracy, "you are on trial for your crimes against femininity."

"On trial for what?"

Tracy smirked down at him. "Anything you say can and will be held against you in this court. So, we recommend you shut up."

"If this is a trial," said Michael, "where is the jury? Where are the lawyers?"

"This is your courthouse," said Tracy, waving her gavel around, urging him to see for himself. "You built it, brick by brick. So, you tell me."

He said nothing for a minute, as he looked around, locking eyes with several of the women his subconscious had invited to render his verdict. His jaw went slack, his lower lip drooping. Tracy couldn't tell if he was staring in disbelief, or if he was ogling them.

"You're the judge?" he said, still not looking at her.

"Apparently," she said. "And, if you don't mind, I'd like to call my next witness."

Now he looked. "Wait," he said, "the judge doesn't call witnesses."

"In here she does," said the two bailiffs.

Tracy was amused by this. All the power rested with her, except for the final judgment. And maybe that was her call, too. After all, the jury was fiction; she was reality.

"OK, fine," said Michael. "But don't you mean first witness, not next?"

She wasn't sure what she meant, so she embellished: "We're halfway through this trial already, Mr. Silver. Have you been asleep this whole time? Is this matter not worthy of your attention? Did you not see me, right here in front of you?"

"No," said Michael. "I, uh..."

"How typical," said Tracy.

"How unsurprising," said the bailiffs.

"Tracy!" shouted Michael. "Wait a minute. I—"

But Tracy ignored him. She looked down at the notes in front of her, scribbled so many days ago now, back when the potion was still brewing, when it wasn't even certain when Michael would be in town, when it seemed like there would be more time to plan, more time to prepare the case. Tracy looked at the notes and saw her mother's name—Veronica—and that's who she called first.

In the real world, she felt her hand sliding up the fader for a second pool of light, off to the left, but she didn't see the mannequin there that she was expecting. She saw Veronica, a younger Veronica, five and a half months pregnant, in a godawful prom dress the color of a pistachio. Tracy closed her eyes, tried to remember what was real, and then looked down. There was no fader anymore. There was nothing more real than the young woman beside her, nothing closer to the truth than the gavel in her hand.

"Please," Tracy said to Veronica, "state your name for the record."

"Veronica Amelia Silver," said the young woman—younger, Tracy realized, than she was herself.

"And what," said Tracy, "is your relationship to the accused?"

"I'm his cousin," said Veronica.

"Could you please explain the scene we are about to see?"

"Scene?" said Michael. "Is this a courthouse or a playhouse?"

Tracy realized how preposterous it sounded, but scene was what she had meant to say, what she felt compelled to say. She pointed down at him with her gavel. "The accused will remain silent until spoken to."

"This is absurd!" said Michael.

"Guards?" said Tracy.

The Gunslinger drove the butt of her rifle into Michael's stomach, and he fell to his knees. Then the Swordswoman grabbed a fistful of his hair and yanked his head backward. She put her sword to his throat.

"The accused will remain silent until spoken to," said Tracy. "Do you understand."

Still on his knees, Michael nodded. A drop of blood traced its way down his neck, from the edge of the blade and onto the collar of his jumpsuit.

"Ms. Silver," said Tracy, "please continue."

"This was the night of our prom," she said, and suddenly it was, the courtroom replaced with a school gymnasium all done up in maroon and white, the DJ playing a schizophrenic mix of Nirvana and Michael Jackson. "I didn't want to go," said Veronica, "but my dad didn't give me a choice. He decided it would be best for the family's good name if I went with the baby's father, my soon-to-be husband, to keep up appearances."

Out of the darkness beside Veronica appeared Tracy's father, the

Runt, dressed in a tuxedo, a green cummerbund at his waist to complement the dress of the awkward girl beside him. They looked so strange, so young. Not that they were old now—they were the youngest parents in her grade, in fact—but the idea of them creating her this early in their lives was harder to stomach in reality than it had been in theory. Even the photo albums didn't do this scene justice. Somehow, by the time it came time for photographs, the two of them would figure a way to at least look like they liked each other. But now, standing on the edge of the dance floor, not quite an arm's length apart, his hands clasped behind his back, hers folded underneath her breasts and above her belly, they looked like they had never touched each other before, let alone touched enough to—

Tracy shook her head to rid the thought from her mind.

"Meanwhile," said Veronica, "the person I wanted to be with, Desiree, wasn't going to go at all."

"But she did go," said Tracy, "didn't she?"

"Yes," said Veronica. "At the last minute, my cousin Michael asked her."

Michael stood, shrugging off the bailiffs as if they were ghosts, which is what they seemed to be now. He looked all about the room, searching, it seemed, for Desiree.

"And she said yes?" asked Tracy.

"Yes," said Veronica.

"Ms. Silver, is it true that your cousin was a freshman on the night in question?"

"Yes," said Veronica.

Tracy scribbled on her notepad, pencil scratches echoing through the chamber. "Do you have any idea then," she began, "why Desiree, cheerleading captain, star of the field hockey squad, lusted after by hundreds of her schoolmates, would deign to accept Mr. Silver's invitation?"

Veronica looked over at Michael, who was still looking around for Desiree. She shook her head, sighed, and then said, "She felt sorry for him."

"Why?" said Tracy.

"Because," said Michael, still looking, about to step from his circle of light, "because I'd had a crush on her from the moment I first met her."

"Mr. Silver," said Tracy, "I will not warn you again. I'm not interested in your version of things, however truthful you might swear it to be, whatever excuses you might have for—"

From the shadows came Desiree's voice. "Let him tell the story," she said.

Tracy had heard it all before, the awkward circumstances under which Veronica's cousin had once crushed on her future wife. Back in the day, Michael swore he was in love with Desiree. At fourteen, maybe he didn't know what love was, but he knew for sure that he felt something. And it wasn't just 'the hots.' He had more than just 'the hots' for her. As his grandfather had so eloquently put it, at that year's Christmas party, Michael lit up like Rudolph's nose at the mere sight of Desiree. And if that wasn't love, then what the heck was it?

What was it about Desiree, in Michael's opinion, that made her so combustible? Well, you had to look at it this way: she was a senior, and a cheerleader, and far prettier than any cover girl he'd ever seen, and yet, despite all that, Desiree still said "hi" to him in the hallways at school. She was Veronica's friend—what a fucking idiot he was, Tracy thought, if he didn't see they were more than that—and that meant she knew Michael by proxy, and kinda-sorta had to be cordial to him when they bumped into each other at parties and whatnot. But she was under no obligation to acknowledge his existence within the hallowed halls of the high school. And even if she was so obligated, she surely wasn't required to give him a smile on occasion, or a wave. Acknowledging a freshman's existence, let alone a freshman boy's existence, was tantamount to social suicide. And yet—

Desiree danced with him now, stunning the room in her scarlet satin shift. "I didn't go to prom with you because I felt sorry for you," she said. "I said yes because I wanted to put a smile on someone's face, and if it couldn't be Veronica's, if it couldn't be mine, then why not yours? You were always so sweet."

"Objection!" shouted Tracy, ready to hurl her gavel at the pair of them.

"Tracy," said Veronica, off dancing with the Runt now, making a fool of her pregnant-ass self. "Give him a chance to defend himself."

"No!" said Tracy. "I will not. That's all he ever does: defend himself. All those pre-emptive strikes to keep us feeling sorry for him and stop us from asking the difficult questions. Like this one," she said. "Mr. Silver, do you recall where you were on the night of December 31, 1991?"

Michael ducked his head. In shame, Tracy happened to know.

"Where were you?" said Desiree.

"I repeat," said Tracy, "do you recall where you were on the night of December 31, 1991?"

"I was at home," said Michael, still not looking up, which was even more incriminating than perhaps he realized, since his eyes were now focused squarely on Desiree's chest. "I was at home," he said again. "In bed."

"And do you recall what you were doing that night," said Tracy, "alone and in bed?"

"I plead the fifth," he said.

"There is no fifth to plead here," said Tracy. "You will answer the question!"

"I was jerking off, alright?"

"To what?" said Tracy.

"To a picture of Desiree," said Michael, "from the yearbook."

Tracy knew just what picture it was, the page dog-eared in Michael's copy of the yearbook, which he'd given to Veronica and Desiree as a wedding present after learning they'd both burned theirs in grief during the years of their separation. The photo was of Desiree in her field hockey uniform, smiling for one of the many cameras that followed her that year—one of the guys on the school newspaper took it upon himself to get a photo of her into every issue, even if there was no legitimate reason to do so. She had her white shirt on, her plaid skirt, and her knee socks of course, and every piece of her ensemble was a bit dirty, as if she'd just finished up a game. But the pièce de résistance was the hockey stick she clutched to her chest, between her breasts to a certain extent, a happy accident that had been the impetus for many happy "accidents" on the part of Mr. Michael Silver and his perverted fourteen-year-old imagination.

"It's okay," said Desiree, blushing, smiling, lifting his face up by the chin.

"It is not okay!" said Tracy. "Mr. Silver, are you aware of where Desiree and your cousin Veronica were that night?"

"Tracy," said Veronica, "what does the one thing have to do with the other?"

"Mr. Silver," said Tracy, "are you aware?"

All at once, the dancing stopped, the lights faded, and the record stopping spinning.

"I am," said Michael, walking away from Desiree.

"Where were they?" said Tracy.

Michael looked over his shoulder. Veronica and Desiree were side by side now. "They were at a party," said Michael, "at Veronica's house. They were drinking and playing spin the bottle."

"And?" said Tracy.

Michael looked away from them again, staring off into the

distance as he said, "After Veronica spun the bottle and it landed on Desiree, it caused quite a ruckus. They kissed, and that was enough to cause all of the hornballs at the table to pair off."

"And did Veronica and Desiree pair off?"

"No," said Michael. "They didn't."

"Objection!" said Veronica. "Relevance?"

"Overruled," said Tracy.

"Tracy," said Desiree, "what is the point of this?"

"The point," said Tracy, "is that your quote-unquote sweet prom date was no better than the hornball who took you to bed that night, no better than the runt who got my mother pregnant. And yet, he consistently tries to pass himself off as sensitive and—"

"No," said Desiree, storming back toward Michael, the lights and the band and the crowd returning as she did. "Do you know what he said to me that night? Prom night?"

"Thank you for saying yes," said Michael, as they began to dance again.

"I'm having a great time," said Desiree.

"It must suck," he said, "to see her with him."

They both glanced over at Veronica, who stood against the far wall, nodding along as she listened to the Runt. She tried to get a word in, but failed.

"I don't know what you mean," said Desiree.

Michael said, "I know how much you both like—"

"You're wrong," said Desiree, cutting him off. "I don't know where you got that idea."

"I'm not wrong," he said. "I'm a details guy. You've seen how long it takes me to get anything done. That mural down the hall, the one with the lions chasing the Indians, I obsessed over that for months."

"And?" said Desiree.

Tracy watched him swallow, as if trying to build up some head of steam inside himself to say what needed to be said. For a moment, she saw her uncle again, the man she wanted him to be, the man he was capable of being: a man who said the right thing, who did the right thing. Always.

"And," he said, "I've been obsessing over you for years. I see the way you and Veronica look at each other. And I've seen the way she looks at the Runt. It may take her a while to see what she's seeing, but she will. Eventually," he said, "she won't be able to ignore it."

Desiree ducked her head and nodded. "You're a pretty smart kid," she said.

"Thanks," he said.

Desiree kissed Michael on the cheek and pulled him into a hug. They danced close for a second before Tracy felt the anger swelling in her again, saw the Michael in this moment that she needed to purge, to wipe away. His hand was on Desiree's back, her lower back, not quite where it wasn't supposed to be yet, but getting there.

"The witnesses are excused," said Tracy.

Desiree and Michael parted ever so slightly. They smiled at each other, kept dancing, as if waiting to see how long the moment would last. Waiting to see how long Tracy would *let* it last.

"Guards," said Tracy. "Separate them."

The bailiffs pulled them apart, the Gunslinger shunting Desiree off toward Veronica, the Swordswoman shoving Michael back onto the stand of the accused, all light going out except for the circle that shone down on him from above.

22

A TRAIL OF HONEY TO SHOW YOU WHERE HE'S BEEN

High atop the judge's bench, Tracy was anxious to get on with things. She was on a roll, and Michael was reeling, so as soon as Desiree and Veronica were gone, Tracy said, "The prosecution calls its next—"

"That's it?" said Michael. "No breaks? No res—"

Tracy nodded into the darkness, where she saw light glint off a gun barrel. The Gunslinger stepped from the shadows, slammed her rifle into Michael's head once more, and laughed as he fell to his knees.

Satisfied, Tracy continued. "We call Robin Gates to the stand," she said.

Michael's head snapped up, his eyes still watering, a rivulet of blood on his chin, dripping down from where he'd bitten his lip. "Well that's not possible," he said. "She's... she's..."

Dead was what he meant to say. As a doornail. Just like Marley. Tracy held back a chuckle at the thought. Five years she'd been gone, compared with Marley's seven, and she looked much better than Scrooge's old partner ever had, as if those extra two years were when all the decay happened. No rotting teeth on her, nor crossed eyes, nor festering wounds held together by filthy rags. And, as far as chains went, there were only the ones she wore in life. No, the Robin Gates that walked into their courtroom was like no ghost Tracy had ever seen. She was the spitting image of the girl Michael had fallen for all those years ago, the girl on his best friend's porch, the one he'd painted and drawn again and again.

She looked cold, her thin body shuddering as if still held in the grip of that steady January breeze they'd met in. And she looked just like the pixie Michael had always painted her to be. It wasn't just the way she carried herself, as if, like a bird, her bones were hollow and full of air, as if she might fly away at any moment. It was her hair, too—the short, chunky, playful cut of it. It was her bright, mischievous eyes. And it was the fact that it seemed as if the only things weighing her down at all were the jewelry that she wore, and the leather.

There were earrings everywhere, one dangly one in each lobe, two studs in each as well, and one up near the top of her right ear, right in the crook of a fleshy part, a puncture that made Tracy swoon for a moment at the sight of it. When Robin laughed, Tracy spied a stud splitting through the middle of her tongue. Michael, down below, searching for somewhere else to look, besides her eyes, besides her plunging neckline, seemed to have found the final piercing, or at least the final visible one, a small jewel lanced through the flesh above her navel.

"Ms. Gates," said Tracy, "what is your relationship to the accused?"

"Well," said Robin, fixated on Michael and not on Tracy, "for a period of approximately three years, I fucked his brains out on a regular basis."

Tracy banged her gavel down, half-amused and half-annoyed. She liked this girl, always had, and she thought she might miss

Robin almost as much as Michael did. "Language," said Tracy, admonishing her.

"Which one?" said Robin.

"Excuse me?" said Tracy.

"Which language would you prefer?" said Robin. "I can do French—*J'ai baisé le cerveau hors de sa tête*—or German—*Ich sein Gehirn aus dem Kopf gefickt*. My Swedish is a little rusty, but I could give it a whirl."

Tracy said, "What I meant was—"

"Oh," said Robin, cutting her off. "I got it. *Jag knullade hans hjärna ut*!"

"If we could keep the vulgarity to a minimum," said Tracy, "that would be most appreciated."

Robin laughed, finally looking up at Tracy. "Well," she said, "fuck me in the ass and call me Charlie, I'll sure as shit do my goddamned best."

Once upon a time, she had been called—by the *Phoenix*, no less —"Boston's most notorious rock and roll slut." The mouth on her, Tracy now remembered, was a big part of why.

Tracy looked down at her notes again, trying not to get starstruck by this girl she'd spent her adolescence idolizing. She continued: "You were Mr. Silver's girlfriend from January 1995 through January 1998, is that correct?"

"Oui, oui," said Robin.

"And together you made up two thirds of the popular local band Gideon's Bible?"

"Well," said Robin, "at the beginning, technically speaking, we were one half of the band. But, you know, love triangles and all that."

Tracy knew that. How had she forgotten that? Or had she forgotten? Maybe when she'd written the question down she'd simply been trying for simplification. Maybe—she cut herself off and asked her next question: "Could you describe how you came to be involved with Mr. Silver?"

"Could I?" said Robin. "Man, I remember the night I met Michael Silver so well it hurts."

Tracy listened as she told the story, the third most recounted love story in their house, just after the story of her two moms getting together and the story of Michael and Jenna. They were headed to a Nine Inch Nails concert at the Centrum, Robin and David (the corner of the love triangle since lost to history), and in walked their ride, Michael, a guy in paint-stained jeans and a torn Voltron t-shirt, looking all innocent and unkempt, like he had no idea what he was in for. The way Robin used to tell it, he was the best kind of handsome: the kind that doesn't know it yet, and maybe never will.

"And it was at the concert that he made his move?" said Tracy.

"The concert?" said Robin. "I haven't even gotten there yet."

"We don't require every detail," said Tracy, which was true, though secretly she loved every one of them, from the crazed teenagers leaping over their heads to get to the mosh pit below, to Michael and Robin singing to each other of the tainted touch of each other's caress.

"Well, listen," said Robin, "Ms. Judge, Jury, and Executioner, you need to pipe the fuck down. I'm telling a story here."

"That's not how this works," said Tracy.

"I don't care how this works," said Robin. "This is how it *should* work. You argue against him, someone gets to counter. Basics of academic discourse, baby."

"I understand that," said Tracy. "I'm the valedictorian of—"

Robin shouted, "I'm the valedictorian of life, sweetheart!" and it was as if the judge's bench shrunk as a result, shriveled up a bit, tucked itself closer to the ground. "I know what's what," said Robin. "So, sit down and shut the fuck up for a while."

Tracy stared at Robin and Robin stared back. Robin seemed to be waiting, to see if Tracy would interrupt again. And only after a full measure of silence did she continue.

She talked about the car he drove, a gray Ford Tempo that was falling apart in every way imaginable. She lingered over the lights on the dash that were illuminated when they shouldn't have been, over the noises coming from places that should have been silent. And then she talked about how none of it mattered once they were on the open road, how the stereo drowned out all that was wrong in the world, how they sang along to anything and everything.

Robin knelt down beside Michael now. "And you could sing," she said. "Oh, man, could you sing. Your voice was heavy, and warm, and untrained, and when you hit a note you didn't hit it because it was what you were taught to do. You hit that note because it felt right, because it felt good."

"You can't be here," said Michael, his hand creeping toward her cheek, as if to see if she was real. "You..." he said, pulling his hand back, wrapping his arms around his body, shaking his head. "You're—"

But Robin put two fingers to his lips to quiet him.

"Do you remember the concert?" she asked him.

"How could I forget it?" he said. "So many people were rushing to the floor that security lost control. The railings started to buckle."

"It was amazing," said Robin.

"It was," said Michael.

"And then," said Robin, "do you remember afterwards, when I made *my* move?"

Tracy caught the emphasis, rolled her eyes at it. Yes, technically, Robin had made the first move. But his eyes, the way he looked at her, the way he looked at Desiree—the way he looked at every woman, dammit—they proved that he was just as much at fault.

At fault for what? asked a voice in her brain, a voice she silenced with a shake of her head. *You know what*, she thought to herself.

Michael stood and walked away from Robin, the room transforming into the hall outside the auditorium. It was a zoo of people in black t-shirts and fishnet stockings, their mopey make-up ruined by sweat and post-show smiles.

Robin said, "Good show, huh? They play everything you wanted to hear?"

"I was hoping they'd do 'Heresy,'" said Michael. "It's become my, sort-of... I don't know... my anthem?"

Robin smiled, drawing nearer to him. "God is dead, huh?"

Michael ranted for a minute about how that wasn't what the singer was really saying, how the song was really more about why God sucked. He quoted lines, talked about the presence of the capital H in the song, and Robin ate it up, sauntering up to him, nodding along.

"You're really into it," she said. "I like that."

And then it was his story about his grandfather, the one who'd died the spring before, the first death he'd ever experienced for himself as a grown-up. *Blah, blah, blah*. That was Michael for you, co-opting family tragedies to explain his wild mood swings and his sudden changes in musical taste.

He coughed a little at the end of his monologue and that was when Robin did it, when she sealed the deal. She leaned in toward him, tilting her head, and pressed her lips to his Adam's apple, lingering there for a moment, puckering as she withdrew, as if to suck away the hurt with her as she stepped back.

"All better?" she said.

Michael turned away from her, and Tracy was startled by what happened next. And equally startled that she hadn't noticed it before. The room changed when he decided it should change. Michael was just as much in control as she was. They were back in the courthouse, the jury murmuring all around them, the bailiffs whispering something to each other too.

"Yes," said Michael, "it was all better. Except for the part where I lost my oldest friend over you. Except for the part where you cheated on me with that drummer you met at Berklee."

Robin squeezed his bicep, such as it was. "You do know it wasn't just that drummer?" she said. And then she rattled off the list: the slam poet from Maine, the part-time DJ at BCN, the bi drag queen from Swarthmore, and, of course, the twins from Wellesley.

"They didn't count," said Michael.

"Why," said Robin, "because they were chicks?"

"No," said Michael, "because that was our autumn of anything goes."

"Oh yeah," said Robin.

"Objection," said Tracy. "You're skipping ahead."

Robin scoffed: "I thought you wanted us to skip ahead."

"Only in the places I tell you to," said Tracy.

"Fine," said Michael, standing beside Robin, the two of them a united front now. "Where do you want us to go back to?"

Tracy consulted her notes, though she already knew the part she wanted to hear. "Your first time," she said, more timidly than she wished she had.

"The first time we did what?" said Robin. "The first time I blew him?"

Michael blushed, ducked his head.

"Because," said Robin, "that was a totally different time than the first time he ate me out, which was up in his room while you and the rest of the family were downstairs watching the Pops play the '1812 Overture.'"

Robin turned and squeezed Michael's arm with two hands now. "Do you remember," she said, "how I came in time with the cannon blasts? It was a good thing they had the sound blaring—"

Tracy slammed her gavel against its sounding block, cracking the block in two. She looked down at it, unsure how she'd done it. She was angry, yes, but they weren't even to the part that pissed her off the most. Maybe the stories of their escapades were swaying her, like the always did, convincing her that Michael was just being Michael. Maybe these old stories were doing more harm than good when it came to making her case against him.

"Ms. Gates," said Tracy, after a moment, "I'm not entirely sure we need any more of your testimony. If you can't control yourself, then you'll have to head straight back to where you came from. Is that what you want?"

Robin looked sobered by the threat, the first time she'd looked defeated since she'd entered the courtroom. "No," she said.

"Then, please," said Tracy, "describe for this courtroom the first time you and Mr. Silver had sex."

"It was Easter," said Robin, "just a couple of months after the concert."

The Gunslinger stepped out of the shadows with a gift-wrapped box in her hands. She gave it to Robin, then disappeared again. And, as she vanished, the room began to transform. Tracy knew this place all too well: the old footlocker and the strong scent of its cedar lining, the plastic bins full to the brim with Cabbage Patch Kids and Care Bears and Pound Puppies, the beat-up plaid couch with the thick wooden arm rests. It was the rec room of the Cape house, and it looked almost the same in 1995 as it did now.

"No one else was awake yet," said Robin. "And the first thing he said to me, when I gave him his present was—"

"Oh no, you're turning into the batty neighbor."

"What do you mean?" said Robin.

"You're confusing holidays," said Michael, "just like she does."

"How so?" said Robin.

"It's Easter," said Michael, "and you're giving me a present. Presents, as you know, are for Christmas."

"You're ridiculous," said Robin. "Just open it."

Michael sighed, then started in on the package's ribbons, its bow.

"Just out of curiosity," said Robin, "how is it that she's mixing things up?"

"You didn't see it?" said Michael.

"See what?" said Robin.

"Oh, Christ," said Michael. "Let me finish opening this and then I'll show you."

He finished opening the package and his face was all mirth and mischief as he pulled from it a plastic baby in a burlap swaddling cloth.

"Is this what I think it is?" said Michael.

"Yep," said Robin. "I stole it from her yard this morning."

Tracy had heard stories of this doll, of where it came from. The next door neighbor, Mrs. Doris Brown, before she passed away, had kept a nativity scene in her yard year round. But Michael, the family atheist, didn't buy that. Since the only time he saw it was at Easter, when he came down to visit, he swore up and down that the woman was just losing her marbles and mixing up her holidays.

Michael contemplated the baby. He paced with it, holding it by the feet and tapping its head against the palm of his free hand. Then, suddenly, he stopped and removed its swaddling cloth. He stared down at the naked doll, dumbfounded.

"No dick," he said.

"Excuse me?" said Robin.

Michael held the baby close to his face, inspecting its crotch.

"No dick," he repeated. "The son of God has no dick. Now I get it. Now I know why we're all so sexually frustrated."

Robin guffawed, then covered her mouth, looking toward the stairs, maybe to see if anyone was coming, if they'd woken anyone.

"I mean, shit," he said. "I knew they cut off the tip, but this is a bit much, don't you think? We are definitely not converting to Judaism."

Michael hoisted the baby high above his head and bellowed, "I have seen the loins of Jesus Christ, and they have shown me the light!"

Robin held a finger to her lips, trying to shush him, but she had the giggles now, and her attempt didn't last long; soon, she was doubled over with laughter.

Michael shook the baby at the window that overlooked Mrs. Brown's yard. "I don't know how many times we've told that woman that the nativity scene is for Christmas and not for Easter. But does she listen?" he said. "NO! I mean, Jesus! Is it too much to ask that, if you're going to put a tacky plastic sculpture on your lawn to celebrate your faith, you at least know what holiday it is? I'm no theology scholar, but this is pretty simple shit we're talking about here. I mean, why doesn't she put a plastic crucifixion scene on her lawn or something?"

"I don't think they make those," said Robin.

"I betcha," said Michael, "somebody could make a lot of money producing plastic crucifixion scenes."

He used the doll to illustrate his point, nodding and pointing as necessary. "See," he said, "you've got Jesus over here, and then you've got the two thieves over here and here. And of course we can't forget about Mary, with the cherry, and Mary Magdalene, and the Romans—"

"Stop it!" said Robin. "You're killing me."

Michael put the baby down. "I'm sorry," he said. "Thank you for my present."

"You're welcome," she said. "Now, sit. I've got something to tell you."

Michael sat on the floor of the rec room. He grabbed a raggedy old Cabbage Patch Kid and held onto it as he said, "I have a bad feeling about this."

Robin sat across from him and took hold of his hand, the Cabbage Patch Kid slumping in his lap now.

"I'm just going to come right out and say it," she said.

"OK," said Michael.

"Carl Jacobson," she said.

"The football player?"

"Just once," she said. "At a party. I was playing my guitar, and he was looking at me just the right way, and there was a lot of Schlitz involved, and—"

"Just once, meaning what?" said Michael. "I mean, you and I haven't even—"

"No, not that!" said Robin. "We just made out for a while."

Michael took his hands back, wrapped his arms around the Cabbage Patch Kid again. Then he reached out and grabbed a Pound Puppy for good measure. "Why did you tell me?" he asked.

"What do you mean?" she said. "I wanted to be honest with you. Isn't honesty what great relationships are built on?"

"Great relationships are built on kindness," said Michael, running the Kid's fat hand over the Puppy's mottled fur. "Consideration," he said.

"And me telling you wasn't kind?" she said. "That wasn't considerate?"

"No," he said. "I know who you are, Robin. I know *what* you are."

Now she seemed taken aback. She scowled a bit. "What am I?"

"A bonafide fucking rock star," said Michael. "Or as close to a rock star as a 17-year-old can get."

"And what does that mean?" said Robin.

"It means," said Michael, "that I knew about Carl, and about the other guys before him, but that I accepted that was part of the deal in being with you. I accepted it and ignored it. And you keeping quiet about your indiscretions aided that cause."

"So," she said, "you'd rather I didn't say anything?"

"Yes!" he said, hurling the toys back in their bins. "I'd rather you let me labor under the delusion that a pretty girl would ever be interested in me, could ever be satisfied by me and me alone."

High above, on her platform, Tracy looked out into the darkness, both to avoid looking at the awkward scene playing out before her and to see how the jury was reacting. But she couldn't see them at all. It was as if they had disappeared, as if maybe they weren't there after all.

Robin was on her knees now, stretching her limber body toward Michael. She wrapped her arms around his shoulders as she said, "You do satisfy me."

He kissed her then, and she kissed him back. They made out with wild abandon as he pushed her backwards and got on top of her.

"Have you no decency?" shouted Tracy. "You're a married—"

But they weren't listening. And was he even the same person now, or was he, in fact, the version of himself from all those years before, the unmarried one?

Does it matter? asked a voice in her head.

Robin began to tug his pants off. Tracy caught sight of the slightest hint of her uncle's ass crack and that was it; she was done. She banged her gavel down three times on the broken sounding block, splintering it further.

"That's enough," said Tracy. "Guards!"

The Swordswoman and the Gunslinger tore out of the darkness, then tore Michael off of Robin, the Swordswoman yanking his pants back up as they did.

Robin stomped over to the Gunslinger and threw a haymaker, dropping the woman to the ground, but stumbling over herself in the process, falling flat on her face.

"Stand up," said Tracy. "All of you."

The Swordswoman grabbed hold of Robin and yanked her up, pulling her off to one side. The Gunslinger, wiping at her bleeding lip, grabbed hold of Michael.

"Ms. Gates," said Tracy, "I have one final question for you, before you're dismissed."

"Yes?" said Robin.

"When Mr. Silver emailed you on the evening of January 22, 1998 to end your relationship, to what did he attribute his decision to call things off?"

"He told me he couldn't understand why I hadn't told him about the drummer from Berklee," she said. "He wanted to know why he'd had to find out from his cousin. Or his cousin's husband. Or something."

"He couldn't understand why you kept the affair from him, even though he had specifically asked you to keep your affairs from him?"

"That's right," said Robin.

"So," said Tracy, "it would be accurate to describe Mr. Silver as a hypocrite, would it not?"

Robin rolled her eyes. "Since when is it a crime to contradict yourself? People change, sometimes from day to day. Hell, I've lived my entire life as a walking contradiction."

Tracy looked around as the rec room faded and the courtroom reappeared, and she found the jury whispering to each other, nodding their approval. *Yes*, they seemed to be saying. *Contradiction is good sometimes. Necessary even.* She was losing them. But they had to see. She had to make them. "But your life is over because of your own hypocrisy," she said. "Shot by a fan you spurned after writing an album of songs begging the masses to adore you." Tracy shook her head, trying to push aside the memory of the tearful, snotty mess she'd been on the day she heard the news. "Ms. Gates, do you wish the same fate for Mr. Silver?"

"No," said Robin.

"Neither do I," Tracy said, and suddenly the courtroom fell silent. The whispers stopped and the gawking commenced. Had she really just said that? Out loud? While trying to win this case? "We're not just here to protect women from him," she said, stumbling for what to say next. "We're also here to protect him from himself."

She banged the gavel down once more. "The witness is excused."

Robin gazed longingly at Michael. Then, with a firm nudge from the Swordswoman, she stepped out of the light, fading back into the darkness from whence she came.

23
THE ATTENTION THE KISS DESERVES

He stared now at two of the more audacious members of the jury. The first was a brown-skinned woman—*not a redhead*, Tracy realized, surprised, having thought the jury was nothing but. She wore a purple bathing suit, the left side of it an inexplicable gash of fish-net, from just below her breast to just above her hip. She had blue hair, green sunglasses, and dangly gold earrings that reached all the way down to the purple choker that held the suit up and her enormous chest in.

Beside her sat a redhead, one of the many, in a white kimono with purple trim, a magenta corset beneath it that was half leather and half skull-patterned lace. She wore a pair of handcuffs on her left wrist, a purple rose and its thorns on the right, and she held matching Comedy and Tragedy masks in each hand. The right half of her face was covered by her hair and three mascara-lined tears rolled down her left cheek. Tracy stifled a laugh. The woman's big 80s hair—that was tragic. But the rest of her get-up, all the half-assed attempts at symbolism, that was almost funny.

Michael shook his head as the two jurors stared at him, their eyes narrowed, their lips pursed. "This is a joke," he said. "How much more of this is there? How long until this shit wears off?"

"This is no joke," said Tracy. "And it doesn't end until you admit your guilt and accept your—"

"Okay then," Michael said to the women he'd been eyeing. "I'm guilty."

"Of what?" said Tracy.

"I don't know," he said, turning to face her now. "You tell me!"

Tracy shook her head. He wasn't ready yet, but that wasn't a surprise. She knew he wouldn't be. She knew it would take the whole journey to get him there.

"I would like to move on now," she said, "to your relationship with Ms. Jennifer Worthing."

"Jenna?" said Michael. "Don't you mean Mrs. Jenna Silver? If you insist on being official—"

"She doesn't belong to you," said Tracy, "no matter what her driver's license says. She was born Jennifer Worthing and—"

"So she belongs to her father then?"

"Excuse me?" said Tracy.

"Worthing was her father's name, and he left when she was five. So, why not give her the name she chose, rather than the one she was saddled with by that good for nothing—"

The lights changed, without Tracy doing anything and without, it seemed, Michael doing anything either. Onto the stage—for it was a stage now, not the courtroom anymore, and not their stage but something bigger—danced someone, a woman, a woman who said, "How about the two of you quit your bitching and let's get on with this?"

It was Jenna and the story Tracy was about to see play out was legend. Michael fell to the floor at the sight of his wife dancing in as her younger self. From his pocket, he withdrew a tiny paintbrush.

Tracy said, "When you met Ms. Worthing—"

"This isn't when I met her," said Michael. "We'd been living in the same townhouse for over two years at this point."

"Okay then," said Tracy. "When you and Ms. Worthing began your relationsh—"

"Why don't you just shut up and watch?" he said.

Michael was working on the last corner of a 48-by-48 foot backdrop with the tiniest brush he owned, a 9/128" red sable that he normally reserved for painting ceramics. Behind him, only Jenna's lingering feet were left, shuffling and skittering across the floor. Try as he might to stop himself, he could not help but glance over his shoulder in between strokes. He could not help, he had told Tracy once, but stare at the girl to whom the feet belonged.

Through the accident of her DNA, Jenna Worthing was possessed of the same idyllic body the Greeks had sculpted two thousand years before. Statuesque, all hips, she was more woman than any girl he had ever known. She spun slowly in her tight black leotard, her arms reaching upward, those full, womanly hips thrust outward, and her head back, her auburn hair falling downward in a matted mess, away from her sweat-soaked brow, from that soft, girl-like face of hers, that face that was, as always, devoid of any of the embellishments—the rouge, the eyeliner, the lip gloss—that might have more fully given her the façade of a grown woman. Wisps of hair clung to each of her apple cheeks, and a heavy, wet lock of it was strewn across those petite lips of hers, which curved upwards at the corners in the devilish little grin that seemed her most cherished facial expression. When she lifted a leg off of the floor, he could see that her foot was dirty, blackened from dancing atop the rubber floor for most of this cold winter's day. He turned away from her once he realized that he'd been staring at the cracks between her toes, and he wondered what he'd been looking for. Some splotch of pure, innocent pink? Who knew? Michael tapped at the bulge in his right jeans pocket, where he kept his wallet, inside which there was still, undoubtedly, a photograph of Robin. Then he painted some more.

Jenna sat down beside him when she was done, legs stretched out in front of her, arms stretched backward to support herself as she stretched. She smelled deliciously awful, her scent a funky potpourri of perspiration and peppermint patties, burnt rubber and Bolognese sauce.

"Nobody," she said, panting in between gulps from her liter of spring water, "is ever going to notice this."

"I will," he said.

"I admire your dedication," she said, laying her head on his shoulder, her labored breath hot against his neck, her hair clinging to his cheek.

"Me, too," he said. "I mean, I admire your dedication. Not mine."

"Thanks," she said. "I wish that it would start paying off. Y'know?"

"You're too harsh on yourself," said Michael.

She patted him on the shoulder as she stood to go. "Aren't we all?"

Michael watched her walk away. Her leotard was riding up in the back, her firm bottom glistening with sweat. Robin, Tracy knew, wouldn't have been caught dead in the same situation. And that was what Michael must have been thinking about: Robin, running around looking for a sweater to wrap around her waist, or walking backwards toward the door, trying not to stumble over her own feet.

Jenna paused at the stage's side door and looked back at him. "You want to walk back to the house together?"

"Yeah," he said. "Yeah."

The bitter December wind whipped at them as they trudged across campus through the freshly fallen snow.

Originally founded when Thomas Jefferson was in office, Kimball College sat atop a wooded hill high above the city of Haverhill. Down in the city, along the banks of the Merrimack River, there had once been a thriving shoe industry. Now, like much of the city, the factories sat boarded-up and crumbling. But up here on the hill, behind the brick and iron fence that surrounded the whole of the campus, there remained a happy, hippy community of bohemians and n'er-do-wells. In the midst of a quiet residential neighborhood, the campus' sprawling lawns served as something of a public park, where children rode their bikes and families walked their dogs and where, from September to May, the student body was like the circus come to town—a rainbow of world cultures, of hair colors, and of sexual deviances in this place that had been, for almost two centuries, nothing more than a coven for rich men's daughters.

It was, Tracy happened to know, one of Michael's favorite places on earth.

The front of the campus presented to bustling South Main Street, and to the rest of the world beyond it, the façade of academia, a trio of harmonious buildings built in the classical style, all Doric columns and red brick, each of them flanking the "sacred sod" of the front lawn, on which you were not to tread until your commencement.

But the rest of the campus, beginning with the modern-looking library, all windows and gray concrete, stood in stark contrast. It was the many faces of Kimball that Michael loved, however: so much history, and yet so much of the here and now.

As the story went, they had crossed half of the campus before his mind wandered back to the girl at his side. Jenna was so bundled up that only a sliver of her face was visible, just between where her purple wool hat ended and her thick green scarf began. Her enormous winter coat added so much bulk to her frame that she more resembled a middle linebacker than a prima ballerina.

He smirked behind his own scarf. She would have beaten him silly had he made that comparison out loud. She was not, she told people early and often, when discussions of her dancing came up, a ballerina. She danced modern, and though she'd never say it out loud, her eyes would always add, "and please don't make that mistake again."

She didn't have the body of a ballerina, she was quick to point out. Her shoulders were too broad, her bust too big, her hips far too wide. Her legs were long enough, sure, but her neck was too short. And her technique—well, that was a whole other story. Her turnout had always been poor, her flexibility was mediocre at best, she couldn't do pointe at all, and she had the worst feet in the entire company. Once, when they'd been sitting around the living room floor of their townhouse, she'd caught Michael flexing his foot and simply marveled at his form, his arches, the way his first three toes were almost all the same length. "I'd kill for your feet," she'd said.

But he'd always taken her criticisms of her body the same way others seemed to take his criticisms of his paintings—they were both too close to their art to have any kind of perspective on it. Her body, in his humble opinion, was quite alright. She was what his grandfather would have called a "substantial" woman, not nearly as substantial as Grammy, but certainly a "healthy young lady," a compliment Grampy could never have paid to Robin.

As they passed over the footbridge, Michael cast a sideways glance over the railing down at the icy pond. The first time he'd brought Robin up here, to show her around, he'd tried to convince her to come up to school here instead of down in Boston, at Berklee. She'd be the star of the program, rather than just another voice in a chorus, just another guitarist in a school full of them. And she'd smiled at that, in that way that she always did, like his mother did whenever his father said something stupid, a sort "Yes, dear" smirk that was meant to end the conversation. But he, like his father, was never good at picking up on that particular brand of smile, at least not until reflecting on it later, and he'd asked her, as they'd walked over this same bridge: "Berklee doesn't have a pond in the middle of campus now, does it?" And she'd nodded along, saying "No, I guess not." But Berklee is where she went anyway.

He hadn't said anything after that, but he'd wanted to. And what he would've said, what he said to her in his head, planning the conversation that he would have with her if the opportunity ever presented itself again, was, "Look around you! Listen! Breathe! There's no clutter here, no buildings all hunched together. There's no exhaust filling your lungs, just fresh air. There's no honking, no swearing at the guy in front of you because he doesn't know how to make a right turn on red—if you want to move fast here, there's plenty of room to go around. I'm peaceful here. I can hear myself think. I know who I am here. How could you love me and not love this place?"

"Has she fessed up yet?" Jenna asked him, her voice still muffled by her scarf.

They passed underneath the glow of the floodlights that hung alongside a dorm as Michael searched for an answer to her question.

"I suppose she wouldn't, would she?" Jenna added.

"Maybe the Runt didn't see what he thinks he saw. He and my cousin don't exactly have a happy marriage."

"I don't think he'd have even bothered to call you if he wasn't sure."

The patch of his scarf right in front of his mouth was wet with saliva, and it chafed against his lips as he said, "I suppose."

A cluster of townhouses loomed in front of them now, huddled around their snowy common lawn like so many vagrants around a flaming garbage can—unapologetically too close for comfort. Their house, the last one on the right, was dark. Their housemates must've been saving their energy for tomorrow's opening night party, for that was the way the rest of them, as non-artists, found a way to share in the whole event.

Michael scowled behind his scarf, recalling Robin's laughter upon first sight of these delightfully derelict buildings, at how they stuck out, even back here on the weirder, non-traditional side of campus. Yes, they were too angular, too seventies in their design. And yes, they were gradually sinking into the mucky New England soil. But they were charming, nevertheless, and oh, how he'd hated Robin that night. He'd taken her right back to the car, driven her home, and promised himself he would never bring her back. But the memories haunted him still, enveloped him in their irksome embrace.

In fact, they so enveloped him that he didn't notice the snowball careening towards his head that evening until it was too late. It hit the side of his head with a splat, the wet and cold seeping right through his hat and into his ear. Jenna was running down the path in front of him, laughing hysterically. He reached down into a towering bank and hurled a clump of snow at her, taking no time to ball it up, but she was out of range, already at their doorstep with her key in hand.

"What do you think I should do?" he asked her as they sat at the dining room table, sipping from mugs of steaming hot chocolate, their coats and scarves and hats draped over the other chairs.

"I've told you," she said, picking at the dried paint that covered his hands and forearms, piling up the flakes on the table in a neat stack. "You should dump her so that you and I can finally, you know, get it over with."

Michael winced as she plucked a huge chunk from his wrist, a clump of hair coming along with it.

"Sorry," she said, frowning for a moment before going back to work.

"What about your boyfriend?" he asked her.

She sighed, rubbing the edge of her thumbnail along a particularly stubborn piece of paint.

Michael ran his free hand along the top of his head, trying to smooth out the hair he could feel sprouting outward in a dozen different directions. He chuckled. "I love how you put it—we need to 'get it over with.'"

She kicked him lightly underneath the table. "I'm not the only one who thinks so."

He grabbed hold of her foot before she could steal it back. When he began to knead at her naked arch with his thumb, she let go of the hand she'd been holding and leaned back in her chair, unclenching.

She moaned, "Mmm. That is sooooo nice..."

Michael shook his head and groaned, "Damn."

"You think too much," she said, flexing her foot in his hand as he stopped rubbing.

"You know what," he said. "I do. I do think too much. But never about the important things. At least not until lately. Now I can't stop thinking about all the stupid stuff she's put me through."

"Like her going and cheating on you," Jenna said, pulling her foot back from him.

"Like her going and cheating on me," Michael said, nodding.

Jenna leaned over the table and smiled at him. "Listen, could you maybe drop her for tonight?" And then, pausing for a moment, she added, "Or maybe for the rest of your life."

He picked up his hot chocolate and sipped from it.

"She was high school and now it's college. I went through the same thing." She held her mug up to her lips and tilted her head back, then set it down on the table, a frown on her face. She'd begun to rub a foot up under the cuff of his jeans, along his calf. "We've wasted too much of our time here," she said, picking up her mug again and tipping it upside down. "Everyone in this house came to college with a significant other, but they all came to their senses a long time ago. Now it's time for us to see the lights."

"You mean, 'the light,' singular, right?"

"Whatever," she said, reaching across the table for his mug, then sipping from it.

Michael laughed. "I just can't believe that a girl like you, a girl so talented, so beauti—"

"Oh, stop it," she said, handing him back his mug, her foot disappearing from his leg. "You're taking me out of the mood."

"You're the only girl I know who gets turned off by compliments about her appearance."

"It's not that," she said. "It's that I get annoyed when you don't give yourself enough credit. You do it with me. You do it with your art." She paused, seeming to consider whether she should really say what she wanted to say next and then, said, "You do it with everything."

"Point taken," he said. "And I guess... baseball teams do carry a personal masseuse, so, even though I wouldn't be on a team in your league, so to speak, I could conceivably become an employee of the league."

She chuckled at him. "You need to learn when to shut up."

"It's genetic."

Jenna stood and gathered up her things. "I'm going upstairs," she said. "Kate is gone for the night. So..." She paused and smiled. "Good night."

"G'night," he said, waving a little wave.

He watched her ascend the stairs until she'd rounded the corner to her room, then looked down the flight of stairs that led to his own bedroom. He tapped at his wallet again, and then pulled it out. He leafed through the photos he kept inside, past his cousin Matt, his sister Ashley, past Veronica and Tracy, past the miniature copy of the poem "Footprints" that his mother had bought for him after Grampy's funeral. The last picture was of Michael and Robin, from senior year, up on stage at the talent show, singing into the same microphone. They had sounded perfect, or so the stories went, so perfect as they sang, in harmony, "You can go your own way." He ran his fingers along the edges of her face, then closed his wallet and put it away.

And this was where Michael broke the fourth wall. Without looking at Tracy, he said, "This is the moment you've been working me up to, isn't it?"

"Yes," said Tracy.

"And are you going to let me have it?"

"Of course," said Tracy. "You need to have this moment. Or else the rest of it won't hurt as much."

Michael stood, then climbed the stairs.

Jenna took her time in answering his knock. She was wearing a longish t-shirt that fell down to her hips. "Are you sure?" she asked him. "Because I don't want to force you."

"I'm sure," he said.

She opened the door wider, took him by the hand, and pulled him in.

Up on the judge's bench, as all light went out, Tracy banged her gavel down three times. Below, torches in hand, the Gunslinger and Swordswoman stood waiting.

Tracy looked off in the direction where the ghost of Jenna's door still blurred her vision. She closed her eyes, pinched the bridge of her nose, hoping to regain her bearings, her focus and purpose. But, in the dark of her own mind, she could now hear the faintest sounds of lovemaking in the distance.

No, she thought. *Fucking! It's fucking. What they're doing is cheating, not love. He doesn't even know how to—*

She opened her eyes, focused on the guards. "We will adjourn for a brief recess," she told the two of them, "I need a moment."

24
SEVEN MEN AT PERFECT HEIGHT, SEVEN NOSES PINK

Up in the house and unaware of what was going down in her barn, Veronica dreamed herself and her wife into the bed of Christy Turlington. They were tangled together under a thin white sheet, underneath the canopy of an enormous four-poster, a gentle breeze playing with the curtains by the window and the curtains of the bed. Veronica had an arm around each woman, their heads resting on her chest, their foreheads nearly touching but not quite. And while Veronica ran her fingers through their hair, they watched *Pretty Woman* on a thirteen-inch TV with a VCR built into the bottom of it. It was perched precariously on the end of the bed and threatened to topple off the pillowed top of the mattress at any moment. Only the feet of Christy and Desiree held it in place.

Why is the TV so small? Veronica wondered. *Surely a supermodel can afford something grander than this. And a VCR in 2011?*

That was when she woke, the logic of the dream crumbling like a leaning tower of Jenga blocks that you've stared at for too long, the mash-up of sexual fantasy and old childhood memory giving her a shiver that woke her from her slumber. She turned from her side to see if Desiree was awake, if there was someone she could share this pleasant but curious vision with, but Des wasn't in bed.

Veronica sat up, rubbing at her eyes, and found her wife perched in the rocking chair by the window, staring out the old dormer and into the night. By the light of the moon, Veronica could see that Des was biting her thumb.

"What?" said Veronica.

"That space bastard," she said, "he killed my pine."

Space bastard? thought Veronica. Was she still dreaming, she wondered.

"*Back to the Future*," Desiree explained. "When Marty first ends up in 1955 and he runs over one of Old Man Peabody's saplings in the DeLorean."

Veronica was confused. "There's a DeLorean out there?" she asked, scooting out of bed. "And a space bastard?" she asked as she knelt down behind Desiree and wrapped her arms around her.

"Tracy's date," said Desiree, pointing at a now-disheveled hedgerow near the edge of their property. "He hit it as he peeled out of here."

Veronica nuzzled her wife's neck, then her ear. "Baby," she said, "how long have you been up?"

Desiree took hold of one of Veronica's hands and brought it to her lips. Then she sighed and leaned into her wife's embrace. "Too long," she said.

"And what did you see?" asked Veronica.

"The kids parking their car down by the beach," she began, "then them creeping up into the barn."

"Tana and Tori were with her?" asked Veronica.

Desiree nodded.

"I love those girls," said Veronica. "Reminds me of us," she said, nipping at Des' earlobe, "when we were their age."

"A long time ago," said Desiree. "In a galaxy far, far away."

Veronica nudged her wife. "So, what happened next, Uatu?"

"Uatu?" said Desiree.

"The Watcher," Veronica explained. "From the comic books? He's a space bastard with a big head," she said. "He watches things."

Desiree smiled and kissed Veronica's hand again. With her eyes still fixed on the window, she continued. "The date, he ran back to his car for something. But then everything was quiet for a couple of hours. By the time I heard the front door creak open downstairs, the porch steps groaning under someone's weight, I was about to nod off. I looked down and saw that it was Michael, headphones in, going for a stroll. And where do you think he strolled to?"

"Shut up," said Veronica, slapping Des on the shoulder.

"Yep," said Desiree. "He went straight for the barn. Couple minutes later, Tana, Tori, and the date come racing out of there—the date tripping over his half-buckled jeans, I might add—and they all make for the car."

"And Michael and Trace," said Veronica, pointing toward the barn, "they've been in there ever since?"

Desiree nodded.

"How long?" said Veronica.

"A while," said Desiree. "Just before you woke up, I was thinking of going down there."

Veronica pulled out of their embrace and shimmied on her knees until she'd rounded the chair and was facing Des. "You can't do that," she told her wife. "You need to let them work it out on their own."

"But you didn't see how mad she was at him," said Desiree, taking Veronica's face into her hands. "Not the half of it. I caught her upstairs after the show last night and she... she's really pissed, Vern. I don't know why exactly, but—"

"It's between them," said Veronica, taking hold of Desiree's hands and lacing their fingers together. "Father and daughter stuff," she said.

"He's not her father," said Desiree.

"He's the closest thing she has to one," said Veronica.

"But," Desiree began, but whatever she was about to say was cut off by the sound of a door slamming open outside.

Veronica spun on the spot as Desiree leaned forward, and the two of them peered out the dormer window to see what was happening. As they did, Tracy came storming out of the barn in a huff. Hands on her hips, she paced the length of the barn as they watched.

"That's a cute top she's wearing," said Veronica. "A hand-me-down from you?"

Desiree nodded, frowning. "It's on backwards."

Down below, as if she'd heard them, Tracy quit her pacing and stared up at the window for a moment. Veronica thought to duck, but Tracy was moving again just as quickly as she'd come to a halt. She shook her head and looked to be mumbling something to herself.

"You think she saw us?" said Veronica.

"I think we should go down there," said Desiree. "That's what I think. Or maybe wake Jenna and send her out, if what you're worried about is us being overbearing."

"She's 18," said Veronica, looking back at Des over her shoulder. "This is the part of the story where she figures things out on her own."

"Is it?" said Desiree. "And if it is, then why is it? Because that's what you had to do?"

Veronica grunted, then said, "I had to figure things out on my own long before she did."

Desiree squeezed Veronica's shoulders. "Right," she said, "but do you want to be your dad?"

Veronica spun around again. She narrowed her eyes and stared up into Desiree's face, determined to find an answer there, a compromise. But she couldn't. So, instead, she held out one open palm before her and then set a closed fist atop it.

"What are you doing?" said Desiree.

"Rock, paper, scissors," said Veronica. "No fairer way to decide," she said.

"Parenting by Roshambo?" said Desiree, shaking her head and smirking despite herself.

"Yep," said Veronica, nodding at her outstretched hands.

"I guess this is what happily ever after looks like," said Desiree, mirroring Veronica's hands now and getting ready to duel. "Dumb and so saccharine it'll rot our goddamn teeth straight out of our increasingly empty heads."

"You ask me," said Veronica, "the Brothers Grimm—"

"I don't think people lived happily ever after in their versions," said Desiree. "Mostly I think they had their eyes put out by ravens, or else they sawed off their own toes to win the love of aloof princes."

"You knew what I meant," said Veronica. "The fairy tale people," she said, "I think they end things too early. I think it's possible, however unlikely, that happily ever after could be a lot more interesting than it lets on."

"Fine," said Desiree, shaking her head and rolling her eyes. "Are you ready?"

Veronica nodded. Then, together, tapping fists against open palms on each beat, they said, "Rock, paper, scissors." But before they could say "shoot," the barn door slammed shut down below.

Veronica and Desiree turned from each other and cast their gazes out of the window again, but Tracy had gone back inside.

"Come back to bed," said Veronica.

"Shoot," said Desiree, shaping her index and middle fingers into a pair of scissors and waiting for Veronica's response.

Paper or rock, Veronica had to decide. She looked into her wife's eyes, as she always did, for the answer.

25

THE LONELY BOY IN THE RAIN

As she stormed back into the courtroom, it was Tracy's nose that stopped her in her tracks.

It was filled, all at once, with the smells of plumeria and pineapple, of sunblock and aloe vera, of a pig roasting on a spit.

Then there was sound: rain pounding down on the roof overhead, rain sizzling as it hit the hot pork, the slap of bare feet racing across cold stone. And, somewhere beyond all that, waves crashing on a not-so-distant shore.

Finally, there was light and a whole lot of it. Tracy blinked her eyes against the burst of color, rubbing them until they adjusted. The room she found herself looming above now was all wicker and white linen, open to the elements on three sides, a collection of Polynesian art on the fourth. Michael's own painting of Pele was the centerpiece, a fierce portrait of the goddess emerging from a lava flow to confront a trio of suit-clad men breaking ground where they shouldn't have been.

She looked around for some sign of Michael, who was the mastermind behind all this. His ability to bend the world to his liking was frightening. Her mother hadn't been able to do this, at least not this well, at least not as far as Tracy knew. They were already in Hawaii, and they weren't meant to be there yet. Michael was in control, and Tracy didn't like that one bit. She remembered her mother's dream about the Salesman, how frightened Veronica said he'd been when she had taken control when she wasn't supposed to. It was happening to Tracy now. But she couldn't let it. She had to find a way to turn things around.

A board game sat open, in mid-play, on the dining table. It was Risk, if Tracy was right, a game of military strategy and world domination. She wondered at the significance, beyond the name of course, which was surely meant to refute her claim that Michael didn't make choices in his life.

"Mr. Silver!" she shouted, hoping her voice would draw him out. "What is the meaning of—"

"I'm defending myself," he shouted back, as he strode into the room. He looked confident, victorious even.

Tracy said, "The prosecution hasn't finished its—"

"Whatever rules this farce might have had," said Michael, "you broke them first!" He waved at someone in the hallway and then, through the doorway, walked Jenna and Veronica. Veronica strummed a happy tune on the ukulele and they both sang along. Then they seated themselves and looked at their cards, examined their positions on the board.

Tracy threaded her fingers together and pushed her thumbs together, trying to keep her composure. This looked good. This looked like he had something. She breathed, then said, "You try this court's patience, Mr. Silver. But, given how unlikely it is that your evidence will sway us, we'll allow it. Would you care to set the scene?"

"It was the summer of 2002," said Michael, "a little over a year after Jenna and I were married. We'd moved to Hawaii after honeymooning there and your mothers decided to pay us a visit."

"And where was I?" said Tracy.

Michael sat at the table, picked up a pair of six-sided dice. "Back in Massachusetts," he said, "with your father."

"He's not my—"

"Oh," said Michael, "that sniveling little coward is your father, alright. The family resemblance has never been clearer than it is right now."

Tracy banged down her gavel in anger just as Michael rolled the dice. That was when the ladies at the table started speaking.

"How big are the needles?" said Jenna.

"Wait!" said Michael. "There are needles?"

"Yes," said Veronica. "There are needles. Two different kinds, actually. Subcutaneous and intramuscular."

"And which kind is it that Desiree is on now?" said Jenna.

"Intramuscular," said Veronica.

"Intramuscular?" said Michael. "As in inside the muscle?"

Veronica smirked. "Yep."

"Egads," said Michael.

"What are you squirming about?" said Jenna. "You're not the one who'd be getting the shots."

"Yeah," he said, "but I'm the one who'd be administering them."

"You can't do them yourself?" said Jenna.

Veronica shook her head. "Desiree did the subcutaneous ones herself, from time to time. But not the intramuscular. Too much contorting."

Michael raised an eyebrow. "Where do you have to stick them?"

Veronica said, "The upper outer quadrant of a buttock."

"Ouch," said Michael, rubbing his own ass.

"Oh, quit your worrying," said Jenna. "I've survived being

married to you for a year. I know how to deal with a pain in the ass."

Tracy laughed, in spite of herself. Michael and Jenna's banter had always been her favorite part of having them around. But something was gnawing at her, as the conversation continued: How had she not known about this? How had her mothers kept it all a secret?

"There was no other way for her to get pregnant?" said Michael.

"There were a few," said Veronica. "But, seeing as she didn't want to reenact that Heart song—"

"Which Heart song?" said Jenna.

Veronica smiled and Michael groaned, their typical reactions to Jenna's lack of pop culture knowledge. Veronica illuminated her. "'All I Wanna Do Is Make Love To You,'" she said.

"Which one is that?" said Jenna.

Michael explained: "The one where she picks up a dude on the side of the road for the express purpose of knocking herself up."

"Oh," said Jenna.

"Yeah," said Veronica. "So, that was out. We did try artificial insemination, but it didn't take."

"Didn't take?" said Jenna. "You mean, she had a—"

"Yep," said Veronica.

Jenna grabbed hold of Veronica's hand. Up on the bench, Tracy wished she could do the same. She braced her upper lip against her lower, thinking of what her mothers had lost, of who. A face came to mind, a little old man's wrinkled, toothless face, but on a cherub's soft pink body. She squeezed her eyes shut.

"I'm sorry," said Jenna.

"Water under the bridge," said Veronica, as Tracy opened her eyes again. Veronica addressed the game, waving a hand over the board. "Whose turn is it?"

"Mine," said Michael.

Veronica said, "Then what's your move, Professor?"

"Shh!" said Michael. "Don't jinx it. I haven't graduated the program yet. And, even if I do, I'm not sure I would want to be a profes—"

"Waitaminute," said Veronica. "You haven't wowed them yet with your thesis on those perverted pin-ups?"

Michael's thesis! It was one of Tracy's favorite texts, both the spiral-bound review copy he gave her the day after he successfully defended his dissertation, as well as the version that the University Press of New England published a few years after that. The premise, as famous now in the art world as it had been for years in their family, was that Nick Gold, a pin-up artist and comic book penciller from the 1940s, was actually an alias of Michael's Great Aunt Dottie. She was a lesbian trying to break into a male-dominated industry, and Michael posited that it was only because of her male pseudonym that her drawings of half-naked women were as popular as they were. Michael said that, if readers knew it was a woman drawing the stuff they were jerking off to, it never would have worked.

"Oh, please don't get him started," Jenna begged Veronica. "Can we just play?"

"Of course," said Veronica. "What's your play, Prof?"

Michael winced at the nickname, just as Veronica might wince if the name of Scottish Play were mentioned within fifty feet of the barn. Then, he said, "I'm invading Camel Crap."

"Camel what?" said Jenna.

"Kamchatka," said Veronica. "It was the nickname our fathers had for Kamchatka."

"But," said Jenna, "Kamchatka doesn't sound anything like—"

Together, Michael and Veronica said, "We know."

"Did you roll?" said Veronica.

"Sure did," said Michael. "Beat that, cuz."

Veronica picked up the dice and rolled. Then she smiled as Michael jolted back away from the table.

"Damn!" he said. "I never win, dude. Never."

Veronica plucked several pieces off of the game board tile representing Alaska and deposited them back into the game's box. "And," she said, "the mighty army of Camel Crap beats back the pitiful Alaskan hordes once again."

As Jenna picked up the dice to roll, Desiree crept into the room, lingering in the doorway. When the rest of them turned to face her, she manufactured a smile, but the craftsmanship was shoddy and Veronica saw right through the façade. Up on the bench, Tracy did too.

"Hi," said Desiree.

Veronica rose from the table and made her way across the room. "What happened?" she said.

"What do you mean?" said Desiree. "Nothing—"

"Des," said Veronica.

"We can talk about it later," said Desiree, taking a step toward the table.

Jenna rose, pushed her seat back, and tapped Michael on the shoulder. She said, "We can give you guys some privacy."

"No," said Desiree. "No, I don't want to... Not right now."

"Is it the baby?" said Michael.

Tracy wanted to leap down and smack him, to pummel him with her fists until he was weeping on the floor, weeping the way she wanted to weep now. First, he had to show her this in the first place, another piece of him she didn't want. Then, he had to say that, to ask that stupid question, in that stupid way. She wanted to rip at his neck until she could pull his larynx out of there, then to stomp on his voice right in front of him, until all the words he had left to say were nothing but a bloody mess on his tile floor.

Desiree broke down and began to cry into the crook of

Veronica's shoulder. Veronica held Des tight, held her own tears back.

"It's not because you flew," said Michael, "is it?"

"Michael!" said Jenna. "Let's go."

Now Michael began to tear up. He turned to Jenna, said, "I'm the one who convinced them to fly out here."

"It's not because we flew," said Veronica, guiding Desiree out of the room. "It's not your fault."

Jenna turned on Michael. She said everything Tracy wanted to say, which was the only thing keeping Tracy where she was. "It has nothing to do with you," said Jenna. "How dare you inject yourself into—"

"Did you see how crushed she looked?" said Michael. "If there's anything I could have done, Jenna. If—"

"There's nothing you could have done," said Jenna. "It has nothing to do with you."

"Why," said Michael, "are you so mad at me for caring?"

Jenna stalked away from him. She stood by edge of the lanai and held a hand out into the rain. Then she brought that hand to her forehead, used it so push her hair back, away from her face. She closed her eyes, breathed.

Tracy admired this woman so much, pitied her. The things she put up with, even from perfect, sensitive, gentlemanly Michael.

"I'm not mad at you for caring," said Jenna. "I'm mad because you're falling apart, and it isn't even your baby."

"Yeah," said Michael. "But it's my cousin's, and—"

"Yes," she said. "It was your cousin's. And what would happen if it were yours?"

Michael said he didn't understand.

"Michael," said Jenna, "you're a sensitive soul. I get that. I love that about you. But in this situation, if we're going to go through this, one of us needs to be strong. And I'm telling you right now, it can't always be me."

"But we know this wouldn't happen to us," said Michael, standing, going to her. "I mean, the women in your family pop out babies just by thinking about it. I'm the one with the problem in our equation."

"So," said Michael, reaching for her hand, "if all we need is to give my guys a little guidance, then—"

"Then it could still fail," said Jenna, pulling her hand away, not yet ready to give it. "It could still fail. And what happens then? Do you turn into a blubbering mess when I need you the most?"

Michael walked away from her, went to the wall, and plucked the statue of Haumea off of the shelf. *Of course he did*, thought Tracy. *The fertility goddess, the most obvious prop in the room.*

"You want kids," he said to Jenna, turning to face her again, clutching the statue to his chest. "Don't you?"

"Yes," said Jenna.

"Then why are we even having this discussion? Why are we pretending like not doing the IVF is an option?"

"Because," said Jenna. "It is an option."

"It's not!" said Michael. "You want kids. End of story. We have to do this."

"No," said Jenna. "We don't. If you can't handle it—"

"I can handle it!" said Michael, setting Haumea back on her shelf. "Find me one of those needles," he said, heading back to the table, grabbing the strap of Veronica's pocket book. "I'll show you. I'm not gonna pass out at the sight of—"

"OK," said Jenna, "you'll get over your fear of needles. But what about everything else?"

"What else?" said Michael.

Jenna sat back down at the table. She said nothing for a moment, began to clear the board of the game's pieces. Then, she looked at him. She said, "What about the fact that you might not have a choice about that theoretical professorship Veronica was teasing you about? One of us is going to have to get a job, the nine-to-five kind, the kind with health insurance attached."

"Oh, man," said Michael, "you know I hate talking about that shit. I mean, why do we need health insurance? Plenty of people—"

Jenna sighed, leaning back in her chair. She rubbed at her temples, probably trying to keep her head from imploding under the sheer weight of his idiocy, his naïveté. "Oh, Michael," she said. "Jesus Christ! Have you read any of the emails Veronica has sent us, looked at any of the websites?"

"We're not going to be able to afford it without insurance?"

"No," said Jenna, "we're not."

Michael ducked his head, something finally sinking into it. "I didn't realize that," he said.

"There's a lot you didn't realize, apparently."

"But I want kids," he said. "I do."

"I know you do," she said, reaching for his hand, squeezing it. "We all want a lot of things in life. But there are only some wants that we actually get."

He turned away from her, pulled away from her grip, but she held on.

"Maybe," he said, "you should go out and make like that Heart song then? Find a dude by the side of the road and—"

Jenna stood, pulled at his hand, and spun him around. "I don't want a dude by the side of the road," she said.

Michael leaned his forehead against hers. "But the one thing I can't give you," he said, quoting the song, "is the one little thing that he can."

"Yeah," said Jenna, "but all I want to do is make love to you, you idiot. You, not someone else."

Tracy looked down on them for a moment, frozen there in their dining room. It had been nearly nine years since this moment, and she'd never heard of it. So many things about it stunned her, kept her tongue in her mouth and her mind inside itself, but the thing that shocked her most was that Michael had managed to keep something secret, that there was something she hadn't uncovered in all the digging she'd done.

"I didn't know," she said, as she tapped her gavel against the podium and washed the courtroom in darkness once again.

Michael stepped back into his pool of light. He stared up at her. "You think I can't make decisions?" he said. "Well, there you go: the toughest decision I've ever made."

"Except that you didn't make it," said Tracy. "Your wife did."

He shook his head, stomped from one edge of the circle to the other. "We made the decision together," he said. "That's how marriage works, you little—"

Tracy banged the gavel down. From the darkness on either side of Michael came the guards, each brandishing their weapon of choice.

"One more insult," said Tracy, "and I'll find you in contempt of court."

"I have nothing but contempt for this court!" shouted Michael. As he did, something rather odd happened, something he seemed to notice almost as quickly as she did. The darkness around him flashed, for the briefest of moments, to a scene from some cartoon. There was a robot, a car rearranged to look like a man, delivering the same line Michael had just spoken. The first robot, all orange and gold, the hot head, stood beside another robot, all blue and gray, who was complaining about not being to transform. Above them, an egg-shaped robot with many faces was passing judgement. Below them, a school of robot sharks circled in a yellow-green pool.

Michael raised an eyebrow as the image faded away, then closed his eyes tight, as if in concentration, as if maybe trying to conjure another image.

Out of the darkness came the briefest flashes of other courtrooms, other scenes. There was a battle-hardened Marine losing his shit on the stand while being grilled by a punk-ass Navy lawyer, a Spartan king kicking a Persian messenger into a vast pit upon his warrior queen passing judgement, a city kid using the Bible to convince a small town's council members to let him and his friends dance, a bespectacled district attorney playing a horrifying film of an assassination over and over again to make a point.

This was getting out of hand. Michael knew. He knew now that he wielded as much power as she did. "I am trying to help you," she called out to him, hoping to break his concentration, to get a reaction out of him, any reaction. "I'm trying to reform you."

Michael's eyes shot open. The visions stopped and the darkness returned. "Reform me!?" he said. "There's nothing wrong with me! Have you seen any of these women complaining about who I am or how I treated them? You're the one with the complaint. So, out with it! Quit dancing around the fucking subject and tell me what I did to you."

Good, she thought. *Crisis averted.* She spoke. "I will get there when I'm good and ready," she said. "But first, one more thing."

It was time, she knew, for the big guns. She shuffled through the papers in front of her. From the stack, she pulled a multi-page document that looked like it had been torn apart and taped back together again.

"Do you know what this is?" Tracy asked him.

"I have no idea," said Michael. The gulp of air he took after he said it said otherwise.

"It is a print-out," said Tracy, "of a message you composed. Composed, but never sent."

"Where did you get that?" said Michael.

She had hacked his email account, easy enough to do when his idea of a password was his wife's initials and her date of birth.

"I was hurt when I wrote that," he said. "Things were rough."

"But you don't deny writing it?" she said.

"I don't even remember what I wrote," he said. "But I never sent it. I made a *choice* not to."

"You don't remember what you wrote?" said Tracy.

"I don't," said Michael, though the color of his skin was growing paler and paler.

"Well then," said Tracy, "let me remind you."

26

WHO YOU WANT TO TAKE YOU HOME

Carrie,

The photo is of you, you sitting on a rock on the beach we all drove to on the final afternoon of the Boston conference. It was hot, and we'd known we were headed for the ocean, but none of us had thought to wear shorts (or maybe we had packed none). The cuffs of your jeans are wet, your feet are bare, and you're leaning back, supported by your hands, your ring finger not yet naked. You don't see me taking the picture. I didn't remember taking it until now.

I have a computer now which organizes my photos for me, which searches long forgotten corners of my hard drive, pushes aside digital cobwebs, and pulls eight-legged memories into the light. The program that does this is connected to a World Wide Web where I can set these spiders free, if I choose, and see if they are squashed as pests or made pets by button-clicking arachnophiles.

Oh, what a terrible metaphor. How is it that I, with paragraphs like that, was a prize winner, and you, with your ability to turn a phrase, were but the lowly administrator?

My mouse cursor hovers above an upload button as I wonder about you and the baby in your belly, about my wife and the womb I've left barren, about what could have been different, what would still be the same. If only. If.

This program sorts photos by location too, and my first discovery gets me wondering if there's more evidence of what happened in those six cities, over the course of those six years. So, instead of saying the hell with it, instead of clicking the button and seeing what happens, I go exploring.

WE MET IN NEW ORLEANS, on Bourbon Street, the year before the flood. I'd been nursing Diet Cokes and listening to the house band at a little joint called Fritzel's, way down past the strip clubs and the sports bars. My colleagues, who'd been hammered since halfway through that evening's banquet and keynote address, and who hadn't heard a damned note of the music since we'd arrived, had finally driven me off. I hadn't gotten out much since the conference started on Friday afternoon, and now that I'd presented my paper and the nerves were gone, I'd been hoping to get a taste of the real N'awlins before flying home. That they'd ruined that for me, as they'd ruined so much else for me that weekend, with their shoddy second-rate scholarship during the conference and their meandering, misogynistic anecdotes after hours, that was unforgivable.

So, I left Fritzel's and started back down Bourbon, headed in the direction of the Monteleone, where we were all staying. I made my way past Big Daddy's, where a pair of fishnet-clad mannequin's legs swung in and out of a window; past a karaoke club where some unseen gentleman screeched his best impression of Jon Bon Jovi; and past a sports bar where the New England Patriots, my hometown team, were on the TVs, beating up on the Buffalo Bills. But, despite the fact that a visit to a kitschy strip club probably would've sated my desire to see the real New Orleans just as much as listening to some European jazz, despite the fact that "Living on a Prayer" tops my list of guilty pleasure songs, and despite the fact that I hadn't missed a Pats game since they played in a blizzard three years before, I did not stop. The night was ruined. It was irreparable.

And then I spotted you, the prim and proper administrator of our young organization, your hair down both literally and figuratively, walking out of the Gold Club, your face flush, your body too, skin all aglow from your plunging neckline to your sweating forehead. There was an immense smile spreading across your face, and it only spread wider as you saw me draw near.

"Having fun?" you said.

"Trying," I said.

You shook a thumb over your shoulder, back at the club. "I was just leaving, but if you want to go back in, I'll buy you a dance."

"I doubt my wife would approve."

You laughed. "My husband would shit himself. But that's the whole point. Why else do we go to conferences?"

"The scholarship, I would hope."

Even me, at my most morose, could not bring you down. You shook your head at me. "You headed back to the hotel?" you asked.

I nodded. "I'd been hoping to catch some jazz, but—"

"You try Fritzel's?"

"Yes," I said. "I remembered your suggestion. Trouble is, so did everyone else."

"Yeah," you said. "That's the trouble with conferences. You have to discover something early, before all of your friends ruin it."

"I wouldn't call them friends," I said. "At least not at this point."

"A wise man," you said. "But, anyway, about the jazz: follow me!"

You grabbed me by the arm and led me off, past the hotel, down one side street after the other, until we found ourselves across the street from a run down sandwich place that was just closing up shop, the sign advertising authentic Po-Boys flickering from bright white to dull gray. The lights went out and then, just as they did, a mournful horn sounded out from inside. You laid your head on my shoulder as we eavesdropped on what seemed to me like a very private lament. I began to ask you if maybe we shouldn't feel wrong about this, but you shushed me before I was through.

"You don't blow like that if you don't want to be heard," you told me later.

IN BOSTON THE NEXT YEAR, I sat with you in the dark, at the registration desk, as you ate the dinner you'd been too nervous to touch during the banquet. The keynote, given by the eldest scholar of our bunch, had descended, during the Q&A, into a drunken argument between the group's two belligerent factions. You cut into your re-heated steak with murder in your eyes, and as your meat spilled its juices onto the gleaming white plate, I imagined you imagining your knife slicing through the necks of those argumentative assholes.

"At least it's over," I said.

"It shouldn't have even started," you said. "The way these people can make anything political. Christ!"

"This stuff matters to us," I said. "And when something matters to you this much, and you get together with folks who care about it just as much as you do, arguments are bound to—"

"It's just a bunch of stories!" you shouted. You blanched as you looked around, searching the hall to see if anyone else had heard you. Then you set down your fork and knife, dabbed at your lips with your napkin, and whispered, "All they're arguing about are words and pictures on a goddamned page. The little things, the stupid things—that's all anyone ever argues about."

I didn't know what to say. You were right, of course. But I couldn't say that out loud, and I had to stop even thinking it before I drove myself nuts with the thought. So, I said, "You want to go to the beach tomorrow and cool off after everything's wrapped up."

You smiled. "Sure," you said. "That'd be nice."

IN SAN FRANCISCO, you didn't want to leave the hotel, but nobody could figure out why. This was your city, after all, and there was an expectation—and not an unreasonable one—that you would be our guide. But you shunted those duties off to an intern and stayed indoors, dashing between sessions, checking in on the volunteers manning the registration desk, disappearing into your room for hours on end.

It was before dawn on the last day that you collected me from my room and decided to spill the beans. We walked out of the Sir Francis Drake, away from Union Square, and headed north on Powell. Up hills we went, and down them, and up them again. For the most part, you said nothing, the only sounds you made the grunts you directed at the billboards hanging overhead.

It was only once we reached Fisherman's Wharf, when you'd grunted for the seventh time, that I commented on this, that I asked you what was wrong.

"They're everywhere," you said.

"Billboards?"

"Those billboards," you said, pointing.

The sign in question was one of dozens I had seen and immediately forgotten about over the past year, not just there in San Francisco, but back home as well. It advertised a ubiquitous gadget of the moment with a dancing silhouette set against a pastel backdrop. I had no idea why the signs bothered you so—these things were so omnipresent now that they just blended in with the scenery for most of us—but bother you they did. I was about to ask when you spoke up again.

"He makes those things," you said. "My husband."

"Your husband?"

"Yes," you said. "Or, well, my ex… or soon-to-be… Or, well…"

"Oh," I said. "And these billboards, they're the reason you haven't gone out?"

"Do you notice what's wrong with them?"

I turned my critic's eye to the billboard, trying to spot something.

"Her ribcage," you said. "She's been Photoshopped, and her ribcage is slightly out of proportion. Slightly," you said again.

"I know Photoshop," I said, squinting. "Like, I *know* Photoshop. But I don't see it.

"No one does," you said. "No one except him. And now me. He made me stare at it until I couldn't help but notice it, until it was all I noticed."

"The little things," I said.

"The stupid things," you said, pushing the palm of your hand into the corner of your eye, wiping away something you didn't want me to see. "Anyway," you said. "Want to go see the Golden Gate?"

In Chicago, we shared a deep-dish pizza the night you told me that it was finally over, that the papers had come through and you were officially a "free" woman. But you didn't want to talk about it. You were ready to move on. And so, before I had a chance to ask you how you felt, or what was next, you asked me, "Why sausage?"

"You don't like sausage?" I asked.

"No," you said, taking a bite of the pizza and speaking now with your mouth full, "I was just wondering."

"Well," I said. "Me and some of the other guys in the department back home, we go to Uno's a lot, and we order the Chicago classic, which—"

"Has sausage on it," you said, cutting me off. "I get it."

"So," I said, "I figured I might as well see how the real thing compares."

"And?" you asked.

"It's good," I said. "Hearty."

You smiled, kept eating.

On the way back to the hotel, we passed by a store that was selling the latest version of your ex-husband's gadget. You paused there and said to me. "I appreciate you not asking me about it. I appreciate you not digging."

"You're welcome," I said, responding to the thank you that was said but not spoken.

We shared a cab out to O'Hare a couple of days later for our flights back home. You laid your head on my shoulder again, for the first time since New Orleans, and I think you fell asleep for a spell, but I didn't look. I closed my own eyes instead, and breathed in the scent of your hair—lavender and jasmine—remembering the conversation we'd had in the Crescent City.

"I doubt my wife would approve."

"My husband would shit himself."

Only one of them remained an obstacle, I thought to myself, before pushing the thought aside. An obstacle to what, I wondered. An obstacle to what?

PHILADELPHIA WAS BEDLAM. Or, well, the most memorable night of it was.

It was pouring rain and the two of us were out in it, trying to find a town car in which sat our keynote speaker for the evening, down from New York just for the occasion and trapped inside that vehicle with a driver who refused to take directions.

You were on your cell, trying to calm the poor woman, trying to, through her, convince the driver to just pull over. "A moving target," you said into your phone, "is only going to make this more difficult."

I checked my watch. We were already half an hour behind schedule. I asked you if you wanted me to head back inside and say something to the crowd.

You said, "I want you to keep looking for the car." So that's what I did.

It was a few minutes later that, patrolling the corner of Dock and 2nd Streets, I spotted the car a block north, driving west along Walnut. I screamed, "STOP!" at the top of my voice and the driver seemed to have heard me, even at that distance, for stop he did. You ran to me as I pointed.

"Look," I said, as one of the rear doors of the town car opened.

"I could kiss you," you told me. "And, in fact," you said, grabbing hold of my face in both your hands. "Why not?"

You pulled me in and laid one on me, a kiss that was trying so hard to be chaste that the effort involved erased any chance it had at innocence. You pulled back, held my left hand in both of yours, and fiddled with my wedding band. You stared at it for a moment but then, down the street, a door slammed, and that noise broke you from your reverie.

"Gotta go," you said, looking up at me.

And then you were gone.

It was in Denver that we said goodbye, a three-day-long goodbye that began with Hawaiian fish flown in that day to the most expensive seafood place you could find; that continued with a drunken evening of spoken word poetry in front of a pop art mural of a pair of puckered red lips; and that ended, with more drinking, in front of the hotel's piano at two in the morning the day that you handed in your resignation.

You played the opening riff to a song we had both known in college, and you sang, "Closing time. One last call for alcohol, so finish your whiskey or beer."

Then you pointed at me and I followed up, "Closing time. You don't have to go home, but you can't stay here."

We laughed, collected ourselves, then gulped down the seventh and eighth of the ten pancake shots the bartender had laid out for us.

"He had a crush on you," I told you. "No way he would have laid out this much otherwise."

You threw back the orange juice chaser. "It really does taste like pancakes," you said, licking your lips. "How does that work? I mean, seriously: how does that work?"

"I know not," I said. "I know not."

Out of nowhere—or at least it seemed like it came out of nowhere—you grabbed my leg and squeezed. "Have I told you?"

"Told me what?"

"I've met someone."

"You have?"

You bit down on your lower lip, tucking it underneath teeth

tinted yellow by all the orange juice we'd been drinking, and you nodded, blushing.

"Me too," I said.

Your eyes widened and you looked down at my left hand, checking to see if the ring was still there. "You have? But wait," you said. "What about... what about—"

"Only a matter of time," I said. "She hasn't been happy in years. Nor I."

"Who?" you asked.

"A student," I said. "A former student, that is."

"For real?" you asked.

"Yes," I said, though every word of this was a lie.

"Wow," you said. "I'm glad. I was worried that... well, given what happened in Philadelphia last year. I..."

I ran a consoling hand along your shoulder. "I'm a big boy," I said.

"How big?" you joked. "After all, I've only just met the other guy."

We roared with laughter, falling into each other, into a hug that told the truth that I could not tell.

After a few moments, you pulled away and looked at me. You looked and you waited. And when still I said nothing, you tucked your bottom lip up under your teeth again and squinted at me. Then you grabbed the ninth of the shots that had been laid out for us and handed me the tenth and final one. We threw them back, then the chasers, and it was as you were wiping your mouth with the back of your sleeve that you asked me if I remembered *Top Gun*.

I nodded as you stood, as I looked up at you and tried to puzzle out what you were playing at.

You ran your fingers through my hair and I melted into you, closing my eyes as I rest my head against your stomach. You asked me, "Do you remember what Meg Ryan says to Goose? When they're in the bar?"

I couldn't. I shook my head no, the wool of your skirt scratching against my nose as I did.

It was as you slipped a hand down my neck and underneath my loosened collar that you said it. "Take me to bed," you said. "Or lose me forever."

I waited for you to laugh, to feel against my face the ripples of you busting a gut. But you didn't.

I remember fumbling up the escalator behind you, sweaty hand wrapped around sweaty hand. I remember looking down at the moving stairs to keep from looking at you, and then catching myself staring at your skirt instead, staring and thinking the drunken and/or juvenile thought that the view would be so much better from a couple steps further back. I remember punching myself in the thigh with my free hand, just for thinking that thought.

But I don't remember much after that. I think we opened your mini-bar for a bit more courage, but I'm not sure. All I do know is that I woke up in your arms the next day, that our shoes and socks and bottoms littered the floor around the bed, but that our shirts and underwear were still on.

"Did we?" I asked you as I sat up and rubbed at my temples.

You shrugged and smiled. "Does it matter?" you asked, and you patted a hand on my pillow, willing me to come back. When that didn't work, you held out your arms to me and gave me your best puppy dog eyes.

But I couldn't, and I told you as much as I dressed. I just couldn't.

I'M STILL WITH JENNA, and you must know it; all it would take to know it is a glance at my status on this web that connects us ever so slightly, ever so completely. Things are better. We're getting there.

But I can't stop thinking, as I look at the photo of you and your swollen belly that ornaments your own corner of the web. I can't stop wondering if maybe it does matter what we did that night, if maybe it matters more than any other thing I've ever done in this world.

It wasn't supposed to happen. The doctors told me and Jenna as much. Told us again and again. But what if it did, Carrie? What if it did?

I can't stop wondering.

Yours,

Michael

27

A DOG WHO HAS EYES FOR EVERY BITCH

Tracy folded the pages of the letter in half, then ran a finger along the crease, waiting for Michael to do something, to say something. But he didn't move. Though the rest of the scene had disappeared, he was still sitting up in bed, eyes on his laptop, its glowing screen all that illuminated his weary face. It was a long time before he said anything, but for the first time since they'd begun Tracy had no urge to fill the silence. She would wait, and wait she did.

He closed his laptop, the glowing apple on its backside blinking out as he did. Then he stepped out of bed and trudged back toward the defendant's platform, where the light shone down from above once more.

"So that's it?" he said, holding a hand to his stomach as if he'd been punched in the gut. "That's what all of this is about."

It was the beginning of it, she told him, but not all of it. "Mr. Silver," she said. "Do you recall where you were on the Tuesday evening before Thanksgiving this past year?"

"That was the night before your college visit," he said. "Right? When you came out to see the Manoa campus?"

"It was the night I arrived," said Tracy. "I flew in early."

"No, you didn't," said Michael. "We picked you up at the airport the next day."

"I came early," said Tracy, "to surprise you. But I was the one who was surprised."

"Waitaminute," said Michael. "When did you come? What did you see?"

Tracy banged her gavel down one last time, the judge's bench melting away as she did. The guards, too. She was on Michael's level now, where, she now realized, she should have been all along. The theatrics, the long and winding road to get here—they had been all for naught. He had scored just as many points as she had, maybe more. What mattered, all that mattered, was this: the confrontation. It was good that it would happen at the scene of the crime, rather than in any old room, but that was about all the magic was good for.

Hawaii was back, but not Michael's paradise. Not anymore.

Tracy stood in the shadows at the edge of Michael and Jenna's lanai, seeing but unseen. A real trick, that. But high atop the hill, with so much ocean to look at on two of the veranda's three open sides, wasn't it understandable that they might spend the least amount of time examining the side by the trees? If Tracy's mother had been with her, there might have been cause to look over here; they might all have been focused upon Veronica at the piano, the palms swaying in the breeze behind her as she made a requiem out of some piece of Top 40 schlock. But Veronica was not here. Tracy was alone, a backpack slung over shoulders slick with sweat from the climb, her suitcase leaned up against the side of the house. And before she could jump out from the trees to make them jump from their skins, she was stopped dead in her tracks by twin tableaux that made her own skin crawl.

Jenna was sitting on the chaise longue, her head hung low, a letter and an envelope clutched between trembling hands. Another woman, a lithe figure Tracy took to be one of Jenna's dancers, had her muscled arm around Jenna and was running a consoling hand up and down Jenna's shoulder.

Just a few feet from them, though it might as well have been at the other edge of the deep green sea, Michael was seated opposite a third woman. The two of them sat in wicker arm chairs and looked deep into each other's eyes as the woman held a baby in her outstretched arms, waiting. Waiting, it seemed, for Michael to take hold of the child himself.

This, Tracy would discover only later, was Carrie. And the child —the way that Michael looked at the child as he took it into his arms, his smiling face stained by tears; the way Carrie's concerned countenance twitched between Michael and Jenna, Jenna and Michael—Tracy decided that it had to be his. It wasn't possible—everyone knew he couldn't have kids—but here it was.

Tracy sank back further into the shadows, steadying herself on her suitcase and praying that none of them had seen her there. She closed her eyes, thought of the Michael she knew instead of the one before her now. Michael hadn't started things with Jenna until long after it would have been clear to anyone else that his relationship with Robin was over—it wasn't fucking, she finally admitted to herself; it was indeed making love. And then later, despite what happened, when the press dubbed Robin "Boston's most notorious rock and roll slut," Michael was the first person there to defend her and to call them out on their bullshit. When Veronica was pregnant with Tracy, and he wasn't even 15 yet, Michael was the one who stood up at Easter dinner and said it should be Vern's choice about the baby and not her father's.

Michael was a legend to Tracy, the perfect father figure for a girl who already had two awesome parents in the form of her moms. He was the cool rock and roll dad, but without all the bullshit baggage. He answered every email you sent him with an ass-kicking anecdote, he swooped in twice a year from 5,000 miles away with a new portrait of you gussied up as the bad-ass heroine du jour, and he was there when you and your moms needed him but got the hell out of the way when you didn't. When her mothers told her that Michael and Jenna weren't going to have kids, she cried because of how unfair it was that nobody would ever get to call him Daddy.

And yet—she opened her eyes again—here he was. Here he fucking was.

Tracy looked at Jenna again and began to cry for her now. Tracy knew how Jenna doted on her nieces and nephews up in Maine. She'd seen photos and videos of Jenna dancing with the tiny little girls and boys who took her creative movement classes back home in Hawaii, a line of smiling children bedecked in grass hula skirts and nearly fluorescent leis, each of them swaying their hips slightly out of time with the kid next to them. Jenna would never have any of that, thanks to the man she married. But now *he* had it! Now there was a baby falling to sleep on Michael's shoulder as he ran his fingers through its mop of brown hair.

That was enough for Tracy. She ran into the woods, down the hill, and out to the main road. She grabbed a taxi back to the airport, slept on a bench there, and waited to put on the show that she knew she must, the performance she'd been giving ever since.

"And that's all you saw?" said Michael, once they were back in the courtroom.

"Did I need to see more?" said Tracy.

"Yes!" yelled Michael. "See, the trouble is that, so far, you've only seen what you wanted to see. Let me show you—"

"What I wanted to see?!?" she shouted. "I didn't *want* to see any of it."

Michael stepped off of the accused's stand and, with a swift kick, sent it crashing into the darkness. "If it pleases the court," he said, "I'd like to submit a scene from the spring of 2010. It had been a month since I composed the email referenced by the prosecution, and several months before the scene we've just been made to watch. I was hosting the bachelor party for a colleague from the university."

As he continued speaking, the scene formed around him. He was in a hotel room, a half-dozen easels standing between him and a naked woman sprawled out on a couch. It was Jenna's dancer friend, Tracy realized after a moment of gawking, the one who had been consoling her. Tracy scoffed, wondering how this scene would help prove his innocence. Then Michael's clothes disappeared, save his boxers.

"Christ," she mumbled. What the fuck was this meant to prove?

"It was only once we were alone together that I began to sweat," he said. "Half the guys had left by midnight, thanking me for the invitation and for the entertainment. The groom-to-be had left for the next room, led off by the bustier of the two performers. And the last guy, a gay poet whose motives for coming had been unclear all night—once he'd finished counting out the five hundred-dollar bills he had agreed to leave for the groom's seductress, he stepped out into the yard with a couple of cold ones to chat it up with the security guy, who, it turned out, was gay too.

"That left Amber and me—"

Tracy scoffed again. The stripper's name was fucking Amber? Of course it was.

Michael ignored her and continued. "That left Amber and me, and now she was asking—"

"Where do you want me?" said Amber.

Michael scanned the room, then pointed. "Over there, on the floor, against that bare wall. And you'll need..." He looked around again. "Your stockings. Your stockings and shoes."

She pushed herself off of the couch, then navigated her way through the maze of easels toward where'd directed her.

For the first time, Michael seemed to notice his own near nakedness. "Shit," he said, "you don't mind that I'm down to my—"

"All's fair in love and Strip Pictionary," she said.

"I know," he said, "I know. But I did take off my shirt of my own free will after the beer-induced hot flashes began. I can put everything back on, if it'd make you feel more comfortable."

She shook her head, chuckling. "This has to be the strangest party I've ever done."

Michael searched the room for a clean canvas as she pulled on the first of her stockings. "Only one should be all the way on," he said, not even looking at her. "The right one. The pose will be you pulling on the left one."

"Got it," she said.

He set the last blank canvas on the easel he'd been using all night.

"Do Isis and I get to keep any of these?" she asked as she sat down.

"To be honest," he said, "most of them are crap."

"Not yours," she said.

"Even mine aren't all that—"

"You're too damned modest," she said.

Michael blushed. "Okay," he said, getting back to business. "Lean back against the wall. Keep your right leg flat on the floor, and lift your left leg up."

She nodded, then did just as she was told.

"Right," he said, "that's great. Keep your knee at about the same level as your chin—yes, bring the chin down if you need to—

and keep your eyes focused on the stocking as you're pulling it down."

"How far down?" she asked.

"About mid-calf," he said. "And make sure you're using both hands to pull it down. But gently," he added. "Slowly, I mean. You're not in a rush."

She smiled. "You needn't be in a rush, either, Mr. Silver. I can't leave until Isis is done in the other room. We've got plenty of time."

"I don't know about that," he said. "This is only my friend's second or third time. He's only a PhD candidate, after all. They were probably done before she got his pants down."

Amber chuckled.

"Sorry if I seem frazzled," he said. "I just want to get this one right."

"You apologize too much, too," she said. "Your wife the cause of that?"

"No," he said. "That'd probably be my sister."

"Your sister, the stripper?"

"That's the one," he said, beginning to sketch the line of Amber's arched back. "She's been making me feel like I have something to apologize for since the day my parents brought her home from the hospital."

"And she's the reason that this evening was about easels instead of dildos, right?"

Michael nodded. "The others had him convinced about the traditional bachelor party, but I've never been one to keep things traditional. And, I mean, when your sister's in the profession..."

Amber said, "She the reason you're so afraid of looking at me?"

Michael stopped sketching. "What do you mean?" he said.

"You haven't looked at me all night," said Amber. "Not really. At least not since I took my clothes off. The sketches you've done have been great, but they've all been from memory. Haven't they?"

Tracy watched the lump form in Michael's throat, watching him swallow it back. He was caught. Guilty. Again, Tracy wondered why he was showing her this scene, what it was meant to accomplish. A stripper calling him on his subterfuge? This was meant to make him look *less* guilty?

"This one's a Nick Gold," he said. "From an old trading card set of her best pin-ups."

"Her?" said Amber. "Isn't Nick a man's name?"

Michael put down his pencil—in order, it seemed, to pontificate. "It was a pseudonym," he said. "Nick was actually a woman by the name of—"

"Pick up the pencil," said Amber. "Isn't that the rule, that you never take your pencil up off the page?"

In spite of herself, Tracy was beginning to like this one. She'd comforted Jenna at a critical moment, or, well, she was going to eventually, and she was giving Michael shit when shit was what he deserved—why should Tracy let Michael's infatuation with this woman influence her opinion of her?

Michael began to sketch again. "How did you know?" he asked. "How did you know I was doing it from memory?"

"I saw how nervous you were when one of your buddies picked a pose early on, when he set up something you had never seen before."

Michael snickered. "I don't think that pose had been seen by anyone on Earth before."

"It was pretty hard to hold," said Amber.

Michael smiled, lightening up. His hand flowed across the canvas now, no longer skittish and uncertain. He captured the arc of her back, the slight roll of flesh at her midsection, the way one breast drooped just a smidgen more than the other. He seemed the least certain of his work on her feet; an old insecurity, Tracy happened to know.

"Can I be honest?" he asked her.

"Absolutely," said Amber. "Lay it on me. I did take one semester of psych at U of H before dropping out."

"It's all about something my sister said to me once. Or, well, something she said about me."

"And that was?"

Michael worked fast now, as if the conversation had drowned out the nagging voice of his inner critic. He said nothing for a moment as he captured her pouty lips, the severe line of her bangs. Then he said, "My sister once told me I'd never been able to say no to a pretty girl in my life."

"Wow," said Amber. "Harsh much?"

"Sure, but it's also true," said Michael, sketching now the parts of her he might have been embarrassed to approach earlier: her nipples, her narrow strip of pubic hair. "And it makes me worry," he said."

"Looking at another girl isn't a crime," she said. "Neither is thinking about one."

"But acting on those thoughts," said Michael, "acting on those thoughts *is* a crime. The worst crime. Isn't it?"

Amber broke her pose and turned toward him, but it didn't matter now. He was almost done.

"Have you ever done that?" she asked him. "Do you have any real reason to be worried?"

"Kinda," said Michael. "Yes."

"You've cheated on your wife?" said Amber.

"I cheated *with* my wife, back in the day. Or, well, the other relationship was pretty much over. So—"

"OK," said Amber, "so that doesn't count."

"But there was this woman that I met while attending conferences over the last couple of years..."

As he trailed off, Tracy leaned forward in her seat. This was it.

Was he going to admit to this stranger what he couldn't tell her. What he *wouldn't* tell her?

"We had this one night," said Michael.

"And what?" said Amber. "You fooled around a little? She sucked your dick?"

"I don't know," said Michael. "We had a lot to drink."

"Well," said Amber. "That doesn't count. Or, well, you can't be sure. So what the hell, right? Give yourself a break!"

"But I wanted it to happen," said Michael. "I wanted it to happen so Goddamned much."

"And have you ever felt that way before?" said Amber. "About anyone else."

"I feel that way right now," said Michael.

"Oh," said Amber, smiling.

"But I don't want you to," said Michael, putting his hands up in front of him. "I want you to ignore that, to resist—"

"I don't know," said Amber, staying put, heeding him in action if not in speech. "You're looking mighty cute in your underwear there, Mr. Silver."

"You mean you would?" said Michael. "If I wanted to, right now, then you—"

"Of course I would," said Amber. "But you don't want to."

"But I do," said Michael.

"If you wanted to," said Amber, "you'd be over here right now."

Michael wove his way through the easels to her. And, as he did, she stood to receive him. They moved ever so close to each other, ever so close, but still far enough away that he could feign innocence if they were caught. Then they drew closer. His hands hovered over her hips; hers reached for his ass. Their fingers curled in anticipation, the two of them ready to puncture that final invisible barrier. He pressed his face close to hers, their eyes closing, their mouths opening. Tracy caught sight of the head of his penis, that awful, deceitful creature rising from its slumber, seeking out the fertile ground it could smell, could almost taste.

Then, at the last minute, Michael pulled away. He shoved his dick back into the folds of his boxers and stalked back across the room. "I am such an asshole," he said. "I love my wife, but—"

"Does she know about these moments?" said Amber.

"Every single one," said Michael. "I haven't been able to keep a secret from that woman since the day I met her."

Tracy found this hard to believe. Did Jenna know about the email yet? Would he tell her about this night, the one he was showing Tracy right now, or would it be Amber who did that? How could Jenna know all of this and still hold his hand? How could she know this and still laugh at his jokes—his *terrible* jokes?

"So, she knows," said Amber. "Key question then is, is she OK with it?"

"She says she's fine with it," said Michael. "She says she understands. But how can she? Does she really understand how close I've come?"

"Close only counts in horseshoes and hand grenades," said Amber.

"What if I *am* a grenade?" said Michael. "What happens when I go off?"

Amber crossed to him and grabbed ahold of his crotch. She pulled him close, pressing her breasts against his naked chest, rubbing a thigh against him, pulling his package toward her own groin. It was an invitation she was waiting to see if he'd RSVP to. But he gave no response, neither accepting nor declining.

Instead, he blurted out "I'm worried I got her pregnant."

Amber let him go and laughed. "Who?" she said. "Your wife?"

"No," he said. "The other woman. Carrie."

Amber nodded. Then she held up a finger and crossed to the

door that led to the other room. She held an ear to the door for a few moments, smirked, then nodded again.

"There are tests," she said, as she collected her clothes from the floor.

Michael, taking her cue, began to get dressed himself.

"Have you asked her to get the baby tested?" she asked. "I think it's pretty simple. You swab the inside of your cheek, she swabs the inside of the baby's, and you send the swabs off to a lab."

"I wrote her an email," he said as he zipped up his jeans. "But I never sent it."

With her hands behind her back to fasten her bra, Amber couldn't throw anything at him, but it looked like she wanted to. Instead, she rolled her eyes and sighed.

"How do you even broach that subject?" said Michael.

"Is the other guy still around?" asked Amber as she stepped back into her dress. "Or other guys, plural?"

"Only one," said Michael as he pulled his shirt back on. "And no," he said. "That dude split the moment she told him she was pregnant."

"Mind giving me a hand?" she asked him, nodding over her shoulder at the zipper to her dress.

He had a bit of trouble with it and he asked, "How did Isis do this with her teeth?"

"Girl's got skills," she said. "Anyway," she said, turning around to face him, "way I see it is that you want to let this woman, this—"

"Carrie," he said.

"Carrie," she said. "You want to let Carrie know that you're not like the other dude, right? That you're *not* going to duck your responsibilities."

"Right," he said.

"And your wife already knows?" she said. "She knows all of it?"

Michael nodded. Tracy couldn't believe it, but Michael nodded.

"Then it's settled," she said, pulling a phone from her purse and swiping its screen to unlock it. "Give me their numbers. I'm going to make shit happen."

"You?" he said with a snicker. "I didn't see 'making shit happen' on your menu. What's it going to cost me?"

She shook her phone at him. "Phone numbers," she said. "And no more stalling. Like your sister said, you can't say no to a pretty girl."

He took her phone and tapped away at it for a minute. Then he handed it back to her. She stuffed it back into her purse as the door to the other room began to creak open.

"Why would you do this for me?" he asked, slipping his coat back on. "We just met."

"*Almost Famous*," she said. "Or *Elizabethtown*. Or any Cameron Crowe movie you'd like, really. See," she said, smiling as she straightened the lapels of his jacket, "I've been one cliché for most of my life. I've always wondered what it would feel like to be a different one."

He smirked. "The manic pixie dream girl," he said. "You do look a little like Kirsten Dunst."

"All I need is a beret," she said. "Right? And then the picture's complete."

"And a quirky saying," he said with a laugh. "You need a quirky saying."

"It's all happening," she said, kissing him on the cheek as Isis emerged from the other room. Then the scene faded away and Michael and Tracy were back in the courtroom, the jury abuzz with hushed conversation, a hundred redheads whispering into each other's ears about good old Michael Silver. His dream come true.

"She made good on her promise," said Michael, still lost in the memory and not looking at Tracy. "She made shit happen. On the Tuesday evening before Thanksgiving, this past year—"

"Waitaminute," said Tracy. "You mean to tell me—"

"Oh yeah," said Michael, turning finally to face her. "The same night you thought I ruined my marriage for good was the night that Amber helped me make it all better. I was just coming back from my last class before the Thanksgiving break. And when I walked onto my porch, what did I see?"

He snapped his fingers and they were back on the lanai. But this time it was earlier, and it was his story, and the sound was on.

28

TEARS ON THE SLEEVE OF A MAN

When Michael walked in, Jenna was just finishing the tale of a camping trip she and Michael had taken some ten years before with her dance company back home. The girls in the company had left clumps of sodden toilet paper and spilled dog food behind for Michael, the conscientious former Boy Scout, to clean up, and he had grumbled about it the whole time, wondering aloud if the toilet paper was wet because of the rain or because of what it had been used to wipe, but somehow over the course of that chore, or during the drive home afterward, he had convinced himself to ask Jenna to marry him.

"And he says to me," said Jenna, "'I hope this isn't considered some form of infidelity, me touching the TP they used to wipe their pee-pees and all.'"

Amber and Carrie laughed and laughed, spilling wine in the process, as Michael, pale as a ghost, said, trying to make a joke, "Honey, I'm home."

The three women turned to face him, silencing their laughter.

Jenna finished off her glass of wine, then stood up, wrapped her arms around him, and planted a big kiss on his cheek.

"Hello, dear," she said. "Surprise!"

Amber stood to hug him next. And, as she did, she told him that she and Jenna had picked Carrie and the baby up at the airport that afternoon.

"The baby," Michael mumbled as Jenna stepped aside to let Amber hug him.

"Logan," said Carrie, who stood now too, and who nodded at a cloth play mat that had been laid upon the floor.

As Amber drew back and Carrie waited her turn to greet him, Michael looked down upon the sleeping boy who might be his son. It was a different look than the one Tracy had seen, not yet that mash-up of sadness and joy that would be playing upon his face when she snuck through the trees in just a few minutes. It was a look of pure wonder.

"He's beautiful," he said.

"Thank you," said Carrie as they hugged, as they held each other for the first time in over a year. Tracy watched them, waiting for some sign of... of what she wasn't sure. But some sign of something.

"We have the results," said Jenna as Michael and Carrie parted. She held up the still sealed envelope, a nervous smile on her face.

"You got any more wine?" he asked.

Jenna poured them each a glass and they took up their positions in the tableaux that Tracy was about to walk in on. Jenna and Amber sat off to the side, giving space to the other two. Michael held the envelope in his hands, but they were shaking so hard that Tracy didn't see any way he could open it himself.

And that's when he, weakling that he was, asked his wife to do it for him.

"I wasn't weak," he said aloud, addressing Tracy as if he had heard her thoughts. "She had asked me if she could open it when it came. It was as much her right as it was mine."

But Tracy didn't care. She didn't want to hear any more. She just wanted to see. She wanted to see it happen, the moment she had missed.

Jenna slipped a finger under the sealed flap of the envelope and tore it open. Slowly, she removed the single sheet of paper that was inside. And even more slowly, she unfolded it. She read silently for a moment, and then the first tear slipped out of the corner of her eye.

"He's not yours," she told her husband.

Tracy gasped. She felt her body quiver at the sound of the words. Her arms began to tremble first, then her legs, and then something deep in her chest—her heart, she supposed—began to shudder from the effort to keep her upright and conscious. She doubled over just as Jenna bent forward, just as Amber wrapped her arm around her.

Then the baby let out a soft cry. He was awake and his mother was picking him up.

"Would you like to hold him?" Carrie asked Michael.

"But he's not," Michael began, then trailed off.

"Does it matter?" asked Carrie, holding the baby out for him to take.

Tracy looked up and caught sight of herself creeping through the trees. She studied the look on her face, the anger there, the incredible sadness. Then she watched herself disappear.

"I held him for a few minutes," Michael told her now, as the scene began to fast-forward before them, "before he fell asleep again on my shoulder. Then I brought him to the other room, to the pack-and-play crib Carrie had brought with her. When I came back, the girls were drinking again, trading more stories about me, and they had come up with an idea."

Michael returned to the scene and stepped into the room. The women looked back at him with conspiratorial smirks upon their faces.

"What?" he said, taking a seat and running his fingers through his now-disheveled hair.

"I've had an idea," said Carrie. "Something we're going to do to turn this night around and turn that frown upside down."

"Please don't tell me we're going for the *Chasing Amy*," said Michael. "Because, as hot as that scenario was in my mind's eye like thirteen years ago, the realities of it, now that it's right in front of me, are too Goddamned weird."

"Nope," said Jenna. "We're going to recreate a painting."

And Tracy knew just which one they were talking about. There was a Nick Gold pin-up called "The Temptresses," one of Michael's favorites—the one he'd referred to the most in his thesis, as it happened—and it involved three naked women surrounding a dapper young man in a suit. There was a blonde, a brunette, and a redhead, just as there were here and now, and they each draped themselves over or wrapped themselves around a different part of the dude, trying to draw his attention away from the painter, the viewer, who he had locked his eyes on.

"And you're okay with this?" Michael asked Jenna. "Me, surrounded by three naked women?"

"We're not the ones who are going to be naked," said Amber.

"Wait," said Michael, fidgeting in his seat, "what?"

"It's a reversal," said Carrie.

"So get up," said Jenna, gulping down the last of her wine. "And get naked."

"Uh-uh," said Michael. "No way."

Amber laughed, reminded Michael that he was outnumbered, and then gave him some speech about how torturing himself wasn't doing him any good, wasn't doing his marriage any good. She intimated that maybe them torturing him instead would be a bigger help.

Michael folded his arms across his chest, defiant.

"Who do you think is going to do this more gently," said Carrie, "you, or us?"

He shook his head.

And that was Jenna pulled him to his feet. As she did, Amber raced over and tugged at his shirt, untucking it, trying to get it off of him. But then he skittered away, putting the table between them. Then they chased each other, taunting and teasing each other as they ran.

"You've probably jerked off to this very idea at least a half dozen times," Carrie told him.

"Only once," he said.

Jenna caught her husband and got his shirt up over his head. He blushed and looked down at the floor. Amber poured him a glass of wine—quite sloppily, Tracy noted—and handed it to him.

"Is this really going to solve anything?" he asked, in between gulps from the glass.

Jenna lifted his chin up before he could have himself a good and proper sulk. "It will if you let it," she said.

Michael took a moment to think, then nodded, convinced. Amber yanked his pants to the floor and he stepped out of them, clad now only in a pair of SpongeBob SquarePants boxers emblazoned with the words "It's a Yellow Thang!" Amber laughed at them.

"My niece bought them for me as a joke one year," he said. "Though she was little, and probably didn't get it, and it was probably her mothers' idea."

Jenna latched her fingers onto the waistband of Michael's underwear now, as if to pull it down. "You ready?" she asked him.

"Who's going to paint it, anyway?" said Michael, stalling.

"You, silly," said Amber. "We'll shoot reference photos, and you can get started as soon as we're done."

"I don't have to do it tonight," said Michael, trying, as always, to get out of anything uncomfortable.

"Oh yeah, you do," said Jenna. "That's part of the plan. Operation Catharsis. We're going to stay right here and watch you do it."

"This is ridiculous," said Michael.

"No," said Carrie. "Living the way you live, like guilt is some cologne you put on, or a body wash you scrub into your pores every day—that's ridiculous."

Jenna's fingers were still latched onto Michael's underwear, ready to do the deed, a deed she'd probably done hundreds of times before, but never, Tracy thought, in front of a third party, let alone a fourth.

"Jenna," said Michael, "I—"

Jenna took his face into her hands. "What?" she said.

"Can't I just paint in the naughty bits later?" he asked.

"Do you really think that would have the same effect?" said Jenna.

"I know what my dick looks like," said Michael.

"Yeah," said Carrie, setting up the camera now, "but we don't!"

Michael and Jenna stared at each other for a moment, until Michael blinked and looked down.

"I promise," he said. "I promise—"

"I know," she said, giving him a kiss. "I wish you wouldn't."

Tracy cried at this, at Jenna's generosity, her understanding. How could she forgive him, not only for the betrayals gone by but for all those yet to come? Tracy could never do that, *would* never. She wiped at her eyes with the sleeve of her judge's robe. Was Jenna the better woman, or the worse?

Jenna stepped away from Michael, then looked over at Carrie. "Where do you want us?"

She waved them into position, giving them instructions. Michael stood center. Amber stood to his right, back arched against his side, hand on his thigh. Jenna went behind him, arm coming up over his left shoulder, face pressed against his right cheek. And Carrie, once she'd finished setting the camera, she grabbed a remote and went to Michael's left side, mirroring Amber.

Amber said, "You ready, Michael?"

"As I'll ever be," he said.

Carrie snapped the photo and the world went white for a second, then black. Tracy closed her eyes, opened them. The flash went off again, capturing not the women but the mannequins, not the house in Hawaii but the theater on Cape Cod. Michael was slumping to the floor. Tracy looked around herself. Her judge's robes were gone, her podium. She was back in the lighting booth, looking down at her uncle, who lay on the floor, shuddering, as naked as he had been in the dream, his clothes scattered across the stage. Something flashed before her eyes a third time, perhaps the last of the drugs leaving her mind. She rushed to the stage.

He was shaking, Michael, mumbling something she couldn't make out at first.

"Michael?" she said, kneeling down to touch him, to search his wrist for a pulse.

"Not guilty," he said. "I'm not guilty."

"I know," she said, though she was anything but certain of that fact. She felt his forehead to see what his temperature might be, pushing sweaty, matted hair out of her way.

"Tell me I'm not guilty," said Michael, his shaking calming to a steady shiver.

Despite the fact that she wasn't sure, that she hadn't decided yet, Tracy pronounced him not guilty. *Not innocent either*, she thought, but did not say.

"Good," he said. "Now, go to hell."

He shook once more, a violent shake that ended with his eyes closed and his breathing shallow. Tracy stepped away from him, back into the darkness. She looked at him, sleeping in his pool of light, and then she ran. She ran to the house. She ran to the women who slept there. They would know what to do. They had to.

29

HERE AND BEGGING FOR A CHANCE

The police were not involved, nor the hospital. Michael was brought to the house, to the bed he shared with his wife, and she kept watch over him. Desiree and Veronica sent Tracy to bed, told her she'd be spoken to in the morning. And so, Tracy had gone to her room and done as she was told. But she couldn't sleep. And the moment that the sun began to rise over Nantucket Sound, a moment in their family that was understood to be the earliest one should ever rise, she snuck out the back door and made her way to the barn, to the theater.

She dressed in her stage blacks, though it was hours before the call for that day's matinée, and she pulled her hair back into a severe ponytail, yanking a stray hair out of her scalp when it dared to fly loose.

Once the chair and the table were set, she sat and worked at stuffing the bloodied and muddied boot into the box from which it was meant to be withdrawn. It was a tight squeeze, the box not built for the task—it was a holdover from a production of *Alice in*

Wonderland, in fact, meant to be used for the largest size cake and nothing more.

The front door creaked open out in the hallway, but she didn't look up, didn't want to know. This was going to be bad, whoever it was.

"How you feeling?" asked Veronica.

"Sore," said Tracy, trying one last time to shove the damned boot into the box.

"Sore how?" said Veronica. "Emotionally sore?"

"No," said Tracy, giving up, slamming the lid of the box down upon the twisted leather of the boot, half of it still hanging loose. "I'm sore sore," she said. "I can barely walk straight."

"Wait," said Veronica. "Why—"

Tracy looked over her shoulder to see the look on her mother's face, to see if she was trying to pull one over on her, but Veronica looked genuinely mystified.

Tracy said: "Don't tell me Desiree actually managed to keep the secret."

"Oh," said Veronica, "your date."

Veronica sat on the arm of the chair, looking off into the middle distance. She breathed in deep, let out a heavy sigh.

"Don't worry," said Tracy. "He didn't hurt me. Or, well... I'm hurting, but... Forget it."

"Forgotten," said Veronica, squeezing Tracy's shoulder. "Too much information, anyway. I assume you were safe about it. And that you know it doesn't *have* to hurt. Not always."

"Of course," said Tracy.

"Do you want to be even safer?" said Veronica. "I mean, we can go to the doctor, get a prescription."

"I've already set up an appointment," said Tracy. "For Monday."

Veronica looked down at her, looked her right in the eye, and stared. She seemed to see something in Tracy that Tracy couldn't see herself. Veronica didn't seem to want to look away. She didn't blink, she didn't flinch; she just stared. And, after a minute, it was too much. So, Tracy looked away. She looked away, fiddled with the boot again—which cooperated this time—and then stood.

"Did Michael and Jenna leave?" said Tracy, walking away.

"They're packing the car now," said Veronica. "They're headed up to Maine to visit her family before their flight back to Honolulu."

"Did he say anything?" said Tracy, plucking props from her milk crate and setting them.

"He said a lot of things," said Veronica.

"About what happened last night?"

"And the night of my own fucked-up dream, too."

Tracy turned to face her mother again. "I was little," she said. "I didn't know what I was—"

"I know," said Veronica, standing now, crossing to Tracy, "but you knew what you were doing last night."

"If you'd seen what I saw," said Tracy, "wouldn't you have wanted some answers?"

It was a dumb question to ask. Of course Veronica could understand the need for answers. She woke to the sound of her parents screaming at each other at least once a week when she was a kid, her own mother yelling at her father, "Why don't you run away then, if that'd make you happier?" And he'd yell back, "You wouldn't understand." But, try as they all did to understand, he never did give them answers.

"I should've stayed quiet?" said Tracy. "I should have let that image fester in my mind?"

Veronica said: "You could have just asked him."

"But," said Tracy, "look at the men in our family, Mum. What reason did I have to expect he'd tell me the truth?"

"Because Michael isn't like the rest of them," said Veronica.

"You knew that before this all started and you know it now. Why you ever thought—"

"I thought it," said Tracy, "because they all let you down, eventually. Your father left—"

"Actually, my mother left him."

"My father left," said Tracy.

"He's not your father," said Veronica. "He never was."

"And, yeah," said Tracy, "maybe Michael has resisted every temptation, up until now. Maybe he didn't fuck Carrie. But maybe he did. And, even if he didn't, then someday, someday he might—"

Veronica shook her head. "Do you have a crystal ball I don't know about?"

"What?" said Tracy.

"Can you predict the future?" said Veronica, grabbing her daughter's arms, looking her in the eyes again in that way only mothers seemed capable of doing.

"Oh, give me a break," said Tracy, shrugging off her mother's hands, turning away. "I can make an educated guess, Mum, based on the evidence. And there's a whole lot of it."

"Whatever happened to 'innocent until proven guilty'?"

But she had already proven him guilty. Maybe not of the big crimes, but what about the fact that he'd fessed up to so many of the little ones? This wasn't the trial anymore. This was the parole hearing. This was about his likelihood to offend again. But Veronica couldn't see that.

"This is about something bigger than Michael," said Veronica. "In your mind, this is about whether or not any man is likely to offend, isn't it? Michael's just the scapegoat."

"Not a scapegoat," said Tracy. "A representative. He's the mean, the average. And if he can't be trusted..."

"He's one man," said Veronica. "Just like the Runt is one man. And my father, too."

"But together, they're a pattern," said Tracy. "Together—"

"Christ!" said Veronica. "Did we ever tell you that all men were evil? Or is this just what happens to the daughter of dykes, that you grow up thinking—"

"Not all men!" shouted Tracy. "I had this one hope, this one shining example. And now it's gone. Now he's gone! Off of the pedestal I put him on, his visage shattered on the cold, hard ground."

Veronica chuckled, then composed herself. "His visage?" she said.

How could she laugh, even for a moment? Yes, it had been an obnoxious choice of words—*Visage, Tracy? Really?*—but the truth was that Michael *was* a hero to her, as much a hero as Zeus was the Olympians, or Helios to the Rhodians. But he was more in her world, not one of seven wonders, but *the* wonder, and he was never supposed to fall, not him.

"If you don't understand how much it hurts," said Tracy. "If you don't understand—"

Tracy broke down as her mother wrapped her arms around her, the tears flowing, the snot clogging her nose, sobs choking back the words she wanted to say, but could not.

"I do understand," said Veronica. "Fathers are never what you want them to be, not forever at least. None of them are perfect."

"But he was supposed to be," said Tracy, stuttering through her tears. "Goddamn it."

They held each other for a moment more, but Tracy soon pulled away and wiped at her face with the long sleeves of her stage blacks. Behind her, she heard Veronica pick up the teacup from the table, then a sploosh of something hitting the water within it.

"Here," said Veronica. "Have some tea."

Tracy turned around and gave her mother a weak smile. "It's not tea, Mum. It's just water."

Veronica showed her a small vial, rolled it between her forefinger and thumb. "I put some chamomile in it. I think that'll take the edge off, either way."

Tracy took the cup and sipped.

"Got anything stronger," she said. "I am 18, after all."

Veronica smirked. "You don't need anything stronger, Trace."

Tracy sat in the chair, sipped again.

"Am I in trouble?" said Tracy.

"I don't know," said Veronica. "You tell me."

They stared at each other for a moment before Tracy spoke again.

"Did you get what I was saying about the boot? My theory?"

"Sure," said Veronica. "It's a metaphor."

"Are you making fun of me?" said Tracy, setting the teacup down on its saucer. "I mean, I'm serious: doesn't it represent the life he wished he had?"

"It was just a boot," said Veronica, running her hand over the top of the box it was now hidden in. "It's what mariners wore."

"You don't think it meant anything?" said Tracy.

"The boot was all they had of him," said Veronica. "His wife hid it beneath the floorboards of the kitchen because she couldn't bear her children looking at the nightmare of it, but also because she couldn't bear to part with the only piece of him that she had left. It was only a piece, and it might have been the piece she detested the most, but it was him, the one she loved. So she kept it. Because it reminded her of all the other pieces, which, though they were lost to the world, belonged to her forever."

"Oh," said Tracy.

"Do you understand?" said Veronica.

She nodded.

"You going to chill out in here for a while?" said Veronica.

She nodded again.

"Okay," said Veronica. "Take a nap. You could use one."

Veronica bent down and rubbed her nose against Tracy's. Her forehead pressed against Tracy's as she gave her daughter's neck a quick squeeze and a rub. And then, Veronica was gone.

Tracy took one more sip of the tea, then set it down on the table. She opened the lid of the box, the boot popping free and landing with a thud on the table. She stared at it for a moment, and then, just as she had the night before, she took off her own shoe.

The boot slid on without a struggle; it fit. Well enough to walk in, she imagined, though she wasn't going to try. She was too sleepy.

"You had a small foot, old man," she said, yawning.

Tracy picked up the tea, leaned back into the cushions of the chair, and put her feet up on the table. She took a final sip, then set the now-empty cup upside down on her belly. She watched it rise and fall, rise and fall. Her eyes began to flicker closed, first on the rises, then on the falls as well. She felt the cup there, on her belly, for a moment more, felt a leftover drop seep through her shirt. But then that was gone, too. And she was somewhere else.

Tracy stood outside a courthouse now, looking up at a piano falling from the sky.

Beside her, someone said, "You might want to move."

It was a man in paint-stained jeans and a torn Voltron t-shirt. On his head, he wore an off-white hard hat emblazoned with a bell inside a circle. He smirked at her, rolling up a comic book and slipping it into his back pocket.

"Just a suggestion," he said.

And because she wondered what he might say next, because she wanted to know, she did move.

"What's with the helmet?" she asked him.

"Oh this?" he said, as he rapped a fist against it. "I fell in love with long distances." He smirked. Then, with a tilt of his head, a raise of his eyebrows, and just the slightest quaver in his voice, he added, "That is the line, isn't it?"

She laughed at his joke, his dumb reference—the best olive branch he had to offer—and she walked with him, happy to have some part of him back, the part that was true and always would be.

AUTHOR'S NOTE & ACKNOWLEDGMENTS

If asked when I began work on this novel, I could answer quite confidently "Fall 1997." And a great many people have influenced the development of the book in the twenty years since. But, rather than rattle off their names in quick succession and leave it at that, I'd like to offer a brief tour through the history of this text and thank each of these wonderful people in the context of when and where they came to help me make this book a reality.

I.

It began with the writing of a one-act play for the Spring 1998 Bradford College Student Theatre Festival. Submissions were due sometime late in the fall semester of 1997 and I did at least some of my work on the script during my work-study shifts at the basement computer labs in Hasseltine Hall. It was in this sex farce, titled *A Lick and a Promise*, that the characters of Veronica, Desiree, and the Runt were born. A fragment of this play, with the character names changed and the gender of the Chinese food delivery person altered, can still be found in the chapter titled "DiFranco-Maguire." And the central conflict of Veronica's life in the play—stay with the Runt or run off with Desiree—that, of course, is still at the heart of the novel today.

Scott Stroot and **Peter Waldron**, the theater professors at the time, accepted my play into the spring festival as a workshop production. And the crowds who saw it over its two-night run in February 1998 laughed their asses off. **Pat Vogelpohl**, the playwright of the play that *Lick* was paired with for the festival, paid me a compliment about my use of dialogue that made my heart sing, the memory of which still brings a smile to my face today. He was the best playwright on campus, one of the best writers period, and I couldn't believe he liked a thing I'd made.

The cast of that production included **Robyn Blanchard** as Veronica, **Robert DaPonte** as Tim (the Runt), **Amanda Damstra** as Tracy (not Veronica's daughter Tracy, but an early version of Desiree with a different name), and **Chris Larsen** as Andy the Chinese Food Delivery Boy. I directed, with assistance from my good friend **Jim Arrington**.

Over the summer of 1998, bolstered by the success of *Lick* and the confidence that success gave me, I began work on a full-length follow-up for my senior project. It was called *The People vs. Jesus Christ* and it focused on Veronica's cousin Michael, who, yes, was based on me. And who, yes, for the half-dozen people who read my never-published comic book *Nightmare* in the late high school or early college days, borrowed his name from the eponymous superhero's alter ego.

The trouble with *Christ*, from the beginning, was that I had that title and little else. I'd listened to XTC's "The Ballad of Peter Pumpkinhead" one too many times and I set out to create some modern-day Jesus story, something so epic and unwieldy and ostentatious that only a 20-year-old with a 20-year-old's delusions of grandeur could have conceived it. My senior project mentors, the aforementioned Scott Stroot and my undergraduate creative writing mentor **David Crouse**, did their best to steer me in the right direction. But, drunk on the tiny bit of success I'd had with my first play—I've always been a lightweight, and success tasted every bit as sweet as the fruity cocktails that were my staple then—I didn't listen very well.

Little survives from *Christ* in the book you're now reading, but it did have its influences. The earliest drafts of *Christ* involved a trial and the later drafts introduced the character of Jenna Worthing for the first time. The speech about the baby Jesus that Michael gives to Robin in the chapter titled "A Trail of Honey to Show You Where He's Been" was also almost fully-formed in the play.

The cast of the March 1999 production included Robert DaPonte as Michael, **Jonathan Martin** as Adam, **Trish Ruppert** as Jenna, Amanda Damstra as Maggie, and **Tori Ryan** as Mary, with Chris Larsen reprising his role as Andy the Chinese Food Delivery Boy. As with *Lick*, I directed. **Nikki St. Pierre**, **Heather Thatcher**, **Lissa Brennan**, and **Matt Perrone** were our crew.

In the years between the end of college (1999) and the beginning of grad school (2003), I tried my hand at expanding the universe of these characters in a few different ways. I adapted *Lick* and *Christ* into screenplays and added a third script, *Just Like Family*, to round out the trilogy. Not many people ever read these, except perhaps my friend Jon Martin and my wife **Stephanie**, but the screenplays did have a profound impact on the story you've just read. The screenplay version of *Lick* is where the character of Desiree really emerged, a friend from high school who Veronica had a crush on (later to be merged with the original "Tracy" character). It's also where the idea of a pregnancy first entered into my imagination, though it was Desiree who was pregnant and not

Veronica. The screenplay version of *Christ* is one of the first times I floated the idea of Veronica and Tim living in the apartment building where Aerosmith once lived (an idea still explored in "Eliot, Tallarico & Hook"). And *Just Like Family* finally introduced the character of Michael's sister Ashley, along with proto-versions of the rest of the extended family, only alluded to here in *Missing Mr. Wingfield* but a vital presence in other stories and a key factor in developing Michael and Veronica into the characters they are today. *Family* is also the first place I dramatized Michael and Jenna's wedding and the weeks leading up to it.

It was also during these years that I wrote a novel titled *The Legend of Zeema Zalowicz*, as problematic a piece of writing as I've ever composed (and something I can't believe I have never obliterated from my hard drive out of fear of it being read). No one has ever read that either, but it is notable because it's the first place I remember developing the idea of Michael Silver as something of a celebrity (at least in his own small corner of the world). The main character of *Zeema* is a student at the college Michael used to attend. And he looks up to Michael, who is already a bit of a legend on campus even just a couple of years after his graduation.

It's amazing to me now, looking back on these early years of development (1997-2003) and reflecting on all of the building blocks that were already there in these pieces of writing that I find mostly cringe-worthy today. These disparate, unrefined elements weren't quite a foundation yet. To extend the metaphor, they weren't yet even concrete. But I was about to whip them into shape and pour them into something solid I could build upon.

II.

I spent my first semester in the Lesley University MFA in Creative Writing program working on stories that had nothing to do with the Silver family (at least at the time). And though I don't remember that being an intentional choice, it was one of the best things I could have done for myself as a writer. I spent four months working with my first grad school mentor, **Michael Lowenthal**, on writing new stories and revising them. Revising them and revising them and revising them again, until I couldn't revise them no more. I turned in revisions of one story, "Ian," nearly every month that Lowenthal and I worked together. He'd send me a letter back telling me how much better I'd made the story that month, paying me endless compliments, and then he'd tell me how much further he thought I could still go with it. Much like the only great physical trainer I've ever worked with, Lowenthal knew that I was the kind of person who needed to be pumped up about himself before he was told what he still had to work on. And to this day, my muse, when it speaks to me at all, sounds an awful lot like him.

Toward the end of my semester with Lowenthal and into my second semester in the program, the one I spent studying under **Christina Shea**, I started to feel like maybe I was ready to get back to the Silver family. After a while away, I at first only dipped my toe into their gene pool (with short stories about Michael's father, Albert, and his high school girlfriend, Robin). But by the end of my semester with Christina, encouraged by an independent study I did with **Sharlene Cochrane** on placing my family's history into the broader historical context of American history, I decided to take a stab at turning all of my old Silver yarns into a novel. Inspired by my family's lengthy history on Massachusetts' Cape Cod, and not yet having learned my lesson about titles from my experience with *The People vs. Jesus Christ*, one of the first things I decided about the novel was its title: *Down the Cape*. And that was the title of this book you're reading for far longer than it should have been. But I don't want to get ahead of myself.

In my third and fourth semesters at Lesley, I studied under

Tony Eprile and Tony was the one who pushed me to finish a draft of the novel for my thesis (**Rachel Kadish** would be my second reader). Though I'd spent nearly half of my time in the program working on short stories, it quickly became obvious to Tony (and to the classmates in my workshops) that I had the drive to push through to the end of this thing in the time I had left. Those classmates included **Shera Palmer**, **Scott McCabe**, **Jill Vora**, **Sara Oliver**, **Mary Verdier**, and **Erica Thinesen**, among many, many others. I also met the talented writer-artist **Bryan Ballinger** during my time in the program. And though Bryan was in the Writing for Young People concentration, the program was small then and we saw each other a lot. I know I must've bounced ideas off of him at some point. Bouncing ideas off of each other was just something we all did for one another—the line about "the products of conception" in the chapter about Veronica's abortion anxiety ("Eliot, Tallarico & Hook") was a gift from one of the women in the program, a sentence that had once been uttered to her. That we shared such personal stuff with each other—I will never forget their generosity.

During that second year I churned out chapter after chapter, writing more in the second half of 2004 and the first half of 2005 than I ever had before and probably more than I have in any similar period since. It helped that I lost my soul-crushing technology job and picked up a gig at a literary non-profit instead, and that I was only part-time during my first year there. My boss at that non-profit, **Michael Gouin-Hart**, was incredibly flexible and incredibly supportive as I finished up grad school. And the fact that he trusted me to help him run the association's annual conference in New Orleans just a month into my tenure there—that was a huge boost to my confidence during a time that, at least professionally, I was feeling pretty low about myself.

The intensity of those annual conferences, mingled with the

intensity of the twice-a-year residencies I attended during my MFA program—these experiences formed the backdrop for the chapter on Michael's infidelity ("Who You Want to Take You Home"). Though I never succumbed to temptation the way that Michael did, it was easy to imagine how, in such an overwhelming environment, the right person at the wrong time in their lives could make those choices.

Though I came into contact with literary luminaries during my time at the non-profit—having a drink with Edmund White and Joyce Carol Oates after a reading, helping to rescue Jhumpa Lahiri from a Philadelphia rain storm and an inept cab driver—it was the staff members and student volunteers I worked with who had the most profound impact on me and my work. I can't go any further without thanking them, in particular **Richie Hofmann**, **Leslie Harkema**, **Beth Stone**, **Lisa Grove**, **Tonya Serra**, and **Chelsea Bell**. Someday I'll write about all of the folks I worked with during those years and the impact they had on me—it was the best job I've ever had, aside from the one I have now—and maybe then I won't forget anyone, as I surely have done now.

In the years between 2005 and 2009, I revised the novel about once a year, cutting huge bits of it along the way as I searched for the right shape (many of which made their way into my 2010 collection *All He Left Behind*). I pitched it to agents twice during those years and got great feedback but no bites.

As a side gig, I started teaching (first English Composition, and then eventually the Advanced Fiction Seminar). My students were, in general, amazing. I was helping them to create great works of their own while struggling to do anything substantive with the great work of my life. It was a confusing time.

Frustrated by the novel's lack of traction, my attention shifted to a pop culture website I'd started under the name of *Geek Force Five*. In my years of networking to promote that site, I spent a great deal of time at the New Hampshire Media Makers meet-up and at PodCamp events throughout the northeast. I met **John Herman**, **Leslie Poston**, **James Patrick Kelly**, and many more during these years, each of them offering invaluable insights about my creative work. I worked on all sorts of projects with them, all of which fed back into the novel in some way. **Phil Kliger**, a musician I met during those years, once helped me write a soundtrack for the novel, including a song called "Sing, Angel. Sing." that would be pivotal in its future development. It was a great time, even if I did more *talking* about the book than I did writing it. I got back into theater after a long absence and started to write short plays for evenings of theater that John Herman put on. When an actor dropped out of a play I was directing at the last minute, I ended up getting back on stage again too. This led to good reviews, which led to more roles, which led to a reputation in the theater community of the New Hampshire seacoast. And all of this time away from the novel actually set up the third and final act of its development.

III.

It's September 2011 and I'm sitting with my friend **Crystal Lisbon** and her friend **Mary Casiello** in Simon's Coffee Shop on Massachusetts Avenue in Cambridge. We're working out details for a collaboration and discussing the duality of artistic life and "real" life as a possible subject. My mission, should I choose to accept it, is to write a brief script that will be paired with a musical performance by Mary. Crystal will produce and direct.

It's a month into the fall semester, I've just started a new part-time job in retail, and I'm rehearsing for a small part in an upcoming Christmas play. Things are busy, and I probably shouldn't be taking on the writing of a script at this particular moment, but I'm a sucker for cool ideas, and I have a slew of material I can pull from if nothing new suggests itself. Plus: when an old friend from college asks you to help her fundraise for her new arts organization, when she trusts *you* to help pull off something that important, you find a way.

It's either at that meeting or shortly thereafter that something new does suggest itself, something structurally new that's made up of something that's, creatively speaking, very old.

By the time Crystal, Mary, and I are done producing the one-act *Crossroads (or The Piano of Death)* in early 2012, I have reshaped half of the novel I've been working on for years into a succinct but beautiful yarn about the struggle between art and obligation.

The cast of the Winter 2012 productions includes **Bridgette Hayes** as Veronica, **Rachel Kurnos** as Vern, **Bob Mussett** as the Salesman for the Portsmouth production, and **James Bocock** as the Salesman for the Cambridge production.

I go on to produce a subsequent production of the piece at the Players' Ring in Portsmouth, New Hampshire that summer. During development, because I'm in love with all of the actors who audition, I write a new scene that sees Veronica and the Salesman attending a dramatized version of Veronica's life. By doing so, I'm able to reintroduce some of my favorite characters and scenes from the original *A Lick and a Promise* script, albeit with a few twists.

The cast of the June 2012 production includes Mary Casiello as the Busker, **Paul Strand** as the Salesman, **Elizabeth Locke** as Veronica, **Cassandra Heinrich** as Vern, **Teddi Kenick-Bailey** as Nica, and **Elise Williams** as Andy.

Playwrights and actors I admire from the Seacoast scene, **G. Matthew Gaskell** among them, come to see the show more than once. They suggest that I should write a full-length as a follow-up.

This, of course, gets me thinking about the half of the novel that I haven't yet reshaped.

Later that summer, my short play "The Boot" is produced as

part of John Herman's *An Evening of Grand Guignol*. It's a story about a heretofore minor character in my Silver family mythos, the great-grandfather of Michael and Veronica Silver. The actors of that production of "The Boot," **Chuck Galle** and **Erika Wilson**, provide crucial rewrites of the then-very-rough script and remind me of how useful it can be to get outside eyeballs on my writing (inspiring me to get outside feedback on every subsequent draft of the novel, after years of not doing that). A plot point in the play, that one of the great-grandfather's wives was a witch of some sort, sparks an idea about that full-length that everyone is telling me I should write.

Over the next couple of months, I reshape the second half of the novel into a full-length play that will come to be called *Temptress*. Inspired (and not for the first time) by some lucky math provided by dates I'd written into previous stories, I realize that the baby Veronica had in my earlier work is now just about old enough to have her own adventures. Tracy Silver's point of view will prove to be the crucial ingredient I've been looking for to make her Uncle Michael's story interesting to the audience.

When a call for quirky performances goes out from my NH Media Makers pals in late 2012/early 2013, I write to Mary Casiello and ask if she'd like to follow up on *Crossroads* collaboration with something new. I'm already sensing that by combining the *Crossroads* script with the *Temptress* script and returning them to prose form, I'll have the best version of the novel I've ever had. But I have a sense that some connective tissue is missing. So, for my second big collaboration with Mary, I write the short story "After All the Kisses Had Failed," which survives mostly intact in the novel today as the chapter titled "In the Mood for a Melody."

Crystal Lisbon, Mary Casiello, Jonathan Martin, **R.T. Tompkins**, and **Jena Marie DiPinto** read drafts of *Temptress* and offer invaluable feedback. I pitch it to the Players' Ring for their

2013-2014 season and it lands a January 2014 slot. While I wait for that production to come together, I get to work on taking my two scripts and turning them back into prose. By the time the show closes in early February 2014, I gift to each cast member a mostly complete draft of the novel you now hold in your hands. I still think it's going to be called *Down the Cape*. Chuck Galle, Mary Casiello, and Lissa Brennan provide invaluable feedback on this draft, including pointing out to me where I used *the exact same description of breastfeeding* in two different places. I am further reminded that one must always have beta readers.

The January 2014 production of *Temptress* is directed by my longtime friend Jonathan Martin and stage-managed by the incomparable **Michelle Blouin-Wright**. My NH Media Makers pal **Sean O'Connell** designs props for Tracy's guards that he calls the Atlas Vulcan Railgun and the Doomslayer Maximus. Another Media Makers pal, **Jeremy Couturier**, designs the poster. And another Media Makers pal, **Kathleen Cavalaro**, shoots the promotional photos. Kathleen, it should be noted, had cast me in my first lead role in a full-length play a couple of years before this. The bit with the SpongeBob boxers in the chapter titled "Tears on the Sleeve of a Man" is an homage to that play, *At My Window*, which Kathleen wrote.

The cast of *Temptress* includes me as Michael; Crystal Lisbon as Jenna; Liz Locke as Veronica; **Meghan D. Morash** as Tracy; **Jennifer Henry** as Desiree and Carrie; **Lizbeth Myers** as Robin and Amber; **Samantha Bagdon** as Tana, Guard, and Student; **Gwyn Codd** as Tori, Guard, and Student; and **Michael Lavoie** as Tucker, The Runt, and George.

Published reviews of this production of *Temptress* are not good, and I am crushed by this. But audience members begin to come out of the woodwork to tell me how much it meant to them. My old high school friend **Beth Pariseau** sends me an extraordinarily kind and thoughtful email about the show, how much she loved it, and what it meant to her. Her email is something I think about constantly in the years that follow, as I pitch and pitch and pitch the novel to agents and small publishers without any takers.

In November 2014, I launch a project initially called "Draft a Day," the goal of which is to make my writing my side gig. At this point, my only job is teaching and I decide to see if I can get by with only teaching and writing money. I monetize "Draft a Day" with a patronage system through a site called Patreon. And among the first batch of stories I write is one called "Missing Mister Wingfield." It's about Tracy Silver getting called to the principal's office for pantsing a kid at school.

I have no idea that this is the story that will eventually bring the novel to its completion. Earlier in the year, over a couple of beers in Portsmouth, my friend Lissa Brennan suggested to me that I might tie the novel together better if I wrote the whole thing from Tracy's perspective. It'll take me a couple of more years to realize it, but by adding the "Wingfield" story to the novel in the right place, I'll have finally figured this thing out after 20 years.

Sometime late in 2014 or early in 2015, I add the "Wingfield" chapter to the novel. But I add it in the wrong place. It ends up going where it should go chronologically, acting as a sort of bridge between the Veronica and Michael sections of the text. But it's needed elsewhere, and I won't realize that until 2017.

In the meantime, I keep pitching to agents. In mid-2016, after having been connected to her from two angles (our mutual friend Jena, who we both knew from our Chelmsford High days, and a former student of mine by the name of **Rachel Simon**), I ask **Jen Petro-Roy** to review a new query letter I've written. She gives me glowing feedback on it and I feel super-pumped because Jen is someone from my hometown who is about to be published traditionally herself and she likes my silly pitch.

Unfortunately, the new query letter doesn't get me much more traction than the previous one did. In June 2016, around the same time that Jen is looking at my query letter, I write a piece for my blog called "Whatever Happened to the Book?" where I first float the idea of putting out this novel on my own. I'm still hopeful that traditional publication is an option, but there's a part of me—the part of me that self-published a comic book when I was a kid—who is itching to put this thing out on its own and finally close this chapter of his writing career.

By early 2017, I start to realize that I want the kid to win out. The responsible adult part of me, the one that's invested nearly $50,000 in creative writing degrees and who demands the validation of traditional publication—I want him to lose. So, I begin making plans.

I finally realize that the "Wingfield" chapter has to be moved. It has to be the first chapter, so that everything you read after that is colored by the fact that Tracy is the first character you meet. Then, round about May, I realize that something needs to go in the hole the "Wingfield" chapter has left. I write the section titled "Those Worn-Out Records" as my new bridge between the Veronica and Michael sections of the book. It comes fast, but it feels as authentic as anything I've ever written, so I trust myself. For once.

I send the book out to beta readers over the summer, including former students **Ali Russo** and **Viktor Herrmann**. Ali gives me the single most important note I've received on the book in years, plus a bunch of other easier-to-implement minor changes. But the big note that Ali gives me completely reshapes the ending and gets me more excited for the book than I've been in ages. As a way of thanking her, I work in a reference in the courtroom scene to a redhead we both admire who I can't believe I hadn't already included.

Then the book goes to **Abbie Levesque** for copyediting.

We've worked together on my *Geek Force Five* magazine before, and she is one of the most brilliant students I've ever worked with, and there's no one I trust more to help me put the final polish on the thing.

And then it's done. Finally, after years of saying that it was and failing to deliver on that promise, it's done.

IV.

This is way longer than I meant it to be, and I think it could be longer still if I really took the time to chart out all of the drafts over the years, all of the major and minor suggestions that completely reshaped this thing, but there are some other people I've got to thank before you quit reading this (if you haven't already).

When I started my Patreon fundraising efforts in November 2014, the response was phenomenal. And it's really thanks to those patrons, past and present, that I finally found the courage to put this book out into the world on my own. So thank you to **Susan Clark**, **Kathleen E. Shepherd-Segura**, Lissa Brennan, **Benjamin DalPra**, Mary Casiello, **Erica Collins**, **Rob Luhrs**, Chuck Galle, Abbie Levesque, **Amanda Giles**, Jim Arrington, Jonathan Martin, Leslie Poston, **Matt Gold**, **Mary Ann Spilman**, Beth Pariseau, **Bethany Snyder**, **Becky Gissel**, **Roger Goun**, **Carla Jean Lauter**, **Shem Tane**, **Jasmin Hunter**, Sean O'Connell, and **Sara Benincasa**.

Thanks also to **Ad'm DiBiaso** for his feedback on my initial cover designs, which were improved immeasurably by his notes.

Thanks to my students at Lesley University, both past and present. I hope you've learned as much from me as I've learned from you.

And thanks to my colleagues at Lesley, both my fellow teachers in the College of Liberal Arts and Sciences and the folks who I support in my role as administrative coordinator over at the Division of Interdisciplinary Inquiry at the Graduate School of Arts and Social Sciences. I've been with Lesley in some shape or form (student, alum, teacher, and now staff) for most of the development of this book, and there's no workplace that's been more nurturing than this one.

Many of the people I've already mentioned are friends, but there are many more that I haven't had the opportunity to name-drop in the narrative above who deserve to be named. Here are just a few: **Rachael Cook**, **Andy Hicks**, **Monica Johnson**, **Stacey Kerrigan**, **Angela Santos**, **Donna Bungard**, **Brendan Mahan**, **Deb McCullough**, **Scott Mortimer**, **Beth Musser**, **Jason Prokowiew**, **Zeke Russell**, **Louann Santos**, **Gradon Tripp**, **Todd Hunter**, **Constance Witman**, **Shawn Crapo**, **Maggie McAleese**, **Jess Rizkallah**, the **Savages**, the **Baringers**, the **Bowkers**, **Evan Leah Quinn**, **Sara Clark**, **Ken Mills**, **Gary Locke**, **Jackie Benson**, **Callie Kimball**, **Joi Smith**, **Matthew Schofield**, **Julie Krzanowski** , **Diane Griffin**, **Rob Killeen**, **Steve Woodbury**, and **Barbara Newton**. (And hey, if I didn't mention you by name, that doesn't mean I don't love you; I just have a memory like sieve, especially when it comes to important moments like this.)

Thanks to my parents, **Earl** and Sue, my brother **John**, and to my extended family, the descendants of Clark and Niemczyk and Tebo and Johanson, who each informed the cousins and parents and aunts and uncles in my book to one extent or another.

Thanks to my mother-in-law **Julee Applegarth** and her husband **Mike Foster**; my sister-in-law **Anisa Woodsum** and her son **Liam Alexander**; my brother-in-law **Nate Woodsum**, his daughter **Lindee**, and her mom **Amy-Lin Thompson**; my brother-in-law **Alex Cunningham**; and my mother-in-law **Lesley Woodsum**.

Thanks to my daughters, **Kaylee** and **Melody**, who find a way to remind me that family is what's truly important to me, whilst never letting me forget that their dad is a capital A Author (even when he doesn't feel like one).

My wife, **Stephanie**, has been with me for nearly all of the 20 years I've been working on this thing. Every time I was ready to give up on this book, she stopped me.

In the 20 years I've been working on this book, I've lost a number of people who also had a profound impact on me and my writing: Stephanie's great-grandparents, **Eunice** and **Roy**, who said to me, after hearing that I'd given our college's commencement speech in May 1999, that I was "something of a great orator"; my father-in-law, **Stephen Woodsum**, whose ability to captivate an audience with a story was something I still aspire to; my one-time co-worker **Colleen Garvey Kueter**, who was a great friend and confidant during my insecure post-college/pre-grad school years; my middle school friend **John Langworthy**, whose childhood home was my inspiration for Veronica's house when I needed a place I could remember that was just across town from my own; my theater history professor **Phoebe Wray**, who did things her own way, and who once cast me as Crystal Lisbon's drunk husband (the beginning of a long friendship); my aunt **Donna Tebo**, who laughed at every stupid joke I ever told; my mother's uncles **Art Tebo** and **Joe Tebo**, who stepped aside to let me give the eulogy at their brother's (my grandfather's) funeral when I was just 16 and not yet a proven public speaker; and my grandmother, **Josephine Clark**, who was like a third parent to me growing up, who I lived next door to when I finally got a room of my own as a teenager, and who read my filthy first book and didn't disown me (and told me, as a matter of fact, that she quite liked it). She was a reluctant storyteller, Grandma, but once she got going—let's just say that I'm thrilled I had an iPhone with a Voice Memos app handy in those last years. Someday, I'll write down her stories as best I can and hope I do them justice.

For most of the first 15 or so years of this book's development, I was certain it would be dedicated to my grandfather **John Tebo**, who died in 1994 when I was 16 going on 17. His death had a profound impact on me and my view of the world. The earliest versions of this book were, in some ways, my attempts to deal with his absence through my art. The book you've just read is not the book I started out writing, however, and it made more sense to dedicate it in another way. But I cannot let this opportunity pass to honor my grandfather's memory. The minor character of Grampy in this book is an amalgamation of my two grandfathers, a mix of both John and my dad's dad, **Earl Davis Clark**. He's a major character in other works that I hope you'll get to read some day.

And lastly, thank *you*, the person reading this right now. A novel is not as obviously a collaborative art form as a play or a film, but it is a journey that isn't complete until my words roll off your tongue or through your mind. I thank you for taking this journey with me. And I hope you've enjoyed it.

Yours,
E. Christopher Clark
September 4, 2017

A NOTE ON THE CHAPTER AND SECTION TITLES

While a big part of me would like to leave the references in my chapter and section titles up to the reader to figure out, the responsible academic in me realizes that readers might mistake some or all of these great turns of phrase as mine when they are not.

- The section titles—"The Bastard Sons of Bastards," "The Snows of Yesteryear," "Better Off Than the Wives of Drunkards," "Those Worn-Out Records," and "What To Look for in a Man"—are all drawn from dialogue or stage directions in *The Glass Menagerie* by Tennessee Williams.
- The chapter titles in "The Snows of Yesteryear" are both an homage to the firm of "Scrooge & Marley" from *A Christmas Carol* and a play on a line from *Father of the Bride Part II* where, during a discussion of "alternative last names," the proposed name of the soon-to-arrive baby ("Cooper Banks MacKenzie") is ridiculed as

sounding like a law firm. Once I came up with the title of the first chapter in this section, the mashup of Bailey (a reference to George Bailey, the protagonist of *It's a Wonderful Life*) and Scrooge, I sought out unique combinations of names brought up or alluded to in each of the other chapters. ("Odbody & Marley" is perhaps the most obscure, a reference to the figures who help Bailey and Scrooge toward their moments of truth; the rest I'll leave to you to decipher.)

- The chapter titles in "Better Off Than the Wives of Drunkards" are all references to famous alcoholics of history: "The Second Man on the Moon" refers to Buzz Aldrin; "The Old M'am and the Seams" is a play on the title of Ernest Hemingway's novel *The Old Man and the Sea*; "You'll Not Be Buried in My Tomb" is a reference to Ulysses S. Grant and the famous riddle about his tomb; "What An Artist Dies in Me" is a reference to a translation of Roman Emperor Nero's famous last words (Nero, as you may or may not know, was known for his debauchery, so referring to him in this chapter about the Runt seemed only fitting); "In the Mood for a Melody" is a reference to Billy Joel's song "Piano Man"; and "Glory, the Grape, Love, and Gold" is a reference to a quote from Lord Byron that sounded pretty good as the title of a chapter about Veronica playing a guitar solo from the top of a piano in front of the two great loves of her life (Tracy and Desiree).
- The chapter titles in "What To Look for in a Man" are references to quotations, clichés, or song lyrics about men: "Dudes Lining Up Cause They Hear You Got Swagger" refers to a lyric from the song "Tik Tok" by Kesha; "Not Living Up to What He's Supposed to Be"

refers to a lyric from the song "Terrible Lie" by Nine Inch Nails; "Guilty Feet That Got No Rhythm" refers to a lyric from the song "Careless Whisper" by George Michael; "A Trail of Honey to Show You Where He's Been" refers to a lyric from the song "Reptile" by Nine Inch Nails; "The Attention the Kiss Deserves" is a reference to a quote attributed to Albert Einstein; "Seven Men at Perfect Height, Seven Noses Pink" refers to a lyric from the song "Behind Every Good Woman" by Tracy Bonham; "The Lonely Boy in the Rain" refers to a lyric from the song "All I Wanna Do Is Make Love to You" by Heart; "Who You Want to Take You Home" refers to a lyric from the song "Closing Time" by Semisonic; "Tears on the Sleeve of a Man" refers to a lyric from the song "Pretty Good Year" by Tori Amos; and "Here and Begging for a Chance" refers to a lyric from the song "Special" by Garbage.

ABOUT THE AUTHOR

E. Christopher Clark writes fiction about fractured families, lust gone wrong, and memories as time machines. His writing has been published in *Live Free or Ride: Tales of the Concord Coach*, *River Muse: Tales of Lowell & The Merrimack Valley*, and *Literary Matters*, the newsletter of the Association of Literary Scholars, Critics, and Writers. He is also the author of three collections of short fiction published independently: *Those Little Bastards* (2002), *All He Left Behind* (2010), and *Out of the Woods* (2017). *Missing Mr. Wingfield* is his first novel.

Get in Touch:

clarkwoods.com
chris@clarkwoods.com

E. IN YOUR EARS

Horribly Off-Topic is a comedy podcast with new episodes every Monday. It is hosted by author E. Christopher Clark and comedian Steve Woodbury. Subscribe at clarkwoods.com/hot in iTunes, Stitcher, Google, Overcast, or via RSS.

ALSO BY E. CHRISTOPHER CLARK

Those Little Bastards

All He Left Behind

Out of the Woods